BIG SUR TRILOGY

– PART I –

THE

STRANGER

In 1923 Lillian Bos Ross and her husband Harry Dicken Ross hiked from the Hearst Castle, where he had worked as a tile setter, to Big Sur for the first time. They were enchanted by this magnificent and rugged land, extolled by Robinson Jeffers, and settled in for good. The photograph above shows Lillian Bos Ross at work in the kitchen of the Livermore Ledge homestead in 1924. She died in 1959, but Harry Dicken still lives in the area. *(Photo by George Challis.)*

BIG SUR TRILOGY

– PART I –

THE

STRANGER

by

LILLIAN BOS ROSS

Introduction by Gary M. Koeppel

Coast Publishing

LIBRARY OF CONGRESS CATALOGUING IN PUBLICATION DATA
Ross, Lillian Bos, 1898-1969
THE STRANGER IN BIG SUR.
Originally published: The Stranger. New York: Morrow, 1942.
Big Sur (Calif.)—History—Fiction. I. Title.
PS3535.74784S7 1985 813'.52 84-23184
ISBN 978-1-938924-00-2
LCCN: 2012905158

Coast Publishing
P.O. Box 223519, Carmel, California 93922
800-875-1757 • www.cstpub.com

NOTE

These imaginary characters and incidents have been set in a scene of unchanging reality. In the land beyond Big Sur, in the year of 1942, real people still walk and ride the same trails which were used by the fictional Hannah and Zande in 1870.

The Santa Lucia Mountains, harsh and lovely, hold fast to their ancient loneliness by a sheer drop of five thousand feet to a shoreless sea and are still called, locally, the Big Sur Hills.

L. B. R.

Big Sur, California
June 1942

INTRODUCTION

The Big Sur Trilogy is the story about one of the last pioneer families in America who lived freely and self-sufficiently in a remote area of the central California coast the Spaniards called *el pais grande del sur,* or the big country of the south, often called the South Coast and now simply known as Big Sur.

The Big Sur Coast extends 100 miles from Carmel to San Simeon and is bordered by the Santa Lucia Mountains and Pacific Ocean. This remote wilderness contains some of the most rugged terrain on the American continent. From the beginning of time the south coast was accessible only by foot, mule or horseback. Originally inhabited by three nomadic Indian tribes, but the Spaniards refused to travel into the South Coast because the steep mountains were covered with impenetrable chaparral and the water crossings in its deep canyons were inaccessible and treacherous.

The three novels of the Big Sur Trilogy depict the hard but rewarding lives of three generations of the Zande Allan family from the 1830's to the 1930's. The Allans were immigrants who became pioneers, plain spoken and hard working. They homesteaded and settled an untamed land, grew their own foods, raised stock and bred families. They relied on themselves and lived simply as they struggled to survive in a land so harsh it took the courage and spirit of an American Pioneer to endure and prevail.

They had little need for the outside world or store bought things of any sort and were insulated from the rapid cultural changes occurring on the continent until 1937 when the last highway in America to reach an inaccessible area was blasted along the granite escarpments of the South Coast headlands, which required eighteen years of convict labor, steam shovels and tons of dynamite to carve out a narrow winding road now known worldwide as the Big Sur Coast Highway One.

Before the road, few outlanders ever visited the South Coast because travel was strenuous, the trail precarious and the homesteads were few and far between, but those who ventured there were greeted with the traditional Coast hospitality of ranch-grown foods, of talking story and lively conversations.

The Big Sur pioneer families worked long hours and full days. They had little time for frills or fancy things, and they had no patience for what was not plain spoken. A cattle drive to the stockades in Salinas took a week-long ride and a trip to Monterey for supplies took three days by horseback along narrow trails at the edge of granite cliffs that fell straight to the sea some 2000 feet below.

Twice a year the pioneer ranchers gathered for a coast barbecue on a beach with neighbors while waiting for the cargo schooner to arrive and winch ashore their load of hard stock supplies too bulky for pack mule or horse. The years passed slowly, filled with the struggles of earning a living from a harsh land and the joys of freedom to live their own lives on their own homesteads, independent and self-sustaining.

The great eagles and condors still soar on the updrafts from the cool coastal canyons and rise effortlessly above to the highest spires of the Santa Lucia's. The Indians and Grizzly Bears are long gone, but the mountain lion still rules the barranca. The few families who scrape a hard-earned living from running cattle in these mountains live simple lives, much like herdsmen in the Bible, with faith in the future by steady work and living each day, simply and to its fullest. Years come and go with little to make one year different from the year before or the one to follow. Years are remembered by rainfall and forest fires, by lupine and new grass in the spring, or by the size of the calf crop or the good honey years. Now and again, a baby is born and an old man dies. —*Gary M. Koeppel*

PART ONE

I

Towns always unease me with all them folks walking around, acting like they didn't see you. Up to that April morning in 1870 you could a counted on one hand the times I'd been in a town size of Monterey.

My buckskins shook in the wind blowing cold off the bay. But underneath them I was sweating. Wasn't all just being in town. Was other things: like being thirty-four years old and never to that day bedded any woman; like standing there in front of the station waiting for the stage to rattle in with my mail-order wife.

I got my eye on her while the wheels was still rolling, before the driver started pulling up. How come I knowed for sure 'twas her, she was the only woman on the stage. The minute I saw her I was sorry I spent money for a hat.

Anyone could see she was respectable and she was American. Trouble with me, all the time I was answering her advertisement, getting her answer, then writing back to Kansas to tell her I'd meet her in Monterey around the first of April—I had to make the thirty-nine-mile trail in town with my young stock about that time anyway—all through that time, I kept thinking about a woman like Maria Demas. But this Hannah Martin coming down the muddy steps of the stage had no look of the honey-pot.

I sized her up careful. Soon as I saw her I knowed she'd lied about her age. "Twenty-five," she wrote in her letter. Her feet was longer and narrower than I was used to seeing; her ankles hadn't broke none but something about her looks said, "Edging into thirty." Said it plain as paint.

She turned around and faced me and I said, "You Miss Hannah Martin?" She answers me, "Yes," and holds out her hand. Her hand was long and narrow, too, a white hand with a few freckles to it and a few faint brown spots that says a woman ain't no heifer.

I never let on that I saw her hand held out that way. Might as well let her know straight off that Coast women don't make up to men. If she was going to be my woman I didn't want her hand-shaking with all the lone-living men down in my country.

I stepped back and told her, "You advertised and I answered you. But before we go further there's things to be talked out."

I saw her face was long and narrow, a white face it was, and her eyes that color of drowned-blue the Mariana flowers get when they bloom in deep shade. Her eyes got a too-bright look and her face pinked up as she took back her hand. Her voice come sort of small and low as she said, "Yes, we better have a talk." She picked up her valise, took the tail of her black skirt in her other hand and followed me without a word into the dining room of the Pacific Ocean House.

I never been inside a hotel in my life but I saw people was sitting around at tables so I walked over to a empty one, pulled out a chair and set down. That fellow in the white coat he come right over, pulled out a chair for this Miss Martin and as she set down he turns to me and says, holding out his hand, "Your hat, please."

I kept my eye on him till he hung it on a deer horn along with some other hats and though I'd never had coffee on the

4

ranch in my life I spoke right up and called after him, "Two cups coffee, boy."

Seemed like everyone in the place turned to gawp at me. I guess I'd spoke out too loud but Monterey was so full of them lazy Spanish I didn't know if this fellow'd understand.

While we waited for the coffee I noticed her hands trembling. I never said nothing, just set there and studied her till the fellow come back and set the coffee down. The stuff was hot so I poured some in my saucer and blew it a while before I said, "Now, you lied about your age, so I'll ask you, did you lie about anything else?"

She jumped like I'd hit her, pushed back her chair with both hands on the table edge, started to get up. All of a sudden she eased back into her chair, picked up her coffee, drank some hot out of the cup, set it down and smiled. That smile uneased me. It come so quick, so bright. 'Twas like looking at one bright spot on a gray ocean when the sun is all behind clouds but for the small break that points all light at that one spot. I saw right then there was sap to this woman. Seemed like it more pleased than troubled me. I knowed I wasn't going to let her get the upper hand.

I never before heard a woman own to a lie, much less do it like this one did. Sounded most like she was pleased with herself as she said, "Yes. 'Twas a lie. You said you was thirty-four and I wanted life—a life on a cattle ranch in the West and—and marriage. If I said I was thirty—I'd maybe scare you off."

"You would a," I told her, "and furthermore, I got no earthly use for a liar." No use soft-soaping anyone, most of all a woman you might spend the rest of your life with. "My idea in getting married is to have a family. I got a big place, a good spread of cattle. I need help with 'em and someone to leave the place to when I'm through."

I set watching her face while I was talking: not a handsome face, but quick, the kind that shows every feeling. Her hands was like that too. They closed tight, her face got whiter'n her tight-closed hands when I told her I'd a scared off if I'd knowed she was past thirty. But when I said about my ranch, my spread of cattle and children then her hands loosened, her fingers curved in a sort of wanting way and her eyes got a soft brightness.

She looked square at me when she told me, "I'd like children. I got good health. There's still time—"

She was too out and open in her talk for a woman. I wanted to get right up, leave the coffee setting there and ride back to my lone house. I had a feeling that if this slim woman ever rode down the trail with me she'd somehow get the upper hand. And that was the one thing I'd swore no one would ever do.

I looked over at my new hat but I didn't get up and go take

it down from the deer horn it hung on. If I'd run from her now she would a had me bested for life. I swallowed the rest of my coffee in one scalding gulp and then I spoke her fair and straight.

"You better know what you're coming to," I said. "It's hard country with never a road, a school, or a neighbor. Us Allans don't neighbor. I live plain. Deer meat, beans, meal and a handful of cress from the creeks now and again when I get a craving; that's how I live and I've no mind to change. When I spend, it's for cattle or for land to feed cattle. I got no time and no leaning for fripperies."

She took her time about answering me. Lifting her spoon she put a mite more sugar to her coffee, stirred it and then tasted it careful before she looked up. Her voice was even and nothing showed on her face, but I got a sudden hot feeling that she was laughing at me as she asked, "Is that all?"

"No, 'tisn't," I said. I was angered to hear my voice going up while she stayed so cool. I looked at the fluff of lace on the front of her black waist and let her have it right out. "I'm minded to marry but I want no foolishness. I expect my woman to mind the house and make a hand with the cattle and comfort my bed. If you start south with me there's no turning back this side of death. We marry for keeps in my country."

She didn't say a word, didn't look at me. I thought I was rid of her. I kept looking to see her get up and skedaddle for the stage and start back to Kansas. She never moved. I got so I could hear my own breathing. I wished I'd never seen that paper with the marriage advertisements in it; wished anything but that I was setting across a table from her. She raised her head and her eyes had a twinkle as she said, "Sounds like a busy life." She took a long breath and her face sobered, her words come deep and straight as if they was from the Book when she looked me square in the eye and says, "I'll go south with you and I'll live your life."

The justice of the peace read the marriage lines over us, took his two silver dollars.

As we walked along the street my new wife was wanting to know how to get her trunk down the Coast, so I had to go with her and hunt up the stage driver.

She was a cool one, all right, but she acted a mite startled when the stage driver took the ticket for her trunk and told her the trunk would come down on the *Sierra Nevada* when the freighter made her trip in November. Her eyes widened and she said, "November? But that's almost eight months—" Then she give a little chuckle and told him, "Oh, I see," and that's all she said.

Not sounding quite so sure of herself she turned to me, asked if there was any way she could carry down a few things that wouldn't go in her satchel. I handed her a empty grain sack, told her she could fill it about half full.

When I tied the grain sack behind her saddle and helped Hannah Allan, my new wife, into the new side-saddle I'd made for the little ginger mare and saw she set a saddle like a sack of meal, I felt better.

It's a hard thing to believe, but it come to me that though she didn't say nothing, my wife was scared of the horses. I hoped she was. She didn't seem scared of nothing else.

The horses' hoofs sucked in the mud as they slogged up the long hill that lay between Monterey and the old Carmel Mission. The slow pull of the hoofs sounded against my ears and seemed like they was saying, over and over, "For better or worse—for better or worse."

I didn't want to talk. My wife had nothing to say, either. Already she was riding pretty far behind, seeming to have all she could do to set her saddle.

We wasn't more than eight miles out, and I'd been think-ing of lots of things aside from Hannah, when I heard her voice and looked around. There she was, hanging to her saddle for dear life as Ginger slid down that steep wet place in the trail at Wild Cat Creek.

She sounded hopeful as she called to me, "Is this the Big Sur?"

She liked to knocked me over. I'd told that fool woman 'twas thirty-nine miles to my place and if she'd bothered to look back she could a still seen the Mission from the lip of Wild Cat Canyon. I yelled back at her, "No, 'tain't," and let it go at that.

I was thinking. Figgering how it was I come to where I'd be riding down the Coast with a wife I'd never saw before.

Nobody ever called me a soft man. Here in the hills of the Big Sur men don't come soft. Them that has a vein of it peters out and ere ever you'd call 'em a man, if they're soft, they've drifted out to the valleys and the flat-lands. I'm not soft.

"Hard," they'd say along the Coast. "Yep, Zande Allan's a hard fellow, but he's a just man." That suited me fine.

Pa's like that, too. Fellow has to be if he's going to scrab a living out of these Santa Lucia Mountains. Pa did better than that, he built himself up a place a man could be proud of and I wanted to be just like him.

Trouble was I was too much like him and no one roof can cover two men that's both bound to the top. We had plenty hard words, blows, too, between us as I started growing up. I was nearing sixteen the morning he went for the ax to pin my ears to the shed door and I knowed it was him kill me or me kill him if we stuck to the same roof.

I lit out.

I'd kept the fires under the sea-water so I figgered I had a right to part of that bag of salt but other'n that I took not one damn thing but my own gun, my powder horn and the two traps that was my own.

I knowed where I was going. A good fifteen miles north from the homeplace there was a homestead and some grazing land open to entry, land far enough from the Coast trail and rough enough to stay unclaimed till I was of a age to claim it. I figgered that once I owned my nine hundred acres I'd have the start of a place and no one to bother me. There'd be one boss on my ranch and that'd be me.

Them days I was starting on my own I never saw a coin, one year's end to t'other, but I was figgering to get a start in the cattle business and I got it.

Must of cut five thousand pickets, packed 'em out of the canyons and over three miles of mountains to get that first start of young stock from Demas. New-cut redwood's powerful heavy stuff but I was strong as the mountains and even Pa always did say I was a fool for work.

Three runty heifers. That's what Demas give me for them pickets. Three runty heifers to stock my nine hundred acres. But it was a start.

Soon as I was twenty-one I rode into town and filed on my homestead and grazing land, got me a brand of my own, registered it in the Monterey County book of registered brands. Wasn't another soul on the Coast registered but me and Pa and that pants-wearing female they called Old Leather Britches, her with the big spread of cattle way down by the Little Sur.

Once I'd got my start I watched out for my own stock and all the other stock roaming the hills unmarked. Them lazy Spanish never give me much as a "Thank you" for what I done for 'em. It got me to brooding. Was how come I clapped my own brand on them twin heifers.

I knowed what I was doing. Them slick little black-and-white heifers was Demas' stuff. Sure they was, but their mother'd slipped off a ledge and they'd a starved if I hadn't got 'em in off the hills. It was hard work to get 'em down to my corral, harder work to get my Rusty cow to take 'em in place of the calf she'd lost.

I clapped my own brand on "em. Was what Demas come riding up to my place about that fall.

I'd been needing new wedges so I was setting there in the chips by the chopping-block, whittling out gluts from a piece of laurel when I heard someone riding up fast.

I didn't have to look at Demas' stiff back or glum face to know he was hot-mad. There was savage temper in the way he sawed at the tender mouth of his palomino as he pulled him to a stop.

He made no move to get off, just looked at me. I give him back his look and went right on with my work, never even asked him to light down and set a spell.

He started in crooked, saying something about him not knowing I had any black stuff with white blazes.

I hefted the glut I was working on, turning it in my hand till I could answer him civil, "I got some now. Got my registered brand on 'em too."

He started screaming, half-Spanish, half-English—mostly curses. That broken lingo them people talk always riles me but I still hung onto my temper as I asked him, "Where's your brand on 'em if they're yours?"

He made like he was going to ride me right down. I believe he would a done it. Was why I throwed the glut I was whittling on; green laurel it was—heavy, too.

Demas didn't bring anyone with him and I had the sense to

push his body over at one of them straight drops on that bad stretch of trail almost a mile further down toward the ocean from where my place is and to leave all them silver trimmings on his saddle.

Hardest thing was getting rid of Demas' horse. With Demas it just happened. It was done and there was nothing could ever get it undone. That fine palomino—but I had to do it.

I'd dropped the reins down in front of him when I'd put Demas over, and he was still standing quiet when I picked up the hardwood maul I'd brought down from my woodyard. Every time I went to raise the maul I sweat till I was sure the handle would slip in my hands.

The buzzards was already circling over what was left of Demas. His horse stood there alive, waiting, on the rim of the canyon five hundred feet above the body of the man he belonged to.

Beyond Big Sur there's no judge, no court. We settle our own troubles. This was between me and God.

I swung the maul.

As the palomino toppled over I heard my own voice echo back at me acrost the empty canyon, "I never wanted no part of this."

I was with the searching party that found Demas and his palomino in the bottom of Devil's Canyon three days later. No finger ever pointed at me and there was never no talk about whether I owned them two black-and-white heifers.

Them white-blazed cattle was a good strain. Good breeders and mixed with my poor stuff into stock with some meat on 'em and still tough enough to make a living for themselves on the rocks and black-brush of the upper reaches of the Santa Lucias. I was started.

I took my share of losses what with cattle sicknesses and dry years but still I figgered that by the time I was rounding into my thirties I'd have upwards of two hundred head; more stock than Pa had.

One thing that worked again' me was I never married. That was bad. If I could a swallowed my Allan pride and took one of the Coast women I'd a had growing sons. Every year went by I was getting more so's I needed hands to help keep up all the branding and cutting and whatever.

Trouble was there was nobody on the Coast to get married with. Us Allans had a right to be choosey about mating. We was real American stock from way back, not a drop of anything but Scotch or Irish blood in any of Pa's, or Ma's folks, either. I wasn't going to take any dark meat into my bed. Sooner I'd get along like I was.

Beside us Allans there wasn't one family in the whole Coast country didn't have some touch of Coast Indian in 'em somewhere. Them that didn't have much Indian was no better for it: they had plenty of Spanish to make up, and that was next thing to worse than Indian. Them Spanish. Plant 'emselves a grape vine, put a piazza to their shack-fronts and when they should a been out riding the hills to keep the lions off their calves, they'd be a setting on their prat on the piazza a playing tunes on a guitar.

Flesh can torment a young fellow though. That Maria Demas now; was something about that girl was juicy as a good steak. Good white teeth she had; good bones too. Spite of the Indian and Spanish mixed in her she could do a power of work and she had the looks. Her Indian grandmother, Old Nacio, she never learned a word of either Spanish or English. Still—

Eight years that girl'd been after me, me wanting her hot as hellfire and still keeping away. I was getting mighty tired of seeing her, in my mind, humped under the covers of my bunk.

13

It wore me down till I was right on the edge of telling her I'd marry her. I'd made up my mind by God I'd do it, and then I happened to meet her when I was riding over to Witch Creek. She stops me on the trail and she says, real soft, "I'll go into the woods with you, Zande."

I says, "The hell with you," and by God I managed to ride away from a thing like that. If she'd go into the woods with me—she would with anyone else. I'd never be sure I had my own brand on any of my young if I married Maria Demas.

But I got a lot of respect for what the Book says and it says, right out plain, "It is better to marry than to burn."

Seems like I took it for a sign, sort of, when that newspaper come wrapped around some stuff the Demas family got in on the winter trip when the side-wheeler put in at the Big Creek landing. Timateo Demas give me the paper mostly because them Spanish is careless with what they get a holt of and anyway none of 'em read English.

Her notice said: "Respectable spinster, American stock, wants life on Western cattle ranch. Wishes to marry."

I cut the notice out with my sheath knife and hid away the rest of the paper, tried to get Maria out of my mind in a lot of hard work. I couldn't make it. Before I give in, though, and wrote to this here respectable spinster, I knowed her notice by heart, backwards and forwards I knowed it.

And that's all I did know. I sent to a box number and I got a answer. Didn't tell much but that her name was Hannah Martin, age twenty-five. I couldn't rightly say I knowed one thing about the woman I rode in to meet. But I knowed it was a tough job, all soul alone, hazing them twenty head young stock over the Coast trail to Monterey. If I'd a had sons I'd a had help holding cattle on trails.

I'd lost my temper so much I was plumb wore out by the time

I met Tony Gallo, that young fellow from Rancho Seco over Jolon way, tiding down the Coast. He about finished me off.

Soon as he saw the side-saddle on the ginger mare he blocked the trail and started talking. "I'm on my way to get a new bull from Old Leather Britches," he said. "Say, that side-saddle looks like you was riding in after one of them mail-order wives. Let me tell you, Zande, my uncle Nicholas got one and she looked first class, but she whetted up the cleaver and damn nigh got him. Crazy as a coot, she was. If it's just a woman you want, why don't you try the wenches down on Crib Street? Only cost you a fiver."

"The hell with that," I said, and he rode off laughing. I was on to him, all right. I still had in mind how he'd kept eyeing me and Maria at the Coast round-up, three years ago. But when I found out yearlin' steers was up two cents, I walked down to Crib Street.

Didn't take me ten minutes walking along, looking in at them women with frizzled hair, wearing short skirts and puffing cigarros, till I knowed I didn't want nothing was for sale there.

I went back to the livery barn where I'd left Ranger and the ginger mare I'd brought in for Miss Martin. It was a good place to sleep and I spread my bedroll on the hay same as I done before.

I didn't sleep much. I kept wondering what a train could look like. I'd never saw a train but this Miss Martin was traveling one clear from Kansas to Gilroy. That was far as the train come—Gilroy. She'd have to change there the Gilroy-Monterey stage.

More even than I wondered what a train'd be like, I wondered what my woman would be like. She might *look* all right and still be crazy; Tony's uncle's woman was. I'd fall asleep.

Then I'd see her swing the cleaver and I'd wake up in a sweat. I was still sweating the next morning at the stage station, waiting for my first look at her...

Sudden it come to me as I rode along that I'd been so busy with my own thinking I'd lost track of the woman I'd married this morning. I looked back but she wasn't nowhere in sight. The trail was crooked as a snake and I didn't think she'd be far back but I pulled up Ranger till she come bobbing around a tangle of wild cucumber that 'most hides the trail there by Rocky Creek.

She was a comical sight. Any two-year-old would a done a better job of riding. I hoped nobody'd see us till I got her up to the ranch.

She was plumb ignorant about a horse, but she was kind of game about it. Her clothes was streaked with dust, and though we hadn't made twenty mile I could see she was fagged out. She had a grin to her face but her voice sort of broke as she called, "I don't think this horse likes me."

She spoke the truth there but I didn't rub it in. I just told her, patient as I could, "That's a *mare* you're on."

As the horses went to their haunches sliding down that steep pitch into Rocky Ford, her hands was like claws on the cantle and the horn and the look on her face was like I'd never seen before. When we was across and going slow up the mountain again I didn't feel for talking at all but I called back to her, "We'll make a long nooning at the Little Sur. Have to rest the beasts." I wouldn't belittle her by letting her know that I was a babying her, Already I felt she was not one for favors but wanted to carry her own load.

Soon as we pulled around that clump of willows at the mouth of Little Sur River I saw the outlander. He was touching off his noon fire. I wished I'd never told my woman I was fixing to stop. If we'd a been a minute later and I'd a seen the smoke, I'd a rode right on by.

I wanted to stop there; 'twas the place I always stopped— about the only spot along this stretch of Coast trail that was wide enough to get off, and that there rock cliff running out to sea broke the roughest part of the wind. It was a good place, a bit of level grass-land for the horses and the wide laguna the river made across the sand was always full of something to add to the meal: wild geese, ducks—even salmon in spawning time.

I told Hannah, "We'll ride on a ways," but she never seemed to hear me. 'Fore I could tell her again, the fellow was right up to us, sweeping off that broad hat and bowing worsen a Spaniard.

"But what fortune," says he. "Now I have the honor of your company for lunch."

"We got our dinner along," I says, but he chirped right on same as if my words didn't count.

"This is wonderful. I have food, everything, ready. Only wanting good company and now—here you are!" That set me on my guard right off. He was a artful fellow, I could see that; knowed how to get his way. Even if it's just a nooning camp by a river, not a house at all, and you ask a body to share food with you, they got to do it or it's insult.

I couldn't make him out. He had camp-gear scattered all around, good stuff, too—saddles, pack-bags, blankets. No horse-feed and not a horse in sight. His clothes was plain crazy. He was rigged out in black velveteen pants, a white cloth shirt, a coat made out of mixed stuff like I'd never saw, and them socks with the stripes running around 'em. It was like he was dressed for a infare 'stead of a pack trip. I didn't take to anything about him.

Then I found out my wife knowed no more of manners than she did of horses. I was studying if there wasn't some way I could put it so's we could just ride on when, without waiting for her husband to speak, she ups and says, "If we ain't putting you out any—it's kind of you to ask us."

Then, like she was bound to make little of me, she tried to slide out of her saddle without waiting for me to get off my horse and help her, proper. She'd a fell in a heap but this stranger fellow was right there to steady her, help her over to a seat on a nearby stump.

He seats her with another of them bows. As he straightened up he give a little, huffling sort of cough, and covers his mouth with a handkerchief so white it still showed the creases of the smoothing-iron.

I didn't like him no better as I watched him fix them eyes of his, eyes with the soft, sad look of a sea-otter, steady on my wife. "Now you sit right there," he twittered, "and I'll fix everything. I know how you must feel after riding over all those mountains."

I couldn't just out and tell him to stop looking at her. Same time I wanted 'em both to catch the idea I didn't like it none. "Well, if you're bound to stay here," I says real loud and rough, "I'll unsaddle and feed the critters acrost the stream."

Little Sur River's only a few feet wide and as the horses splashed acrost I made up my mind I'd tie 'em and feed 'em right by, not clear round behind the willows like I always did.

I give the animals their grain and got 'em rubbed down a bit without missing anything of what went on acrost the river. I couldn't catch the words most of the time, account of the stream-noise, but I could see my wife talking, laughing with this fellow like she growed up with him.

He was busy setting out bright new tin plates and tin mugs,

getting food out of the pack-bags. I reached into my saddle-bag and took out the venison jerky, the corn-dodgers with the wild honey spread on 'em. I'd made a fifteen-mile ride so's I could spread some sweetening on them dodgers. I'd felt pretty set-up when I fixed that snack, but looking acrost the river at the stuff the outlander was spreading out, seemed like the honey didn't look so much. The dodgers was squashed up some, too. I packed 'em careful in the top of my hat.

As I waded back acrost the stream I heard him saying, "Well, you're a long way from home. Kansas is a beautiful state."

I walked right up to him.

"How do you know?" I looked square at him so I'd catch him if he tried to lie out of anything.

But he was smiling. "Oh, I've been there. I've been through most of your great country."

I saw Hannah ease herself up off the stump. "Oh, Mr. Allan," she says to me, as if 'twas good news, "Mr. Avery writes songs, writes 'em himself. And plays tunes to 'em on the flute. Maybe he'll come down the Coast sometime and play for us."

I didn't answer her. There was nothing left for me to say. She'd told it all, our name, everything. He'd quit spreading out food on the flat log so I squatted down alongside it and she come over and got herself settled on a blanket he folded up for her. There was hardtack, bunches of raisins, a lot of truck I'd never seen before. I didn't have no appetite for any of it, not even for the chunk of cold meat, though I knowed it was beef.

This Avery was a spindling string of a man and I could see he needed food if he was ever to amount to anything. But he was so hell-bent for talking, he hardly tasted the stuff on his plate.

He turns to me and asks, "Have you been long in this part of the country, Mr. Allan?"

I took my good time about answering. Then I told him:

"Born here."

"Amazing—"

That's what he said. I had my mouth full of beef. Was just as well. He talked enough for both of us.

"I mean it's amazing to meet a grown man who was born in such a new country—"

The man was simple in the head. "Ain't this here part same age as the rest of it?" I says. "I never heard but how God made the whole business in the first six days."

He had a look I couldn't figger out, but he owned I was right. "Right you are, Mr. Allan," he says. "I meant to say newly-settled country. Such beautiful country, too." He hurried along like I was fixing to argue. I wasn't. All I wanted was to get this meal over and get going toward my own place. I'm no hand for strangers and now I was setting by two of 'em.

I was watching Hannah and I saw she was eating with good relish all the stuff he piled in front of her plate. She hadn't touched the dodgers and I was trying to fix in my mind how I'd get her to try one, when this here Avery picks up two pots of stuff and offers 'em over to her.

"Here's something from your new homeland, Mrs. Allan," he says, cool and easy. "Wild strawberry jam from the Carmel Valley and wild honey from the mountains." My wife put her hands together and leaned forward. "I never liked honey," she says, "but wild strawberry!"

While she was helping herself to the jam, I reached across the hunk of beef and took all the honey-spread dodgers to my own plate.

I et 'em, too.

When I'd finished I pushed back my plate, stood up and give my woman a look. As she got up this Avery jumped to his feet, saying, "I hoped you could give me some advice about school-lands, Mr. Allan."

He fished in his jacket pocket and pulled out a long envelope and tapped it, saying, "I got this scrip in San Francisco. I want to use it in getting myself a small place somewhere along this beautiful Coast. A heart's home, you might say, for I'm not sure the climate—"

He was coughing again. I didn't wait for him to finish. I asked him straight out, "Why you want land, did you say?"

He looks me straight in the eye and he says, "Because it's so very beautiful—I've never seen anything like it anywhere in the world."

That finished him, far as I was concerned. If he'd been honest and said straight out he was hunting a place on the Coast because after buying land rights he'd found all the good flat-land was took, I might of listened to him. I might even helped him. "We ain't got no school," I said. "And we ain't got no school-land. Far as I know all the land hereabouts is took."

He laughed like I'd told a joke and he said, "Well, I won't be too discouraged. The livery people are bringing me new horses in a week. I'll move on down the Coast slowly. Maybe I'll find something."

I said nothing, started over to get my horses ready. My wife was telling him, "My husband says we're short on neighbors. Be nice if you settled down somewhere near. Seems like an empty country to me."

I brought up the horses, led Ginger over to the stump so's my wife could get on without making a show of herself. Soon as she was settled I give Ranger my heel. He rocked off with Ginger hard after him so my wife didn't have no time to be waving any good-bys.

By the time we rode to Hot Springs Creek the moon was high and I could see that Hannah was ghost white. I could a stopped there for the night; it's a good place to camp but I figgered I'd feel easier with this woman I'd married once I got her to my own place. She might as well learn straight off she'd have to be hard to live in a hard country.

I rode on, her following, and when we got to the place where my trail turns off the Coast trail the horses set their shoulders to the steep up-pull.

"It's like riding out of the world."

Above the clatter of falling rocks the horses" feet pushed back, my wife's voice floated up thin, like the hanks of fog that hung from the dripping redwoods.

I didn't answer. My seat was tired and my legs felt it, too, though I'd rode these mountains all my life. The trail up-mountain to my homeplace was steep, even for this country, where any piece of flat-land big as a blanket has a name to itself.

When the horses scrambled the hoof-wide trail among them rock ledges that skirt a straight drop of near a thousand feet, I looked back at my wife.

The fog had thinned out as we climbed and there was a full moon. The ginger mare's reins hung slack and my wife set clutching her saddle with both hands but still hanging on to the end of the reins. Hunched on that saddle, she looked thin and slate-gray as a wasps' nest and not much bigger. It unsettled me, thinking of her as a wasps' nest.

I wished I'd had a dozen women so I'd better know how to deal with this one. Nearer we come to my cabin the more uneasy I got.

We rode in through the first gate and I put the bars back across the trail. When we got to the swinging gate I hoped Hannah'd notice my horse Ranger nose over and push up the catch like I'd taught him to. She didn't. We rode past the one-sided grindstone, past the watering trough and over to the saddling shed but she didn't look at nothing. I got off my horse and waited. If she'd even said, "Help me down," I'd a felt easier with her.

She set that side-saddle like she was growed to it. Her head didn't turn to look at the place she'd come to. She just set, her face gray, her hands still clutching the saddle-horn and the reins.

I give in.

I lifted her off and it hit me like a kick in the guts when I felt how light she was.

For a minute I stood holding her to her feet. Then I let her slide down into the straw litter. I took the bridles in my hand and walked the horses into the shed. I didn't look back.

Never in my life took so much time over unsaddling a couple of beasts. I hung up the saddles careful, carried feed in to the horses. As I shouldered past Ginger, I give the mare the flat of my hand on her rump. Wasn't the mare I was thinking about. I stood there, knocking the last of the feed out of the measure and figgered careful what I'd do: I could feel the muscles stand out on my arm as I jerked her to her feet. I could hear my voice saying, firm:

"Get up out of the dirt. And get to bed. You're my wife!"

Didn't happen so.

Thin fog wisps was still fingering the pine tops but the moon poured full on my woman. As my step come close she looked up and her eyes showed brighter than moonlight. She had two fists full of that litter in her hands, letting it sift through her fingers like 'twas gold.

"Home," she whispered. "Our earth. Our land…forever. No need to move on."

She started to get to her feet, half made it and then fell

forward on her face.

I shook her but she was like dead. I felt so useless, so mad with myself, I could a took the shanty apart with my hands, like the place was paper. I picked her up, kicked open the door and put her in my bunk.

I stood looking down at her, thinking, "Now, what the hell?"

The fog cleared and the moonlight poured full into my cabin through the open door. In all that light I could only see one thing; that little bunch of lace on the front of my woman's dress. I prided myself on living rough, not having one thing unneedful for my work, but I couldn't take my eyes from that fluff of white. It seemed fine and floating as the fog. Watching, it looked like it was shifting like the fog itself. You can't take fog in your hand.

Then I got a thought that set me straight. This wife of mine wasn't stout enough to face life without some geegaw to help her.

Still I stood uneasy, looking down at her. This woman was my wife. I had to take her or she'd know me for a fool. She looked awful narrow, small and white. The clean smell of her made me notice the old smell of my bedplace. It was almost a year since Ma had come over to redd up and cook me a bait of grub.

Ma always growled when she come here. She'd start sweeping bones off the floor with a black-brush broom she cut and tied beside the door, growling, "There's no call for a man to live like a hog. Didn't I never learn you nothing?" She'd still be growling when she doused my stuff in the barrel and took lye soap to it. I never paid her any heed, and when she rode off I went back to my own ways.

I cursed that piece of lace that made me see my shack like this woman would see it. The shakes of the roof and the poles holding it up was all black with fireplace smoke. I saw the spider webs thick with soot, the pans lying on the floor, the straw pillow to the bed with no cover over the ticking, my blankets black and stiff with use. I reached down to open her dress. When I touched the lace it was all crisp and whiter than the edge of a cloud and as hard for me to lay a holt of.

Then she stirred and half turned over on the bed and I saw the woman shape to her. All the life in me I'd fought down for all my years boiled up and set me shaking like a rattle-weed. I grabbed the lace and pulled. The whole front of her dress come open. Under the black waist I saw a underdress thing that was white as the lace and soft as the turn of her breast and shoulder.

She felt my touch on her and like a striking rattler she come awake. She sat up with both hands out in front to fend me off.

"Wait!" She said.

There was no wait in me. I was clear out of myself, like my white-blazed black bull when he corners a heifer. She was my woman, and I had a right to her. If she didn't like the dirty house, the foul bed, she could clean 'em tomorrow.

She pulled back with the strength of a sapling as I ripped off the white thing she wore under her dress with one hand and tore at my own clothes with the other. I held her, like I'd hold a steer I was aiming to cut, till I got my pants off and tramped 'em under my feet. For a minute I was shamed, being in boots and underpants before a woman, and then I lunged at her.

As I grabbed her she softened and went limp in my arms. Scared she'd fainted, I stayed myself. She slipped out of my hands like a wet trout and jumped from the bed. Before I could even turn she was at the door, the fire poker in her hand.

I felt like laughing. The moonlight striking the doorway showed her naked but for a corset and part of her torn drawers. No bigger'n a milkweed, she looked. And the urge to have her was so strong on me I felt I could break that fire hook in my teeth easy as I'd crunch a quail bone.

I laughed out loud and lunged for her again. She never run. She let the fire hook fall to the dirt floor as I grabbed her.

"I came to find a friend," she said, "as well as a husband."

There was that in her voice that sounded like Pa reading the Book on Sunday. I had to listen. Wasn't that the words meant anything, but the way she said 'em made 'em seem to mean a lot. Then my good sense told me it was some sort of woman's trick.

I swung her around to me, shaking her till her teeth rattled. "Damn you!" I shouted. "I didn't ride clear to Monterey and pay out my two dollars for a friend. I wanted a woman. I spoke you fair and straight, told you so and you married me."

I started to drag her over to the bunk.

She fought like a mountain cat, scratching, biting, gouging for my eyes. Twice she slid loose from me, spite of all my strength. The more she fought the more the urge for her worked on me. I wasn't meaning to mark her up, but that slim woman got such strength I fought her like she was a man. And she fought back like a man. Her breath come in quick little gasps, but no whimper out of her.

There was nothing else of man about her. Every touch of her fired me hotter. When I tore her corset off and seen all of a woman's body for the first time in my life, a madness took me. I forgot everything.

I slammed her head against the shelf of the fireplace. Was like she wilted. I followed her to the floor and took her there in the ashes. She lay like dead.

II

There I set, sunning like a trashy foreigner when I should a had eight hours' work behind me. My day was all twisted around and time-wrong but I didn't care. The shortened shadows told me 'twas noon; a plumb-bob would a dropped straight from the sun to Gamboa Rock and proved 'twas noon. I didn't care. I loafed in the sun, my back to the split boards of the hay barn, lazy as a Spaniard.

Something had happened to me. I saw things like never before in my life. That was hard to understand. A man born in the mountains sees everything. A bird, hunched on a dead limb to look like a knot, never fools me. I know it's bird far as I can see it. A stepped-on leaf aside the trail is as plain to sight as a burned-down house. But today—everything looked brighter, softer, sharper.

Everything had more color to it. Color seemed in my bones, in the boards I had my back to, in the ground I set on. There was no will in me to do ought but lay back and soak in this light and warmth.

Always, I well liked the look of the madrone tree beside the meat-safe. Now the red of the new bark had a softer look. The new green leaves was bright as tin. But the one dead limb with a last leaf hanging at the end of it showed bigger than the whole tree. I tried looking away and couldn't. The leaf was raddled with bug-suckings till it was fog-white, web-thin.

A shudder, like when a goose runs over your grave, run down my back. I kept seeing a little bunch of lace lying in the ashes of the hearth. I forced my head around so's not to see the tree.

From up so high, where I set mooning out over my ranch 'stead of looking after my trap-lines, I could see the steep ridges already turning gold with sun-cured grass and between them ridges my stands of redwoods made a purple shadow. Five of them ridges I owned and they was like five spread fingers stretched out to touch the sea four thousand feet below.

Over every ridge and clean down to the Coast trail I could see my own built fences standing strong to tell anyone riding by that this land was already took. Homestead, timber claim, stone claim and grazing rights; I'd used 'em all. My mountains was all held tight to me with fences I'd built while the Spaniards down on the Coast sat strumming guitars and land-hunger grew in the West like a weed.

I was looking at land enough to make a county for them that lived back in the crowded places. I was looking at eighteen years of scheming and working myself to the bone, building up something I'd be proud to pass on to the next Allan man; a place to hand on to a son. My son. The thought was warm as the boards to my back.

A feeling better than warmth spread into my bones. I was of a mind to go into the shack and bring out my wife and show her the land, the far-off black specks that was my cattle. There was such a softness on me I knowed plumb well I'd a liked telling her how I'd built up them herds of fat branded cattle from a start of three scrawny runts.

My eye went down-trail to the spot where Demas and his stallion went over. He was a proud man with life in him and the silver trappings on his saddle was bright as the young leaves on

the madrone tree.

Many times I'd been minded to change my own trail to the Coast trail over to the next ridge. It could a been done easy. I never give in to it. Life had made it so I had to push Demas to the canyon floor. I couldn't undo it by riding around another face of the mountain. It was just, it was right, that every time I rode past that spot in my trail I'd have it rubbed into me that I, an Allan, killed a man.

All the lazy warmth went out of me and with it the thought to show the land to my wife. My eyes turned again to that lacy dead leaf on the madrone tree and anger gripped me. I started toward the house. But I stopped and went back to the tree. I pulled off the leaf and ground it to powder in my hand.

Then I streaked up-trail to the cabin, jerked the door open. I didn't look in, just yelled, "Get the fire built. I want some meat cooked right off!" and slammed the door shut.

Happen my woman might come out of her sulky spell and make the fire like I told her to. A nag was at me to let her be, till she come to her own hunger at least. Women ain't given to thinking straight and simple like men. They let their minds twist and turn till God Himself couldn't get the straight of what they think or why they think it.

I had an uneased feeling not to wait and see if she built the fire and then I remembered that in all the bother of getting her home I'd forgot to take my gun from the boot. It was still on my saddle.

I went down to the meat-safe and shoved a couple sticks of jerky in my pocket. There was blue markings of mold covering the brown of the dried meat but I knowed most of it would rub off in my pocket before I et it. Maybe I wouldn't eat it. She might make the fire. If she didn't then the jerky would stay me for quite a spell.

The same sort of thing that makes a fox smell a trap and walk around it made me know this strange woman was going to come out of bed in a fighting humor.

If she'd a been a Coast woman and fought her man and he licked her, that would a settled it. She never rode all them miles with me, my wife, not knowing I'd be aiming to bed her right off. I told her so, plain and out as is safe to speak to a woman and she answered me, "I'll go with you."

I knowed all along she'd hold me off for a time. All she-critters, the birds in the trees, the fox in the brush, they all act so. It's a regular part of mating.

Come to me I'd shoot a young spike-deer and carry the liver down to her. There was meat in the house but it was dry and anyway 'twas something to do. I saddled Ranger, looked to my gun, put it back in the boot and rode for the high pasture.

It was again' all I'd ever saw and heard of how to get along with a woman. Pa looked to it that Ma kept her place and it worked good for him. Demas was the one man in all these parts never was knowed to raise a hand to his women, and it was the scandal of the Coast how his womenfolks acted. While he lived his wife would set out on the piazza with him, gawping at the sunset, singing outlandish songs, with never a bit of meat in the pot, maybe even the fire out and meal time near. That's what a man gets for being soft. I've seen it, myself.

After Demas was packed out of the canyon and laid away on a plot of his own land with a picket fence around it, his woman acted indecent. She laid flat on her face on that little piece of ground, clutching at the earth and moaning till my people was shamed to ride by the Demas place and see her there. It might be the Spanish way, their ways was mostly heathen. But we was taught some pride and to take death quiet.

Thinking about how to deal with women and counting calves as I rode up toward the high pasture, I didn't chance a look at my shack far down below me. I was sure I'd see no smoke out of my chimney for a long spell yet.

Nearing the big pines I spotted a young buck nibbling the new brush. I was off Ranger and sidling up easy on the fat little spike, getting close, for my gun was not so straight to carry the ball as I could a wished. Then I give in and took a quick look down to the cabin. I eased my gun to the ground and crouched there, spent as if I'd run a mile up-mountain.

Smoke was curling from the chimney. It wasn't new smoke. It was thin and gray, the fire it come from made 'most as soon as I'd started up to the pasture.

Hannah'd give in!

How I felt as I jumped on Ranger made me think of a long-ago Christmas. Pa doesn't hold with Christmas fixings but that year he was storm-bound in Jolon. Ma told us how snowballs and how Christmas was, back in Indiana. She made each of us shavers a Christmas pretty out of popcorn, pine nuts and honey, all stuck together like a white ball.

Heading Ranger down-mountain, I shied a cone at the little buck. As he whistled off through the big pines I thought, Go on, grow up, buck, and mate easy. Females is no trouble if you know how to do with 'em.

I'd bested her. She give in and lit the fire like I told her. I clapped Ranger's neck with the flat of my hand, well suited with my way of handling my woman. I might even come to get a liking for her some day though I'd a never picked her if I'd a had a choice.

I turned Ranger into the corral and when I started up to the house I see the door was still shut. Kind of tickled me. She's a good fighter, I thought. Fighting comes easy to her as it does to a grizzly.

It being a warm day, if she was a woman with no sense and no fight to her, she'd a had the door open. I'd a been able to tell what she was up to before I stepped inside.

Outside the door I stood still, listening. I heard her throw a stick on the fire, heard the scrape of a kettle pulled along the crane by its bail. That sounded all right.

I run my fingers up through my hair to smooth it some, clapped my hat back on and pushed open the door.

She was at the fireplace, setting on the block I used to chop up small stuff on, stirring some meal. I see she'd cut and smoothed a clean stick for her stirring and she'd got the old burned meal scoured off the outside of the pot. She didn't look up. I didn't speak. I stood there, looking around. I could wait as long as she could.

I saw I'd marked her up some. 'Spite of that she looked clean as when she stepped from the stage in Monterey. The clothes I'd tore up was hid away some place. She had on a blue wrapper with little white stars printed all over it. That dress, crisp as a cornstalk, did her up nice but it put her above the house I'd brought her to—above me. As I stood tall above her in my gringy buckskins my mind went back to our nooning by the Little Sur, to Avery and his white folded handkerchief.

I hit the table such a lick with my fist I like to split it. "This place looks like I needed Ma to redd it up," I said. "She's a woman knows how to clean a place. Put some o' that mush you're stirring on the table for me."

That long white hand went right on stirring. I thought she wasn't going to turn her head or let on like she heard me. Then she let go the stick, stood up, looked at me. "Take off your hat when you come in a house," she says, quiet. "And you'll wash your face before I'll put food on the table for you."

I felt my thumb and finger itch to tighten around her neck. I stepped close, my hand reaching for her as I told her, "I'll teach you to answer your husband, you—you—"

She never flinched or drawed back. "Next time you lay hand on me you'll have to kill me. Sure as there's a God in heaven!"

She meant it. She never raised her hand or her voice but she meant it. I could see it in her eyes.

My arm went limp. My head dropped forward like a old bull's head does when he's been bested by one of his own get. The fire went out of her eyes and I saw a strange, lost look come into them.

I couldn't think.

I pulled the damn hat off but it dropped out of my hand. It was the only hat I ever bought. I got it for her. I should a kicked it into the fire but I picked it up, took it with me. I dropped it just outside the door, went and doused my head in the trough under the laurel tree.

The trough-water had stopped dripping across my eyes and my hands was dried in the wind when she stepped to the door. The stirring-stick was still in her hand.

"Your meal is on the table."

"Your meal is on the table." That's what she said, cool as if there was never a word or a blow between us. I couldn't figger her and her strange ways into any trail of sense. I couldn't.

She went back inside.

I watched her through the door. Without a word she set the bowl of corn-porridge on the table and went over to set on the chopping-block by the fire. She set there, her back half to me, her hands folded quiet along her lap, the mush going cold and she not turning her head to see what I was fixing to do.

I hated that woman. She put a feeling of shame on me that was creeping in my butt, crawling up my back. It was like the feeling I had that time when I was a tad and knowed Pa'd caught on to me fooling around with that calf but he hadn't said nothing—not yet. Well, I'd faced Pa. The hell with her.

I walked into the cabin, pulled the stool to the table and picked up my spoon. 'Twas a good horn spoon I'd made myself and I rubbed it on my pants by habit. I liked to rub it to a shine and hold it up and see the light come through.

No sooner had I give that spoon the first rub than my woman was to her feet like she'd been stung. "You've no call to clean that spoon. I scoured it. I scoured the bowl before I set it out for you. And the pot I cooked them grits in. Only clean things in this filthy house."

I picked up the bowl. I should a had it out with her right then; throwing the bowl wasn't touching her. But what I did was hand her the bowl. "Put some more porridge to this bowl and be still."

34

She took the bowl, filled it, carried it over and put it on the table quiet.

I bent over the dish and spooned up the mush. 'Twas a tasty porridge with no lumps, not even no scorched places to it. She set with her face to the fire, her head bent. Even with all the trouble she brought me I found I liked the straight set of her shoulder, the tidy way her hair went in a roll right up the back of her head and no pins showing. Beneath the ruffle to the bottom of her wrapper I could see part of her shoe. The shoe was no good for wear, but somehow pleasing to see. I'd like to have knowed her well enough to go take the shoe in my hand, smell that sort of leather and see how it was the skin of a cow could be turned into something so fine and with a shine to it like a beetle's back.

The more I looked at that shoe, the more I knowed I'd made a mistake. I'd better have married Maria. Her ways in a house, what she wore, how she would fight with her man—all those things in Maria were Coast ways and with her—well, I might a half killed her for being too free when my back was turned. But no matter what she did, she'd never make me feel unused and unable as my new-married wife made me feel.

Hannah told me that if I touched her I'd have to kill her. How could I know if she meant it? First she tells me that, solemn as words from the Book, then sets out food same as any woman would do for her man. Then she tongue-lashes me bolder than Ma would a spoke to me, much less to Pa.

I couldn't figger her out. But I hadn't summered and wintered this woman; I didn't know her. I'd have to bide and watch her.

I set there, thinking how by just saying a few words and giving the justice two dollars, I'd made this woman part of my ranch, part of my cattle, part of me.

"By God," I thought, "she's more like a sore thumb to me, there's no drop of comfort in her."

I got up and went out to my tool shed and uncovered the grindstone. Working over my cutting knives, I tried to think if there wasn't some word in the Book would tell a fellow what to do in a fix like this. I got the wheel started, tried the blade again' it and as the wheel spun it seemed to say, "If thy right eye offend thee, pluck it out."

I run my thumb along the blade I was done with and found it was good, picked up the next one and went at it to the tune of, "If thy right eye offend thee, pluck it out." It was out of the Book all right, and good strong words, but didn't seem any use for my case.

I took a look up to the house and I saw she was keeping the fire like she meant to stay a while anyway. I'd find the way to boss my ranch and her, too, as was right.

I bent over the stone, grinding again, and the Word come back, "If thy right eye offend thee—" Well, my right eye didn't offend me none, my left eye either. I needed both of 'em and maybe a extra one to the back of my head to keep up with this Hannah Martin Allan. But the words had a good swing to them and they seemed to keep my mind often my troubles.

The feeling that clean blue wrapper of my wife's give me, with its white stars shining, made me have to get out all my tools, put them up on the wall to make a better show with the rest of my stuff.

After I'd made red-and-white cowhide holders for my rock hammer and pick to slip into, I fired my forge and took pleasure in the blows of my hammer on that red-hot pick point. When I was hefting it, looking to see if the point suited me, I found my eyes straying to the cabin to see if the door was open.

It was tight shut and I was about to go back to my work

36

Drawing by Robin Coventry

when I see the palomino standing under the willows just outside my swinging gate. The sweat stood on my face before I had
the sense to see it wasn't Demas' stallion. It was the palomino
mare that Maria Demas rode. I'd a better been haunted by the
ghost of Demas' stallion than to have Maria Demas with her
loose tongue sneak into my cabin, talking to my strange wife.

I stood gripping the pick handle so hard my hands went
numb and I threw it from me, cursing the pride that wouldn't
let me wed with Maria or any other of the part-Indian women
along the Coast. I cursed Maria for the lust she'd fired in me,
the feeling that wouldn't let me eat in peace, wouldn't let me
sleep. I cursed her for the aching want that finally drove me to
taking a stranger to wife.

Never before had I asked myself what I was to do, just
knowed my work and did it. Having a wife in the house made
even easy things seem hard to figger out. Seemed like there

was not a single minute of peace, not even a pattern of sense left to me.

Maria'd never dared ride up to my place before. I'd kept her in her place by paying no heed to her and my pride in being white had kept me off her—even though she'd been a bad torment to me these last years. She had no sure way of knowing she worried me. We Allans had our troubles, but none of us was the kind of hound that give tongue to it over the hills and into outside ears.

None of us.

But now there was another Allan. Hannah Martin Allan, not borned into the family but brought full-growed and set in her own ways, to maybe give the lie to the proud lone-living that set us apart from all the easy talkers of the Coast.

For all I knowed, she was telling her story to Maria Demas, making a laughingstock of me right now.

Maria's eyes was sharp as any on the Coast and she would a made a note of every mark on my woman, every spot on the floor—any and everything that would make talk and laughing among my neighbors.

If I'd a had my wits about me, Maria Demas couldn't a come sneaking up the trail on her unshod mare, getting into my house while I was trying to sort out the new feeling my wife had brought with her to trouble my work-time. That thought put the blame right back where it belonged, right back into them long white hands of my wife, Hannah Allan.

I dropped the pick, picked it up and put it in its new sheath and made for the house.

I was halfway up the trail when I heard my wife's voice with the sound of a laugh in it, heard her saying, "I don't know which made me feel worse, falling off the horse onto my face or letting my husband know how scared of a horse a woman from the prairies is."

I stood shamed to my bones. She had no chance to fool Maria. Maria Demas had seen too many men and women marked by a fight to think for a minute them dark bruises on my pale woman come from any fall.

I heard Maria answer Hannah with the cool smoothness of a snake as she said, "I think you should most not like the spots on your face. Zande is young and smooth in the face and a bride should look good to her man. Is my way of doing."

I wanted to slap my leg and laugh when I heard my wife's answer to that one. Smooth as Maria could do it, Hannah says, "Where is your man, Miss Demas? You must bring him along next time you come."

"Ha!" I thought. "There's one for you, you little bitch. "Where is your man?" "For the first time in my life I was glad of an Allan with words quick to the tongue and forgot my shame that I'd married a liar. That could wait.

I pushed open the door and stepped inside the room. My wife looked up and said, friendly, "We got company, Alexander. I'm glad you got back."

No matter what she'd been telling, I spoke the truth, short and plain, "I was no further than the shed."

My wife stepped back from me and got that closed look in her face. Maria laughed. "Is what I told you, Mrs. Allan. A husband is hard to watch in these hills. You never know where he is or what he does. You know he sees plenty things, and be careful."

I didn't know what the hell she was talking about but I saw Hannah had a queer look to her face. It struck me again that my wife took up mighty quick with that fellow Avery. Maybe she'd been talking about him to Maria. Come to me I didn't know all she'd been saying to Avery while I took the horses acrost the river, fed and watered 'em.

I had my mouth open like a fool, as Maria turned to me. "I been telling Mrs. Allan you needed a woman on this big ranch, Zande; telling her she was lucky you was so *good* a rancher."

I took a quick look at Hannah. I wondered was she simple enough to take just the sound of the words and not the meaning behind 'em. She stood cool and mannerly, but seeming far away as the stars on her blue dress.

So I give Maria back as good as she sent, "I needed more'n a woman to my ranch, Maria. Life ain't all just corn and *meat*. I need a wife and I got one."

Maria's face went dark, and for the wink of an eye I thought she was going to take her quirt to me.

Before she could get a word in I says, "I'll go tighten up the cinch for you. The mare's been standing quite a piece."

I went out of the door and down to the willows and she said good-by to Mrs. Allan and followed straight after me. She knowed the man of the place had sent her home and there was nothing for her to do but go. There was no trouble for me in words with this woman. She heard what I meant in what I said and I knowed she would. I guess she even felt the twist that tore through me when I give her my hand and she sailed into her saddle easy as a bird. She did, all right.

She leaned down, showed all them little white teeth and says, "I'll see you some more, Zande."

I didn't answer her. She was a trap. I married to get rid of her and good sense told me I wanted none of her.

But I wished I knowed as much about the one I'd married. My feet went more and more slow up the trail as I walked forward to face Hannah with her lie-telling.

It even come to me that Hannah might a had some fool idea of helping me by claiming she'd fell off her horse. If she thought that was a way to save a mountain man from the laughs of his neighbors, she must a come from a strange country; a queer place. Any man, woman or four-year-old on the Coast would almost rather own to a murder than to tell they fell off a horse.

My ears burned as I thought of Maria riding off to tell that fool story. Thinking of it my hand itched to give Hannah something to make her remember that no Allan was a liar.

Right there I stopped dead in my tracks, helpless. I couldn't hit her. "Sure as there's a God in heaven." That's what she said.

"I'd have to kill her—" There's the words. If I killed her, she'd best me by dying. Well, she wouldn't. I had time to help me break her in, all the time there was to the length of all my days.

A thought can sometimes come to a man like the clear words of the old prophets. I thought about the first runty calves I'd got from Demas.

When them calves was grown ready for the bull, I took 'em clear away from the home range. One I took twenty miles north, another way over three ranges of foothills and mountains to Jolon—the third one I took to the ranch south of Piedras Blancas. That took time, took patience. I was young but I put out the work it took to get new blood into the run-down stock I had. I got what I was after.

From the heifer I took to Jolon I got a bull calf. His father was from a tough strain of Spanish and Mexican cattle, bred to live through the scarce water and scant pasture of Lower California. The stock I bred from that fellow was tough and sure-footed enough to put up with my own broken, rocky land.

From a runty-no-good calf that Demas thought so little of he was willing to trade her to a boy for a three-mile stretch of fencing, from that I got the start of everything I had. What I had put into it was time; and knowing what I wanted.

My thought was, figger she was like them runty calves. Even if she never turned into much, neither did them first calves I had for a start. In the years to come I could still hope to get, out of a bunch of children, one child that would be stout enough and smart enough to take the ranch on from where I'd some day have to leave it.

By that time I come to wonder what it was got me so stirred up. I pushed open the door without a touch of anger left to me. I'd not pull the lines too tight, let the stranger woman have her head for a time and after a while she'd settle to the work at hand. No one looks for anything but stings from the bees after you've moved the hive; why should I look for honey straight off from this here wasps' nest I'd took into my house? Feeling better than I had any time since I'd married, I opened the door, went in and set down on the stool beside the table.

My wife was bending over the bedplace taking off the covers and her nose was wrinkled in a way that said, plain as words, she felt herself 'way above the bed she had to sleep in.

I pulled my knife out its sheath and picked up a stick out of the pile on the floor by the fireplace. I can always find ease for myself in whittling.

Hannah made two heaps of the covers, left one on the straw tick that covered the saplings the bed springs was made of, and carried the others outdoors.

I had my head bent over my whittling. I could see her but I felt sure she had no way to tell that her scorn for my bed had got to me.

I felt peaceful as a basket of chips. The top of the table had been cleared of all the things I found easy to put there, the table had been scrubbed. She'd scrubbed the small Dutch oven and it hung over the fire, looking new as a folded pair of overalls. Now and again the lid bounced up, let out the steam, and I could smell something good cooking.

I leaned my back again' the redwood slabs of the cabin and for the moment I was well suited with my marrying. I had a house and a woman of my own in it. My woman was too lean, too white and used-up-looking. But she had a straight set to her back, a lightness to her step and a lift to her head. I had to admit them things was good markings. She'd round out fast enough, once she was carrying, and by the time she'd bore one or two, she'd settle down to her place.

Like getting a new section of land made me feel good, getting a wife, watching her about the woman's business of doing for her man, made me feel good.

Next time I et I wouldn't be coming in tired out, making up a fire, picking up a unwashed pot and trying to scrape some of the dried stuff off it before I cooked another mess in it. No, sir. I'd have it all done for me and set out on the table neat as Ma could do it. Made me think how easy I might a drawed a sloppy woman out of a marriage advertisement. It wasn't all luck, though. I could tell myself truthful I'd done a bit of picking, even with Hannah clean acrost the country in Kansas. Her name, Hannah Martin, took my fancy. It sounded plain, sensible and all-white. The Spanish along the Coast has fancy names to hand out to their girls but the names don't make 'em no better. Plenty of sloppy Carmens and Juanitas there are, living between Piedras Blancas and Monterey.

I went by Hannah's handwriting, too. A good black pencil she used, and the letters drawed round and smooth so a body could read 'em most as plain as print. Nothing in her letters but plain easy words neither.

I felt my head nod forward and pulled it back with a jerk. I must be getting old if I couldn't come into a room with a fire burning in it and sit quiet without starting to fall asleep. I hadn't slept much for three nights but that was no excuse. No one ever caught me sleepy when stock was being weighed and paid for, no matter how long I'd been in the saddle.

Sniffing what was cooking in the kettle, thinking that by this time next spring there would be a son to my house as well as a wife, letting my hand slide along the clean boards of the table, I was most asleep again when I heard the door open.

"Where is the clothesline?" Straight as a clothes prop herself, Hannah stood in the doorway.

My mind was set to shape my woman to the sort of one I needed and could get on with. I was shaping her up when I sat there, not letting on like I knowed there was a soul in ten miles.

I never lifted my head or turned my eyes but I could see her. She turned pale as evening so her freckles stood out clear. Then a pink flooded up and I saw her eyes bright-misted as she waited for a answer.

Teach her something if she has to ask twice ere I answer her, I thought. Made me feel pretty good to think out a way of handling her without taking my fist to her.

Hannah come inside the door and give me a look. I looked straight at her and she give in.

"You heard me," she said. "I asked where's your clothesline?"

I settled back again' the wall, bending my head over my whittling as I told her. "There's no call for a clothesline around here. If you got stuff to dry, spread it on the brush like Ma does. I told you there was no frills to my living or was there going to be any."

She stood still for so long she got me uneased. When she started in I felt she had a sharper tongue than most women.

"I didn't ask for frills. I don't ask for things to be fine; just to be in my own home, a place where I belong and where I have work of my own to do for my own folks. But I have a right to the few things a woman's work needs. A clothesline ain't a frill, Mr. Allan. You're done with living in the sort of pen I wouldn't ask a pig to live in. Get me a clothesline."

I snapped my knife on the stick and then put them both down to let her know I was giving thought to my words. "I never found it needful to have a line just to hang clothes on. I told you what my ways was and I see no need to change. Like it or lump it; life's going on just the same as it always has around here."

There was a light come into her eyes and her face softened till she was most a pretty woman. It was not all her looks; it was part that blue dress so crisp and full of them little stars, and part a sound to her voice as she stepped closer to me.

She told me, "But things have already changed around here, Zande. You wanted them to change or you'd never wrote me, or come to Monterey for me. It was one thing when you was a lone man with too much work to do; not like it is now. I said I'd be a wife to you and I meant it. To do a woman's work, to make a home, to have children, bring them up clean and good. I'm strong enough to do that and help with your work, too—when I learn how. But you make it so hard."

I kicked the stick over to the fire and answered her, "Go on, put it on me. That's a woman for you. You say I make it hard for you. How do you think a man should act to a wife that acts like you? You fight me like a she-lion and I don't hold that again' you even. But I tell you straight, you're an Allan now and you're the first lyin' Allan—"

She pulled back her hand like she was aiming to strike me and her voice was thin as a locust's cry, "You—you think you're a man! Did you think I'd tell that prying woman you'd raped

45

me? You treated me bad as ever a man can treat a woman and still, because I am your wife, I was willing to stand up for you."

Her voice broke into harsh sobbing and her head went down till the chin of her was sunk again' her breast.

Her saying that her lie was for me because she was my wife made me feel dazed as if I'd run my head into a tree in the dark. I couldn't sit there with her crying that way. I couldn't think of nothing to do, nothing to say. I stood there close to her, looking at her as her sobbing grew softer.

It was no plan of mine. It was the softness. The soft of her dress was near me, the bent head and hid eyes, the smell of starch and clean woman was too much for me. Before she could raise a hand, I'd both arms around her.

She was a little heap of wrinkled calico sunk flat again' the bed saplings when I went out into the evening. She was still crying in a sort of soft, harsh way. I had a word of comfort for her and I didn't grudge it. "I got a length of clean hair rope I'll put up for a clothesline, Hannah," I said.

I did it right off. I went straight to the barn loft, took it down from where I'd coiled it to hang dry and nice and strung it up between a laurel and a oak down by the spring where 'twould be handy to the water.

III

As days wore on everything in the house that could be washed got hung out and carried back in, clean and dry. Every inch of the house was clean as new and I could a found it a better place to live in than in my single days, but for one thing—my wife seemed to have got deaf and dumb.

After I'd put the clothesline up for her like she wanted, I started to talk to her 'most as friendly as if she'd been a neighbor man. She never answered with a word or look and after I'd tried again a couple times, I quit.

That woman moved through her work in the house and outdoors like she was all alone in the world.

She put food on the table, smoothed the bed and kept up her everlasting scouring with lye soap and sand, all the time acting as if I wasn't there.

It wore me down. It got so when I was in her way to the fire or the table, I'd step one side. It was like if I didn't, she'd step right clean through me.

Come back to me about old Nicholas, time I was riding into Monterey to get Hannah, and how Tony Gallo told me them mail-order women was crazy. His uncle Nicholas said his took a cleaver to him and he had to get her committed.

My woman took to looking at me. She'd sit all through meal time, saying nothing, looking at that sharp knife and looking at me. Got so's it was hard for me to eat.

It wasn't the knife, not even the strange look to my woman's eyes. I was scared of trying to figger out how she come to look that way. I remembered the quick way she smiled when we sat drinking coffee in Monterey. I kept trying to put away from me the look to her face when she sat in the litter in my barnyard, her hands full of dirt, saying, "Our land, our place."

That woman, the Hannah Martin I took to wife, she was a stranger to my ways and thoughts, but not like now.

She did her work. She was quiet. The house was clean and the fire going when I rode in from the hills every evening. There was always food cooked and she could do more to make beans and meal and deer meat taste good than even my ma. I felt that for all she couldn't touch Maria for looks, I'd a been well suited with her if she wasn't so brooding.

She got thinner every day, but even so she didn't look a bit like the women hereabout that went crazy from the quiet of the hills. Her hair was as neat as her dress, nothing fly-away or slipshod about her gear.

Come to me that she was taking a slow way to make good her word…I'd have to kill her if I touched her again. I went so far's to tell her I never meant to; that hunger for woman come over me so hard I had to give way to it. I hadn't used her mean, she hadn't fought me, just lay there like she'd give up. That was all there was to it save she'd never spoke a word since that day I put up the clothesline.

Never thought to run up again' a thing like that; a fight that went on and on and never a word spoke or a blow struck.

I couldn't half do my work for thinking about it. It was when I was baiting my coyote traps that the notion come to me. By God, I'd trap her. I wouldn't touch her and still I'd make her so damned mad she'd say something spite herself. If she said even one word she might as well say twenty, maybe that'd

cure her.

I picked out the darkest piece of thin hair rope I had and after she'd went to bed that night I stretched it taut just above the dirt floor close by the bed.

The trap worked, leastwise she tripped on it next morning when she got up. She fell flat and hard on the dirt floor so it 'most knocked the breath out of her. I waited for her to say something. Nothing happened.

She picked herself up, walked over to the fireplace, took the hatchet and knocked out the pegs I'd drove to hold the rope. She never looked at me, stood there winding up the rope careful as I'd done it myself, not even bothering to brush the dirt off her face and hands. She walked out of the house with the rope and I seen she went into the shed.

I was sure that when she come back she'd start scolding. It made me feel right good. I thought of something to please, that's how much she'd got me broke down.

I laid a fire, got it going good before she come in. She never looked at me, and never let on like I'd made the fire. She pulled the meal kettle out over the flame and then she smoothed the bed. She set the bowls and stuff on the table, spooned mush into my bowl and never a speck out for herself.

I slid onto my stool and she crouched on hers. Then she picked up the knife, smoothing the blade with her fingers.

I leaned over, took her wrist in one hand, pried the knife away from her with the other one. I asked her, "Are you sick?"

She got wet and white around her mouth but she never said a word. She didn't try to get the knife back, just sat there swaying for a moment and then she stood up and went outdoors.

She was a modest woman and I didn't try to follow her. If she was going to be sick, or was on her way to the outhouse, I wasn't going to shame her.

When she come back she seemed quieter, didn't make me feel so haunted when she walked past me. I felt the fall must a shaked some sense back into her like I'd hoped it would. When she lifted the lid to the kettle and spooned some mush out into the little gourd bowl and started eating, I let my breath get way down to the bottom of my lungs.

Then I noticed the neck of her dress was rolled up, not the way she mostly had it. No matter how queer she ever acted, her collar was always neat as her hair.

She went to pull the water kettle forward, bent over to put another stick of pine under the kettle and the neck of her dress gaped open. I saw something dark underneath bulged the neck of her dress.

The mush stuck in my gullet and the back of my neck

crawled. That hair rope was fine enough so's she could have a length of it around her neck; enough of it to throw over a low oak limb would not bulge her dress more than it bulged.

I put the knife I'd took from her down on the table careless as if it couldn't mean a thing and told her, keeping my voice low and easy, "Got a lot of work piled up and won't come back till I get it done."

I knowed what Pa'd think of me, telling a woman what I was up to. It was a man's right to go about his business and a woman's place to keep food hot for when he'd get back. But maybe if she thought she was shed of me for a time, it'd ease her.

I filled my two brass cartridges that fit together tight with sulphur matches, put a handful of salt in my skin pouch and walked out. She never turned her head or took no heed of what I was doing.

I saddled Ranger. Since I was doing her no good, I'd light out for a time.

I'd be free of her while I rode my fence line, lived off the country.

I couldn't get free. I mended fence, I tallied up stock, I snared and spitted quail, trying to get back to how I was before I laid eyes on her. It wouldn't work. The thought of the knife in her hand, the rope maybe around her neck wouldn't let me even sleep. Third day out it come to me I should talk to Ma. That was the thing.

Hoping I'd have luck to find Ma home by herself, I kept Ranger moving right along the fifteen miles of trail to the south. Half the time I kept wanting to turn and ride back to my own place, to see if my woman was still setting in front of a dying fire or if...

I was one of them helped cut Ana Bation down and pack her up the canyon to her father's house. Just the loneness they said it was and they buried her right on the homeplace same as she'd died natural. The Coast said there was more to it than that. Nobody ever will know for sure. No sooner got her buried than old man Bation packed up his horses and the rest of his half-breed family and lit out for the valleys in a hurry.

I was fourteen at that time and so green I told Ma I figgered she must a et something bad to be so small and light and yet with such a blowed-up look to her belly. I wondered why Ma laughed so sour and bitter.

Thoughts about Ana kept chasing me along the trail, making me set the spur to Ranger. I'd start wondering if Pa'd sowed the south field to barley or oats this season and then I'd ride up to some oak with a low stout limb and I'd start thinking of Ana again, then back to my woman.

I'd tried talking to her. I'd tried reasoning with her. Nothing did any good. If she had any sense at all, she couldn't help know I took that knife away from her for her own good. She mightn't follow what I'd meant by my plan of tripping her, but if a body won't talk, won't answer, there ain't no good trying to talk to 'em." One thing I was sure of. I couldn't do better than to ride off to my folks' place and get a word with Ma.

I passed old man Bation's place; another four miles would put me at Pa's gate. If there was aught a body could do for a woman that got herself into the state my wife had got herself to, Ma'd be sure to know what it was. She was powerful handy about the sick and knowed as much of the healing in yerbo-pasmo or yerba-buena as any old Indian that ever lived along the Coast.

I'd sit quiet and say nothing about my home troubles if Pa was there. He was always rubbing his ranch into me. I was bound I'd put a good face on my new-married state in front of Pa and the boys. But not with Ma. If it come about right I'd tell

Ma just how things was.

I unsaddled, put Ranger in the shed and then walked uphill to the house. Ma was setting the noon victuals on the table in their kettles when I got to the door. Without a word she pushed the clapper bell into my hand and I started it ringing its call over the mountains like I did countless times 'ere I'd ever left home. Made me feel warm and fond; Ma had a right good way to make a man feel he was homefolks.

I swung the bell till I was sure Ma wouldn't twit me for quitting too soon and then I went to put the bell on the shelf by the door where she always kep' it. "You been prettying up the place, Ma," I said, fingering the edge of the store wrapping-paper that had been cut to scallops and folded neat to cover the top of the shelf.

Ma put her head to one side and squinted her eyes at the paper and I could tell she was proud of the thing, though she said, short, "No doin's of mine. That's your brother Mel for you. Never saw such a one for house fixing. Times I wonder ain't I been fooling myself all these years and got me one girl for all that all seven of you come with tassels hanging to you."

No use to answer Ma back when she gets such a relish on her. I let it pass by and put my hand on a new stool that was all fixed up with a back to it, a deer hide stretched across the back to make it look mighty easy setting.

"Let that alone," Ma says, real short. "That's Pa's, and he's as choice of it as Balaam is of his right stall. I swear Pa gets more like old Balaam every year of his life but he's plumb tetched by this thing. 'Chair,' Mel calls it, though it's naught but a stool with a back to it. We had real chairs in Indiana. Us Jarvises was good people. Well, one real chair, anyway," she went on, "had rockers to it, too. 'Nother ten, twenty years' time, when I start getting old, maybe, I'd like it if Mel made me one of them kind."

She turned her back quick and went over to the fireplace so I knowed something was bothering her. She kept turned from me and she says, "Mel will go out to the valleys before long. Last one I got left to home. The first I borned of the lot not man enough to break in one of these mountains to his use. He's never said a word, but I know. One of these days he'll be gone away."

I never saw Ma soft before. First, the strange ways of my new wife and now my mother gone soft, sticking her head in the smoke and coughing so I wouldn't notice her eyes too bright. And telling me an Allan man was leaving the Santa Lucias.

I wouldn't a been surprised right then if she'd asked me about my wife instead of waiting till it come up right and natural to speak of. But she didn't ask.

I heard Pa and Mel rattling the wash pans on the bench outside the door and I slid onto my old place on the log bench behind the table. Mel kind a grinned as he slid onto the bench beside me, but Pa just pulled his deerback stool to the head of the table and soon as he set, cleared his throat as he always did.

He bowed his head low over his plate and I knowed Mel and Ma would do the same so I got me a good look at my folks. Ma was standing by the fireplace ready to get the plates filled soon as Pa's grace was over. Ma could do a good day's work 'longside any man on the Coast, but I noticed her hands was bad knotted up and while all the rest of her had thickened some, her neck had thinned. Struck me Ma didn't have no twenty years left before she'd be old. Pa's sandy-red hair was thinning and the wrinkles on the back of his neck struck deep dark furrows among the red of his weathering.

Pa's grace was said in his mind and sometimes it took a powerful time.

When I was a tad I used to think that maybe Pa wasn't talking to God about us and the ranch at all but maybe he was spending the grace time counting up the stock or such like. Now, at thirty-four, and having some knowledge of woman's ways and how they could throw a man off in his stride, I thought Pa pulled the grace out to plague Ma and keep her standing there while the food scorched and stuck to the kettles and what was on the table turned cold in the pots.

When Pa finally lifted his head and cleared his throat again to let us know his talk with God was over, I saw a mean spark to his eye and was sure I had the right of it.

Pa was a little fellow. All seven of his sons, even fifteen-year-old Mel, inched way above him. I saw that though Ma might be aging, Pa was powerful as ever he had been. Come to me that Pa was like a mixture of turkey cock and our old bull, Balaam.

After Ma filled Pa's plate with the stuff she was keeping over the fire and set it before him, he stood up and looked into the pots on the table. He put some beans to his plate and took some from the pot of potatoes. Before me or Mel could reach for the pot that had the pig-weed greens boiled with some of the deer tallow to them, Pa picked it up and walked to the door. He threw pot and all out into the yard and come back cackling like an old gobbler. "Told you that slop'd dry the piss 'n' vinegar out o' men. If ever I see it on my table again I'll throw it, pot and all, in your face."

He set down and I felt like I was a boy back home again. When Pa took up his venison ribs and started chawing 'em, I felt Mel, next me on the bench, let loose the breath he'd been holding. I did the same. I knowed Mel was eased that Pa hadn't let loose of his temper. He was eating, so everything was all right.

I let my mind stray back to my cabin and I guess Pa felt it.

He was not minded to let anyone near him get away from right where he was.

"Push them beans over, Zande."

I could speak to him now because he'd took notice of me. Quick as when I was small and scared of him, I pushed the beans over his way, but I proved to him and to the whole room I was a man on my own.

"How's your hay coming, Pa?" I asked him, equal as any man he'd meet riding the trails.

Pa had a real devil somewhere inside him, I saw it look red out of his eye. I thought he wasn't going to take me speaking up that way, but he didn't seem to want to fight today. He just yelled at Ma, "Don't you see my cup's empty? I want some more yerba tea and I want it hot!"

Soon as Ma got his cup filled and went back to her standing place, Pa turned to me.

Mel went red as Pa said, "Looks fair, Zande, looks fair. Mel did his best to spoil it; cut it so's it laid all wrong, but if a fartin' rain don't come along now and rot it, I'll get enough to pay for my time."

Well, I was glad to know Pa had the best hay crop he'd ever raised, liked seeing Ma once more, standing so's to watch what her men wanted before they knowed themselves, but none of it got my deep thoughts away from my own ranch and Hannah.

Pa was eating fast, Mel doing his best to keep up with him. The minute Pa took a heel of corn-dodger and sopped up the bean-juice and grease from his plate he'd always push back from the table and stand up. He never raised no son of his to set eating once his pa was finished. Mel was trying to catch up. Pa watched till the big gawk had his mouth stuffed so full he couldn't talk and then he barked at Mel, "Got that south field done?"

Pa winked at me, his eye bright with that spark of devil, and waited half a second for Mel to answer. He couldn't, so Pa fetched him a box across the face that popped food out of his mouth like it come from the old muzzle loader. It was comical to see. Looked like a lot of chewed-up wadding that had been well rammed down a barrel as it sprayed across the table. Mel's face went redder than a tomato and his eyes was full of tears from his strangling on a bit he'd gulped the wrong way.

Pa stood up and Mel jumped up, too. I could see Pa's shoulder quiver with the laugh he was hiding. Us boys, if we hadn't been so scared of him, might have got on better with him.

Remembering how I used to feel, dragging my bare feet across stubbles, thistles and rocks, and not feeling a one of them because pretty soon I'd have to be in the same room with Pa, I had a thought of telling Mel, but I put it down. Mel was already too soft. There was no use to make him softer.

I stood up same as Mel did. If there was any notice to him he'd learn a lot from the way I answered Pa. Pa sucked at his teeth and then he took his little finger to push a string of deer meat out from his back teeth, chewing on it as he said, "The barley in the top field is ready. You can pay for your victuals by swinging cradle up there this afternoon."

Mel's eyes was out, like snails' feelers when I said, easy, "I'll be swinging back to my own place this afternoon and you can get your victuals back any time you happen up that way."

Ma made a great clatter with the kettles around the fireplace. Somehow I knowed right then, she did it to make my brash talk easier for Pa to take. Seemed like I learned a lot in the time it would take to snap your finger, a deep lot of how things went between men and women that was together for life.

Pa was at the door before Ma got the last of her pots picked up, and I knowed how spited with me he was when he says at me what the Spanish always say to new-married men, "Break your mare in easy and don't try a year's riding in a week."

He'd made me feel as big a fool as he'd made Mel, and so he went off right pleased. I eased my feelings on Ma.

She was standing with her back to me and I could see her move with the laugh she wouldn't let out. I walked over, closed my hand on her shoulder and swung her around to face me. She looked into my eyes and I saw the laugh go out of hers.

"What's wrong, son?" She asked me.

That stopped me. I didn't know. Everything was wrong. Even Ma. She wasn't acting like an Allan ought to act. It's not our way to pry. I'd knowed she was sure there was something troubling me when I come in at the door. But we sort of ease up to things, not go asking a question that is sharp as a knife-cut. My hand was still on Ma's shoulder and I could feel all she'd been hiding under her laughing; something that was life, like the colt at the old mare's tit, like the lone-feeling a man gets when he cuts into the root of a tall tree. But that sort of life ain't something you show or talk about.

"Nothing's wrong," I said rough and loud. She turned away from me and began to spoon victuals onto Mel's plate for herself.

"Seems like you might plant some garden now," she said. "There's a power of comfort to a woman new to these hills in tending something that grows."

I answered, "Such truck is all right for the valleys but this is a man's country. Next thing I know someone will be telling me I ought to keep a cow and pull milk out of her. I got my ranch now just the way I want it." Ma didn't look up. There wasn't a sign on her face you could read any more than you can find a lion track on a smooth rock, but I knowed she was holding to her thought about a garden.

Ma sat there letting her eyes take in her own truck patch, letting me know without saying a word that she'd finally wore Pa down and got her the garden she wanted. Pa got so used to it he et truck out of it without grumbling, only throwing out a potful now and again, more to devil Ma, I think, than to prove he wasn't going soft. But he never give in about a milk cow.

I set there getting more uneasy. I hadn't said one thing of what I come for and it seemed like I couldn't. Ma could take a word, turn it and worry it till she got out everything there was in it and added on everything of woman there was to her.

There was no use to put words to my ma of what was just between Hannah and me. I'd come home and I'd learned that a man and his ma is one kind of thing and a man and his wife is altogether something else. The word that would unknot the rope from around my wife's neck would not be a word from Ma but would have to come from me.

My slow thinking come in good, for it broke Ma down and she put her word in before I spoke of Hannah to her.

She got up and was putting the food back in the pots by the fireplace when she stopped and said, "When the hay's in, if I can get the use of a horse, I'll come see your wife, Zande."

"Do that, Ma," I answered her.

I got up and started for the door. Ma followed me outside and down the mountain toward the barn, stopping when we come even with the fence that held her truck patch.

She held me still with her hand for a minute on my arm and looked across the canyon to watch a buzzard wheeling as she said, "Happens your woman is the sort that catches quick, son, be easy with her. A child still-born does no one any good."

There was a stray spear of grain growing lone by the trail,

its kernels plump and in the milk. I pulled off the head and a mite of the stem and put it in my mouth, started chomping on it like it was something I was craving. I couldn't even a said, "So long," to Ma at that minute. I was so full of something too big for me to hold that it was like a comet shoots across August. It was a better feeling than any of the pretty-moving words Pa sometimes read from the Book, but at the same time made me cold inside my bones like the hell-fire words could never do.

I hadn't asked a thing, just set quiet with my trouble and Ma had give me the very words to make it all seem clear.

Less than the time it takes for a lightning flash, I had the whole thing clear in my mind. I felt to run for my horse and ride off whooping and yelling but I took my time saddling up Ranger.

I rode off without a word. I knowed Ma was dabbing at her eyes with the bottom of her apron, her thought following me across the hills. I had the wish to turn in my saddle and call back, "We'll be looking for you," but it's not our way.

On the home trail my horse stepped along. Steady up the mountain, careful down the canyon, breaking into an easy trot on benches by the sea. It come to me like a song that went along with my horse's feet, over and over. I couldn't stop thinking, "My ranch, my wife, my son." Nothing in wind or rain, in a good crop or even in the sight of a spring pasture thick with strong new calves, had ever give me the feeling that I had now.

My horse wanted a drink at Deer Creek Crossing and I slacked the reins and let him take his time. I set there in the cool of the canyon floor watching how the water swirled over an old redwood log that had been down time out of mind. The log had softened and settled till it was most flat on top and only held together by the thick green moss that covered it where it lay out of reach of the water. Where the log reached the north

slope of the canyon a red huckleberry bush growed up from the green of the moss and where the branches hung almost to the moss a little long-eared mouse was getting himself a meal of them red berries. I set easy in my saddle watching him, feeling no urge to shy a rock at the little beast or bother him any way.

I felt as little like bothering anything as if I'd been peaceful asleep and so I set easy, waiting for the tremble to go out of Ranger's legs. It was a long steep pull down into Deer Canyon and I got the thought that a horse's legs could have the same feeling as my own, like I felt about the mouse, that his vitals might be gnawing at him like mine had plenty times in my life. It never come to me that Hannah might be feeling any other way about a child than I did. I could think about the horse's legs aching him and the mouse's hunger gnawing him, but not that my woman's thoughts about a child might not be my thoughts. It wasn't till I was almost to my house that I got back the memory of my woman, ailing and thinning, looking at me like dead and maybe hiding a rope around her neck.

I almost wished I'd a told Ma about how Hannah was acting, might happen she'd know some yarb was good for a woman took like that. How she was acting when I left was certainly out of nature, nothing about a child growing in her to make her so queer. All the breeding I'd ever saw was simple as sowing grain to a field. A cow goes to the bull and when it's over she goes on about cropping grass and chewing her cud. When her time comes she puts out her calf without any fuss. Now and again some heifer gets an unnatural way of slunking off her calves before their time is done. There's nothing to do with such a one but to slit her throat and make jerk beef of her.

"Be easy with her—still-born child—"

By the time Ranger was nosing at the swinging gate below my cabin, I had nothing left in me of my feeling to sing. I had the memory of Ma's words to go easy with her and my unease at not knowing how. Tied to my saddle and wrapped cool in ferns I had a bundle of cress I'd pulled in the tumbling water of Big Creek, and a hope there'd be smoke coming out of the chimney.

The house door was shut, there was no look of life about the place anywhere. I rode over to the saddle shed, unsaddled and give my horse a measure of grain. I untied the cress from the hanging saddle and stood there eyeing the house. For the first time in my life it seemed to me that a still, quiet place could have more fear-feeling about it than even the close-by scream of a mountain lion.

"This place is already changed—"

"This place is already changed—"

"This place is already changed—"

Clear as if she was there I could hear what my wife had said. She was right, the place had changed, but I liked her no better for having put tongue to it. Allan men don't take right-words from women; they take them from the Book or they take them from learning life on the trap-line, riding after cattle, or making lumber out of redwood trees.

In all the years I'd lived lone on this spot there had never been a lone feeling to it before. There was food-hunger and food to feed it; work-tired and a bed to rest it away, and a drive to get ahead and make the Coast look up to me that made all my strength not enough, made every long work-day too short.

Now I let my eye stray to the low-branched oak behind the house. If she was hanging there, then she'd made a proper fool of me.

I stood there, holding that bunch of green stuff, and the dead quiet of my homeplace got so it was like a noise.

I couldn't start toward the door.

The quiet of the ridge was broke with the harsh call of the blue-jay and I knowed someone, or something, was coming toward the house from the back. A jay-bird is better than any watch dog and quicker 'n a woman at spreading the news.

The jay was swinging in the madrone tree; his crest bristled up, his head turned sidewise, watching toward a rocky barranca which broke the mountainside and creased it toward the creek just about a hundred yards above the house.

The jay didn't call again, but I heard a loose rock move and then bounce off another rock and go crashing toward the creek. It was no lion. Not like a deer either, for they're no foot-loose creatures but walk proud and careful unless a lion or coyote is after them. I figgered on everything but what come in sight,

My wife, Hannah Allan, come around that pile of rocks at

the mouth of the barranca.

She moved slow and careful, like someone learning to walk in the high mountains, but she walked light. There was a little color to her face from the climbing and I could see beads of sweat standing along her upper lip. The branches growing over the trail must a caught her hair, for some of it was loose from the knot she rolled it into and the sun coming through it made it a soft brown web. She had the ruffle to the bottom of her wrapper in one hand and her other hand and arm was holding a whole mess of red and blue and yellow flowers. The flowers covered her clear to the shoulder and I had no way to know if she had a rope wore around her neck. But her face had a look as though she was smiling. It was that same one that had troubled me in Monterey and made me know she was no easy-broke filly but one for spurs and a curb bit. But I had no thought to change that lighted look. I stood there, enjoying for the first time in my life the look of a woman who moved proud and free as a fawn, thinking there was something about her that was both slighter and stronger than pretty. I looked at her like I'd look at a trout when I was neither hungry or fixed for fishing; lust liking the way she moved and not even thinking of her as mine.

It come to me clear and all of a piece what was the matter between me and my wife. She was a thinking woman and I was a acting man. Throw your leg over a horse and you're in the saddle. Put your gun to your shoulder and your eye follows the sight, your finger tightens on the trigger. Your knife is in your hand and you're skinning the game without any thinking at all. You act and you know what happens. Acting is easy and it comes right. But she'd come to see it, too.

I went into the shed and set down on a cut of redwood log beside the door and began plaiting at a horse-hair jacima. I was wondering if she was aiming to cook that mess of stuff she was carrying home for supper. Sort of tickled me, thinking about a new-married pair eating stewed flowers, and so I got to thinking about Nebuchadnezzar. He got a mournful satisfaction out of eating grass and it might be all right to do. Least-ways it put flesh on the creatures. Ma's words, "Go easy," come back to me again, but this time, after all my tangled thinking that got me no place, the words come to me like a good solid gift of gold money Ma had give me. I wasn't going to try to puzzle out what a woman's meaning of "go easy" might be. I'd act. By God, if my wife cooked them yellow monkey flowers I'd not toss the pot of them through the window—I'd *eat* 'em.

As I got up off the log and walked toward the house something inside me prodded me to the memory of my woman saying, "I hoped to find a friend." It was a big lump for me to try to swallow; a woman who had made a bargain to marry and bear children going behind her pledged word, fighting her man with such a empty word as *friend*.

"I hoped to find a friend—"

How was I to tell this woman of mine that here in these mountains you don't find a friend. You earn a friend, hard as you earn your bread. You make a friend out of your neighbor by keeping to your word, minding your own business, not offering to help until there's nothing else to do. There's an old saw for that, not out of the Book, but plain good sense anyway, "Every tub has to stand on its own bottom."

Us Allans never went around claiming friends. We didn't borrow and we didn't lend. Our troubles we kept to ourselves and settled inside our own fences. There was plenty loose-talking ones going around would say the Allans was good friends of theirs, for we never grudged the strength to do whatever they felt was needful for them. But our own notion was they was a shiftless lot or they could get their own plowing or borning or burying done, proud and lone and bow to none.

Thinking on all these things, I was moving along slow. Shadows sharpened the ridges; already the first star showed pale above the Ventanas and the last gold of day darkened out where the sky touched the sea.

When I pushed open the door I didn't know what to make of what I saw. The food was ready all right. The two plates and the pewter spoon and my horn spoon was on the table, winking in the firelight. My wife was bending down to the fire, stirring up the brown crust on the fried beans.

What she'd done with them weeds she'd carried in made my eyes bug out.

She hadn't cooked the flowers. She'd stuck 'em into cows' horns! She'd tied three cows' horns together with a buckskin thong so they braced again' each other, filled 'em full of flowers and stood it on the table. There was a big steer horn each side of the fireplace, hung so's it would hold water and the rest of the flowers was fixed in them.

The whole thing uneased me. I'd never saw flowers put in a house unless they was trimming it for a funeral. But Hannah had no look of grief. She give me a quick look as she dished the beans onto my plate, a queer look but no sadness in it.

I never let on like I seen them flowers, just picked up my spoon and went to eating. My wife sat down but she didn't pick up her spoon and seemed like all the life had went out of her face.

I wanted to ask her who was dead, what was grieving her, but I couldn't. I was bound not to get her stirred up and shaking again like she was when I went off. I didn't know what was the right way with her.

I leaned across the table toward her.

"The beans is good, Hannah. Best eat some and prove you can go your own cooking. Here's some cress I cleaned and brought you." I got it from the shelf near the door and put it down by her.

Her head straightened up quick, a light come back into her eyes and she picked up her spoon. She et beans and cress with good appetite for a time, like 'twas long since she'd et her fill.

Finally she put her spoon down, sort of smiled at me as she reached over to the cow horn holding the yellow flowers, broke off a short piece of flowers and put it in her hair, catching it in the top of the roll with one of her hairpins, smiling right out as she got the pin settled to its place.

That smile shook me till I blurted out, "What's all the fixing with the flowers for, Hannah?"

She looked straight at me. "A beginning of marriage for us, Mr. Allan. We're strangers. A few words out of a Book spoke over us don't get us over being strangers."

She would a said more but I pushed back my stool and stood up. "Strangers!" I said. "The hell we are. I'm your husband and you're my lawful wife. I give you the leave to take me or go back—"

She stood up, too, and answered me. "I'd no choice," she said. "Nothing to go back to. I'm trying to tell you I'm willing to go on."

"Of course you'll go on," I told her, "you're mine. I took you and it's not my way to turn loose of anything I've made mine. Sane or crazy, slut or decent woman, whatever you turn out to be, you're Mrs. Allan as long as you live and I'll stand by you."

She stood looking at me for a moment and she began to laugh. Then I'm damned if she didn't take a deep breath, and turn that lighted look her eyes could hold full on me. She took both my hands in hers and rubbed tears from her eyes on my knuckles as she whispered, "Thank you, Alexander; I believe you...let's be married?"

At first I didn't know what she was getting at, but she kept looking at me with a glow in her eyes that wasn't firelight, and a softness to her mouth that give me a twist. I'd seen that same look on Maria's face. For all the look was the same, there was none of Maria's looseness about the way my woman offered herself. There was a proud look to her. My arms went around her and as I pulled her close, my legs was shaking like I wasn't fit to stand. Her hair with the flower in it was soft to my face. I heard myself whisper, "I had no woman before you."

This strange woman of mine laughed till she shook the both of us. I thought first to shake the laugh out of her, but she says with a sort of a twinkle, "There's no doubt about that, Alexander," and then I did something was brand new for me, I laughed, too! I had to. I was the one who was always sparing words, and here I was saying something I well knowed I'd proved by acts. I never thought to see the night I'd laugh when someone else was laughing at me. She didn't seem like someone else. She seemed, that night, like she was me. So that I had no shame to whisper to her as I fell asleep, "Your shoulder seems small and soft for such a strong woman, Hannah."

She made me no answer, and as I dropped into sleep beside her, I had a hope she hadn't heard me.

IV

When I woke up the sun was already making the dry grass on the pastures atop Old Baldy look like melted gold running down the sides of the mountain, dripping into the shadowed canyons. Our bunk was on the seaward side of the house, but through the one window to the room I could see the mountain tops rough again' the sky.

Hannah had the fire going and the table set. Thinking it was neat that she took time to get her hair smooth and twisted up into the roll which showed the shape of the back of her head, I lay quiet, like I was still sleeping. Through almost shut eyes I could see now and again the way the ruffle to the bottom of her wrapper swung and turned and followed after her steps.

The bunk seemed soft under me, like floating on my back in a warm sea pool. I almost had a wish not to get up, not to go round on my day's work. Like if I reached for my pants and stood up, all of the night before would be gone. Who was this neat woman stepping soft around my house, putting a stick of wood to the fire, shaving jerky into the cornmeal mush? She was so quiet and quick, so sure of herself, so deft with the knife she'd held in her lap as a threat to me such a short time ago. She was right. We was strangers. I got bashful to face her. I couldn't stand that, so I rolled over in bed and reached on the floor for my pants.

Minute I moved, she took one of the waterskins from its

peg by the door and went outside, closing the door after her. I jumped out of bed, and spite of me bulging the muscles on my arms and twisting around to see the good flat muscle that run down my legs, I couldn't make myself think I was a pretty sight. I pulled on pants and shirt, hooked my cartridge belt around me and looked to my gun. I never shot a coyote when I could trap him without cost, but this morning the belt and the gun made me feel good. I stepped outside and doused my head in the trough and was shaking the water out of my hair and eyes when she come up the trail from the spring. She'd been coming fast, but when she saw me, she slowed her steps.

"Good morning," she says, like she was just come a visiting and hadn't not a hour before got out of my bed.

She looked peaceful, half-smiling and clean as the morning, and all the man-urge in me reached toward her, but I had no mind to let on to her.

I spoke short, "I want breakfast ready by sun-up after this. I got work to do."

She gave me a startled look and then went faster toward the house. On the doorstep she stopped and let the waterskin rest on the ground, just holding it up from spilling by keeping the hide strap taut.

Her voice had a hint of laugh as she said, "I see by the tracks around the spring that you was walking in your sleep last night, Mr. Allan."

The door shut after her with a bang and I stood scratching my head, wondering what she was up to now. The door shut, she couldn't see me, so I went to the spring. All about the spring-box was the tracks of the biggest grizzly I'd ever saw on the sea slope of the Santa Lucias. Over on the valley side such big tracks was usual, but not here. I run back to the meat house and put some jerky in my pocket and was halfway to the house

before it even come to me what she was up to.

I opened up the door and I said to her, "Well, good morning to you then, and to hell with it! Ain't you got sense to know that grizzly will raise hob with my stock? Why didn't you say right out there was a bear running over the place instead of singing out "Good morning" like you'd come twenty miles to see me?"

"I come two thousand miles to see you," she says, keeping to her aggravating way of talking in parables, "and I don't think I've seen you yet. I come closer to seeing a grizzly."

I could see that if you gave her an answer, she'd talk a lot faster than I could think, so I said nothing. I et fast and filled up good, for I didn't know how long it would take me to track down that bear. I unbuckled my gun belt and hung it over the bunk and took down the big muzzle-loader. Hanging by it was the hide pouch I'd made for the balls and wadding. The powder horn slipped onto the strap that held my ammunition and the whole thing went over my shoulder and out of my way.

I could feel Hannah watching me, but I didn't mind. Fact is, I was kind of proud of my shot bag, showing it off. I was right handy with leather, it seeming to come to me natural. My *alforjas*, the waterbags, the way I could cover a saddle, always was good.

I looked careful to the sights, the priming, and all the things needful to get big game with an old gun. It'd be a new thing to me, someone waiting in my house to see the grizzly hide when I brought it in. I would liked to ask Hannah did she ever see a grizzly bear hide, but what was the use? I'd find out when I rode in with it tied on behind my saddle.

I had Ranger saddled and was bringing him out of the shed when she come walking out of the house. She stood quiet by the madrone tree, watching me, both her hands hid in the two pockets of the dark apron she'd tied around her waist. I thought she was fixing to tell me something. She'd said nothing yet about a child coming. I fussed around Ranger's gear for a minute to give her time. But she just stood there.

I rode out through the gate and every minute I thought she'd say something. If living on the prairies made her say "Good morning" to someone that lived right in the same house, it seemed she'd expect "Good-by" from me when I left.

She clear fooled me. She never said a word, raised a finger, or turned her head. I should a been pleased, but I wasn't. It didn't seem like even a mountain woman would stand so quiet in a place where a big bear had been nosing around while her man rode off and left her alone so far from any human.

I put her out of my mind. I had business to do. On a little flat below the house, where the spring-water gathered into a marshy place, I picked up the trail of the bear. He was aiming for the pasture my new calves fed on. I touched Ranger with my heel and he settled into climbing. He was wise and I let his head free so he could get it down while he drawed his haunches up and pushed up that almost straight mescal ridge. It looked like there wasn't footing for a mountain goat, but he found solid places and never rolled a rock. I was going right, for I saw where the big claws of the grizzly had slid, clawing for a hold.

Ranger come out onto a rounded knob that held a few feet of level place just below a broken cliff. I pulled him up, to let him get his breath and part because from here I could see my house, half-mile away and a thousand feet down. It was comical to see how small the field around the house looked from here. Like a man could cross it with a few steps and the house not any bigger than a calf pen. The little figure was Hannah still standing where she was when I rode away. I knew she couldn't see me from where she stood. If I'd a been on the skyline she might of, but with the rock behind me, and me and my horse still, even a market hunter couldn't of picked us out. But I had a queer feeling that she was watching me. The minute I looked at her, she lifted her head and turned and went into the house. She put wood on the fire, for I saw the new smoke. In a minute she was back, standing in the door- yard, and she started singing.

The way sound comes up the canyons, I could hear her as well as if I'd been standing in the yard by the madrone. She had a good ear for a tune, and a strong, clear way of saying the words to a song like it was a story she was telling. I could hear every word.

Do not trust him, gentle stranger,
Though his voice be low and sweet—

I'd liked to a heard more of that story, but she didn't tell no more. She sang the same words over, then she let her head come way back till she must have been looking straight up; her arms went out as though she reached for the mountain top and the sea all to once. She turned, went back to the house.

I started Ranger up the slope toward the pasture, thinking that I wouldn't sell the grizzly's hide along with the rest of the pelts. I'd cure it and let my woman use it to spread on the dirt floor between the bunk and the fireplace. I'd make her a chair with a hide back to it, and hide for the seat, instead of a block of wood. A notion of Hannah sitting in that chair with her feet in the grizzly's fur instead of on the cold ground, singing that song over and over while the fire died down, seemed snug as a good roof in February.

Ranger's ears pointing forward, his feet shifting nervous, brought me back to the work in hand. I was almost as close to the pasture as I was to the house, but sound don't travel down like it carries up. Ranger's ears was sharper'n mine but when I listened hard I heard it.

I heeled him and he started up the mountain fast. When I could see over the edge, over to where the mountainside flatted out into rolling pasture, I almost went crazy.

I could hear the wild bellowing of stampeded cattle as they racketed down the far slope toward Lost Valley. Two calves was laying on the ground with their guts hanging out. Some of the young stock was running blind terror, running into each other, too scared to know where their mothers had went or try to follow. The only cow left on the flat was the little heifer with her first calves. She was trying to keep herself between that grizzly and her twins.

Before I could bring my gun up to fire, the grizzly had closed in on her, broke her neck with a swipe of his paw, picked up them twin calves like they was babies. I never heard their last bleat. My gun fired as the bear straightened up and faced me, hugging my good calves to death.

The big gush of blood started down his front and I knowed I'd hit him square in the chest. I grabbed my sheath knife, threw the reins over Ranger's head, jumped for the ground and run over to finish the bear. To cut that bear to pieces no bigger than my fist, that was my crave.

Seemed there was no time, no need to reload. I let my gun drop in the long dry grass.

The bear didn't fall. He didn't let go them calves. Towering like a tree he stood there, blood in bucketfuls gushing down his front, splashing the ground. His wide-open mouth looked like a red door to hell.

I was close enough to feel the heat of his blood, so full of hate for him that I laughed, and my laugh sounded in my ears like a coyote's howl.

Never come to me to watch out for him. Let him stand over me; a shaggy mountain pouring out blood. My knife was long and sharp, my arm hot to drive the point straight to his heart. Long as he stood like a drunk fool holding them two calves I was safe as I was skinning a dead deer.

I was up to him now, right again' him. I drawed my arm back full length for the blow to finish him. My arm was on the down-stroke when he acted.

Quick as a young one'll throw a sugar-tit to the floor, he dropped them calves. Quick as light he swiped me. I felt my jumper pop open and heard, more'n felt, the rack of his claws again' bone. Before I could jump clear, he had me.

Both his front legs wrapped me, hugging me to his bloody breast, my face again' his sticky hair. The wound bled in my face till I thought I'd drown in blood. My arm hung useless but my fingers still clutched my knife.

The grizzly squeezed me till I felt my ribs cracking, my senses going, but my hands acted as by themselves. My good arm and hand felt for, reached, grabbed the knife out of my right hand. I pulled my belly in again' my backbone so's I could get the knife between me and the grizzly, get it pointed up at his heart and make his own strength bury it in him.

I was a goner, but for all the singing sounds in my head and the blackness closing down, I held my idea to take that grizzly down into death with me.

Next thing I knowed I heard voices. The words I heard was, "God A'mighty, he's breathing." I thought folks in heaven or hell, wherever I'd got, must take their own mountain talk along with 'em.

Something harsh and fiery hit my gullet. I was in hell all right. No one in heaven'd be offering newcomers raw stuff straight from the still and that was what I was trying to spit out. I thought if I could tell 'em I was one of the Allans, it might put things straight. I must a said it.

I heard a laugh I knowed belonged to no one but Old Songer. He was a tough old coot who made out to mine over to the Barlow Flats, but his mine never paid out nothing but mountain dew.

He went on laughing till I wished for strength to knock him flat, and he finally gasps out, "Hear that, Bill? This here's an Allan boy. Never thought you was a grizzly, Zande, or I wouldn't a wasted good stuff on you."

Bill Pincus from over Nacimiento way was along with Songer. He's the one that sent the letter over to the Coast asking Demas for his girl Raquel when she was fourteen and Bill was twenty. The Demases give him the girl and a big wedding. Less than ten months later Bill lost the girl and his son died in the borning. Bill was a good catch but he was over forty now and still a widower.

It was Bill stopped me when I tried to sit up. "Take it easy, Zande," he says. "This here place looks like you'd been having *metanza* and you got the worst of it."

"There was a bear—" I was fearful maybe he'd got away.

"Sure was a bear." Songer's beard started wobbling again and he got another of them crazy laughing fits he's always having. Living alone and spirit drinking, both of 'em together queers a man mighty quick.

My head cleared and I saw Songer sitting on his heels, a flat flask in his hand. He took a pull at it and stopped laughing, at least while he swallowed. Then he went on blabbing: "You got so much b'ar hair and blood on you, the b'ar was wrapped around you so, we could a took you for a grizzly cub easy enough. Was a hard job to pry you loose from him. You bad hurt?"

I wasn't going to tell the old fool how I felt. It was my bad luck to have 'em come along and find me. Bill Pincus was all right, a quiet fellow that always smelled of goats. He kept a big herd of 'em on the headwaters of the Nacimiento. He didn't get to the Coast once in a couple of year, seemed like. Even with every bone in my body feeling like I'd been through an arrastre, I did wonder what he'd be doing over to this side, now.

I sat up though my belly had no mind to help me keep my breakfast down. My left arm would lift so I run some of the blood off my face with the back of my hand.

The grizzly, stretched out about ten feet away, was the biggest I ever saw. I was wondering how I was to get on my feet, get him and the calves skinned and the hides packed onto my saddle, when Bill Pincus, who'd been rubbing his chin round and round with his thumb, spoke up: "I'd like to buy that grizzly hide, Zande."

In my head was the picture I'd made of my woman feeling proud to put her feet on that hide. But I set out as if to bargain with Bill.

"What'll you give?" I asked him.

He fell to studying the bear careful, even looked at his claws. "Not much for this hide," he says, fingering some coins I could hear rubbing together in his pocket. "Something wrong with this bear; his claws is gray."

I looked hard at Bill. From the look on his face I saw he meant it. I showed my pride in knowing such a thing when I told him, "That's a habit with bears, Bill. Brown bear, brown claws; black bear has black claws, and these here silvery-gray old grizzlies has the same color to their claws they got to their hair."

Bill was a slow-talking man. He went clear round that old bear and looked at every claw on him, tried his hair some places to see would it shed out, and then seemed to make up his mind.

"What'll you take?" He asked.

I looked at the bear a long time without saying a word. Then I told him, "Seems like I hear them bear hides sells about a cent a pound out Monterey or thereabouts."

Now a cent a pound wouldn't be much even for such a big hide, and I rested myself on my good elbow, my legs stretched flat on the ground while Bill figgered this out.

He finally got around to putting his hand on his skinning knife but didn't pull it out of its case. Bill is a good-mannered fellow, don't help unless he's asked and keeps a close mouth.

"'Twouldn't take me long to skin the bear," he says, "and I'm a fair hand at guessing the weight of things by hefting. If you like, I'd skin him and take a guess at its weight."

"Too much trouble, Bill." I turned on my belly and put my

face on my good arm. "You might go to all that work and then I'd think maybe more of the hide than of the money 'twould fetch."

I'd have to take a chance he didn't make no false cuts to that hide. I shut my eyes and paid no heed to anything.

The blood on my back was getting stiff and the ache in the bone told me the wound had stopped bleeding and took to hurting. But there's healing in sunshine, and as soon as I got home, I'd get Hannah to make a poultice of fresh sage leaves and I'd be all right.

With my head down in the warm grass I could hear the feet of the horses move now and again as they stamped at a fly. I could hear a gurgle as Old Songer pulled at his flask and I could feel myself slipping off to sleep.

I did drift off, for it seemed I come back from a long way when Bill stood over me with the skin rolled into a big bundle and him hefting it doubtful: "I think it runs between sixty-five or seventy pounds.

"I looked at him hard.

"I'm willing to give a dollar for it as it stands," Bill says.

A dollar is a lot of money. Seemed like I was a fool to refuse. That big grizzly hide would hold a power of fleas. I told myself that maybe Hannah wouldn't even want it round the house. But I thought of her narrow feet in the thin shoes.

"Bill," I told him, "this here's the biggest grizzly I ever shot and I sort of feel to keep the skin for myself. I shouldn't a put you to all that trouble, but I'll make it right with you."

"No trouble at all, Zande."

He picked up the hide and carried it over to Ranger. The horse snorted and pulled back, but Bill tied the hide on good and tight. Then he come back and says, "You'll want them calf hides and while my knife's out, I'll get 'em and the heifer skinned."

I didn't answer him. I couldn't. My good little heifer and her twins. Try to figger what her increase and their increase would have meant in a few years' time.

When the work was done and the hides tied on, I said, "You take the meat, Bill. You done me a good turn."

I couldn't see anything else to do. Bill didn't answer for a time and then he says, "Well, if that's the way you want it, I'll share up the fresh with Songer and some of the jerk will go well with my beans next winter. I get tired of goat meat, too much like mutton and a man sickens of it. The veal's a loss. Too young, and besides the bear made jelly of it. I bled the heifer and the dogies soon as we rode up and they're all right."

As I stood up, the whole world was whirling, but I took a step forward toward Ranger and the pain cleared my head.

"Bill, I guess I'm going to have to have help to get on."

He fidgeted a minute, stammered. "We was on our way to your place when we heard the stampede and rode over here, instead of taking the main trail down-ridge. We was fixin' to ask you and your wife to a doings down on the flats. There's a notion to have a big Thanksgiving dance and barbecue and we got to start passing the word along."

I had no notion of going, not with Hannah. I says, "I got too much work to do to be counted on, Bill, but thanks for coming over to tell me."

I thought Songer was too drunk by this time to pay any mind to what was going on, but as Bill boosted me into the saddle, Songer stood up, weaving around and swinging the bottle.

"We won't take 'No' for answer, will we, Bill?"

I said again, "I got too much work laid out this year to take time for visiting. I'll lose time, too, now I got this back bunged up."

Songer acted as if I didn't count. He swung the bottle

round his head and sent it crashing again' a boulder. "Get the nags, Bill," he said. He was so drunk his voice was thick as liver and spit drooled down his chin and hung onto his whiskers. I thought maybe he'd sit down and go to sleep again but no such luck.

"Come on, come on. What you waiting for? Get the nags and we'll go down and see Zande's new wife. I bet we don't have to coax her to go to a barbecue, not when there's dancing."

I didn't want them two riding down to my shack and talking to Hannah.

She was all right when I left, but I don't know what she was up to; stretching up her arms to the sky when she stopped singing. I didn't want her going to barbecues, showing her lack of knowing about our ways. There was no need. She couldn't be lonesome, for she hadn't been in the country long enough, and beside, my mother was coming up when haying was done.

Bill led up his and Songer's horses and I couldn't see any way out of it.

"Never mind riding down, boys," I said. "I'll come to the party and bring my wife. You get that meat cut up and saved from the flies, Bill."

Bill says, "I was thinking about that."

He took a rawhide from his saddle and got ready to hist the little heifer up to a stout limb so he could gut her.

I picked up Ranger's lines in my good hand. As Ranger stepped off slow and careful, my shoulder hurt like blazes, but I had to laugh. Old Songer swayed on his feet, his feet staying put, but his shoulders drawing a bigger and bigger circle till he up-ended himself and fell flat on his face. He never stirred, just acted like he'd fell on his own bunk.

Getting down to the house wasn't easy. Half the time I

couldn't see the sky for the big black spots that come over it when Ranger crab-footed down the steep places. Long streaks of pain went shooting up through my shoulder and then went on turning like wheels. Part of the time I didn't know where I was at.

I let down the first bars in the fence, stepped Ranger through and got 'em back in place. At the fence where I had only one rail to take down I tried to lean over and reach it from the saddle. I got it pulled back all right and Ranger stepped across with me still on his back.

Then I felt Hannah trying to lift me. I was lying on my back alongside the spring-box and my woman washing my face like a baby. I knowed I was thought the best rider and the best hunter in these parts, but that ain't the sort of thing you can tell your wife. When I seen her wrinkling her nose, washing up my blankets, I'd had the thought that I never claimed to be any housekeeper. But I kept my tools oiled, my fences mended, and I could ride and shoot. I'd been thinking she might come to know them things about me.

She'd never think it now.

One thing I had to be thankful for: my woman didn't put on any silly fuss. Hannah acted cool as Ma would of done. Washed off my face and put a wet rag to my forehead, another to the back of my neck, and didn't ask questions.

I hated saying anything. If I could a crawled off till I was myself again, I'd a done it.

I couldn't get the fence to stop flowing past me or the trees to acting like trees ought to and standing still, but I propped myself up on my good elbow and said, "Stop washing at me, Hannah. Get some fresh sage tips and scald 'em down to make a poultice. I'll be up to the house in a minute."

I felt better when my woman says, "Where's the sage?"

I'd heard some dumb things said, but that topped 'em all. The whole mountain was covered with sage. The more I burned off to make pasture land, the more it come back. She was sitting where she could reach out her hand, fill her arms with it. She didn't even know sage.

A woman so ignorant that she didn't know sage when she brushed again' it, likely wouldn't think any less of her man for being too weak to sit his horse. I had a lot to learn her.

"Sage grows everywhere, 'most, and special where you don't want it," I said. I felt like the weight pressing on my chest had lifted. "It's that gray-leaved stuff with the blue blooms on it, right there by your knee."

My wife pulls off the head of a branch of sage that had been close enough to her to tickle her nose, and she looks at it, bruises the leaf, and tastes it. Her eyes wide, she turned to me like she didn't hardly believe it.

"Why, it is sage! It really is. It's got a stronger taste than sage like you put into stuffing, but I could use it if I took less. The flower is purple."

The notion of this old maid from Kansas telling me what color the flower was, when she didn't even know what sage looked like, stirred me up, but I ached so hard I had nothing left to get mad with. I said, "Have the poultice ready when I get to the house and don't bother me." I couldn't even tend my own horse, had to tell her, "Unsaddle Ranger. Turn him into corral—feed him. And rub salt in that bear skin. Rub it in good." She took the bottom of her apron and started plucking tender sage tips, flowers and leaves, and I took no notice of anything till I heard Ranger's bridle shake.

As I inched my way up the trail I could smell the sage boiling. She was putting the scalded stuff into cloths as I reeled toward the bunk. The bunk come up and hit me.

It was dark when I opened my eyes. The fire in the cooking place was bright and something smelled good. My clothes was off and my clean cloth shirt was pulled over my head, buttoned at the neck and wrists. The shirt smelled clean; so did the blankets, and it come to me it was a nice thing when a man is hurt, to have a woman doing things for him.

Whatever my wife was stirring in the black iron pot smelled fine even though I felt too sore to move. I watched Hannah. Her face was turned half toward the bed where I was laying in the shadow and she couldn't see me.

She had a look to her face that was pleasing to see. She didn't look as though fighting come natural to her at all and I was full of doubts she'd ever give growing sons the clouts it took to help their father keep them in shape. I got to thinking the look she had to her face was bright and soft as the flower in her hair the night I'd held her so close and found her soft all over, but still hot and strong…

I got to wondering what she thought about when her face looked smooth and peaceful like it done now.

She suddenly got up, poured the horn mug full of what was brewing in the pot and walked with the dose over to my bunk. She was smiling, bright and warm as the light from the fire, and her voice was soft when she said, "Could you drink some soup now?"

I'd have to watch myself or she'd have me softened down till I wasn't tough enough for living in the hills.

"I couldn't drink it before you fetched it," I grumbled. She paid my growling no heed, but slid her arm under my head and made the drinking easy for me. I never saw nothing like that before, and again it come to me that the ways this woman was raised with must've been nothing like the ways I knowed.

I was feeling weak all right, for it almost seemed, a pity that she'd have to learn new ways. But she'd set her face to the west and her feet to the hills and taken me for her man. She would have to suit her ways to what I wanted.

After I drunk the hot soup Hannah turned the straw pillow, shaking some softness into it and fitting it good around my shoulders so I could lay easy and still have my head high enough to see the room. I watched her fill the mug with soup for herself and then drag the stool over close by and lean her shoulders again' the bunk, looking at me, smiling at me, saying nothing. I wished she would ask me about the grizzly, but she didn't. I admire a woman to be close-mouthed; Ma is like that, but there's such a thing as the right time to speak out. I made up my mind she was crafty, waiting for some reason of her own for me to bring up the grizzly bear hunt. It was like she was measuring her strength again' mine and I thought if it took forever for her to ask me about it, I'd wait till she did and her feet could go cold on the dirt floor for all of me.

She set the horn mug down on the floor beside her. Then she crossed her legs, the bend of one resting on the knee of the other, and she let her foot swing free and sat silent, smiling, smiling. I should of told her not to set that way, but if I did I was going to miss the chance to look at her narrow foot and her small-boned ankle. It was nice to look at, the shining black shoe laced close and neat with black cord string instead of hide strings. Where the string had been tied, the ends were tucked out of sight inside the shoe and there was no loose ends to keep a man's eye from following the leather piece that had been cut in scallops and went around the top of the shoe and then down both sides of the lacings. It was neat enough leather work to have gone good on a saddle and made the paper Mel had scalloped and put on Ma's shelf seem a poor thing.

It was good weather and she could have known enough to put them fine shoes away and gone barefoot till I got her some cowhide shoes made, but if she didn't know sage when she seen it, she just didn't know how things were here, not at all.

She leaned closer to me and her hand touched my arm, went slow down along it and her long fingers closed around my hand. Her head come forward, bent down till it was resting on both our hands. I wondered if she was took sick, but the way her shoulders eased again' the side of the bunk, soft as a fawn curling up for sleep, told me she felt all right. She let the breath out from her nose in a long sigh and tightened her fingers on my hand.

"It's good to have someone to do for, Zande. I'm sorry you're hurt—" Her voice trailed off and then she turned her head and smiled. "But having you here, easy from things I could do for you, gives me the feeling that this is us, this is home."

There was nothing I could put a finger to, but I had a feeling close to tears. I didn't know what sort of answer to make to her. I couldn't say a thing.

The fire was dying down before she went over to the corner where she'd fixed her own things on a couple of pegs. I could make her out some in the glow from the coals. She got into her night-shift so quick I felt cheated. Though I ought to be glad my woman was modest.

Hannah got into the bunk and put her head on the pillow, close to mine.

"Your high wild land," she said, sounding like Mel when he was a sleepy little coot and slept 'longside me. "Seems so close to heaven, the big stars an' all."

I thought she was falling asleep. She laid quiet for a time and then she says, "Zande, ain't we going to be strangers in heaven when we get there?"

She turned her head like she was listening and I tried to roll her off from such notions. "You rub salt in them hides like I told you?"

"M h'm, I salted 'em good, Zande. Hadn't we ought to live for some fun here, so's we'll not be shy of folks when we get there?"

She was beyond me.

"Women don't know nothing about heaven but what their men folks tell 'em," I said. "It ain't fitten for women to expound scripture, that's men's work. Just keep to your own work and get your thought about the hereafter from me. You don't know nothing about heaven anyway; no mortal does."

She was quiet under the covers for so long, I thought she'd went to sleep till she said, "Maybe I don't know nothing about heaven, but I can tell what hell's like. I was there."

I pulled myself back, far as I could, to the wall. Even if I hadn't been all clawed and chewed by that grizzly I wouldn't a took Hannah Allan to myself that night. She was crazier than ever I feared she was.

Took me quite a spell before I could say to her, "Do crazy people have crazy children, do you know?"

She propped herself up on one elbow and seemed like she stared at me a long time before she said, "Well, I hope not. You got any crazy folks in your family?"

It was plain to me she didn't know there was aught wrong with her. I didn't know what to say. 'Twas no use to tell her what I was thinking. I answered, real careful, "Not as I know."

She chuckled till the saplings under the tick was shaking and it uneased me till I blurted out what was top in my mind, "You got a baby yet?"

Much as I knowed I counted on having me a son by next spring, I never knowed how much I'd hoped for him, till she said, short and sharp, "No, thank God!"

The big wound in my shoulder and that deepest one on my leg got proud-flesh to 'em, spite of the sage poultices. When the fever run high, I talked. Could be I talked about Hannah. I don't know. But that wife of mine hung over me day and night, keeping them poultices hot; I'll say that for her.

After the red streaks stopped running up my legs and down my arm, my fever cooled off and I quit brooding. I asked Hannah straight out again, was she growing a baby.

She answered me the very words she'd said before:

"No, thank God!"

When I tried to pull away, she took hold of my good hand and hung onto it. "Don't look like that, Zande. You ain't got no need."

I tried to shove her hand from me. Harsh as I could, I told her, "You don't care how you lie. 'Fore you married me you told me you wanted children."

"I do want," she answered me. Her voice was soft and her words, slow-spoke, like every word had deep meaning. "You got your land, your stock, work. That's life, building 'em. I want life, too. Children—a houseful of 'em" She hid her face again' the covers and her whisper come so low, I could scarce hear. "Rape-children's simple minded. Is what I always heard. You don't want that no more'n I do—"

"It ain't rape when a pair's married."

"Ain't it?"

The way she said that. I couldn't face it. I tried to turn away but I didn't have the strength. She put her hand under my good shoulder and helped me turn my back to her. She pulled the cover straight and tucked it again' my neck, her voice warm and kind-sounding. "Don't turn away, Zande. You think that same hunger never gnawed me? I been lone, too. Only when I come here—I was so tired—I know life's been hard for you."

Know about me? How could she? "I don't need pity," I told her. "I always get what I want. I'll keep on."

She took her hand off my shoulder, stood up. "I guess you will, all right. You're strong. But it's time you started wanting what a grown man'd want."

She give me no time to answer, just plowed straight on. "If I'd got caught that night—" She broke, swallowed like 'twas bitter. "If I had—well, I wasn't going to have no idiot. I'd kill myself first. I was crazy. I know what hell's like, now. I was in it."

I took a long breath, turned my head and looked at her. She wasn't no crazy woman. That was the hell she was talking about the night I'd got back, all clawed up by the grizzly.

She was quiet for a long time. I didn't want her to stop talking. I wished I could a told her so.

Suddenly she shook her head like to shake away whatever she was thinking, lifted one shoulder, let it drop, and I looked for her to let out a long sigh.

She laughed.

I guess I never will know what'll make her cry or what'll make her laugh. That laugh startled me so I shied like a wild colt and then she let out a ripple of laughing. "What a goose I was; thought I'd come to the end of life for sure. 'Twas nothing but fear, making me so sick, so crazy. When I found out, it was just before you rode off and left me to myself. I come round when I run out to the shed with that rope, so I knew I was all right. I hadn't got caught either time you took me against my will. There was still a chance our first one could get a right start."

I wanted to believe her. I couldn't. She wasn't telling the truth.

"What you tie that rope around your neck for, then? Don't tell me you never— I seen it. Not ten minutes before I lit out."

She looked puzzled, then her face cleared and she tipped her head back and laughed again. "I did take a piece of that rope. I thought maybe you wouldn't let me have it so I hid it 'round my neck. It's over there." She pointed to the pegs where her clothes hung. "My good dress was getting all wrinkles."

It was the same thin hair rope, all right. She'd strung a double length of rope between the pegs so's she could put her black traveling dress out flat. Well.

I couldn't say nothing. I looked at her. I looked at her, waiting, and she went on talking:

"It helped a lot, when you went off and left me alone. I never got enough loneness in my life. Always people around, other folks' slops to empty, plates to clean. Other people's children to tend, nothing of my own."

Then she set quiet, thinking, for a long time. Her hands didn't move, her head didn't turn, her breathing seemed stilled as the rest of her. That quiet of hers took hold of the room. When a lizard suddenly run across the doorstep, it sounded loud as a stampede.

Hannah's head turned sidewise to look at the lizard, but I don't reckon she saw him. I thought she must be looking back to the life she'd come from. I wished I could see what she was seeing. But it was a womanish notion and I put it away from me. Her life two months back and two thousand miles off had nothing to do with us. Right there on my place was where we was living, she and me together.

I settled easy again' the bunk, my fears about my wife seeming like a bad dream I'd had. She was a good woman. For all she was eager as myself when she was in bed with me of her own will, and I'd always heard tell that ain't the way of married women, still I felt she was good, as well as natural as the critters.

I was drifting off to sleep when I felt her hand touch mine and looked up to catch her smiling that strange, secret smile of hers. She waited, like she thought I'd maybe say something. She kept looking at me, her eyes bright, waiting. But I had nothing I wanted to say. I might say too much, feeling soft toward her as I done.

I got to wondering if she'd stretched that bear hide out good and well-salted it, but I stopped thinking about the bear hide when I heard:

"I was scared when I come here. This country's all so steep, so big and wild—so close to heaven. It scared me." She leaned over the bed, laughing and close to me as she said, "You scared me, too."

"I aimed to. The man's the boss and you'd best not forget it."

She smiled, like I was funning, and said, "...whatever you turn out to be, you're Mrs. Allan as long as you live and I'll stand by you."

Them was my words. She was saying them back to me like they was such a charm as the Indian women used, like they was the rain-prayer I'd heard my own father say. They come back to me queer, having even deeper meaning than I'd put into the words the night I said them to her.

That was the end of our talk.

As my strength come back, I was well content with her friendly look, her head on my shoulder, and the knowing she was there when I turned in bed and half woke from sleep.

It was most of a month before I was much on my feet and my days of laying-up in the cabin, watching Hannah go around sprinkling the dirt floor, going over it careful with her brush-broom, was days when my thinking habits seemed to grow and leaf out fast as corn grows in good weather.

She was the worst one for cleaning and redding up things ever I see. A man could hardly use a shirt ere she'd snatch it, have it washed and on the line, but the feel and smell of 'em, clean and full of sun and wind, got to working on me. Come to me a house could look 'most as good as a tool shed.

Watching from my quiet corner, I come to sense my wife had a feeling of shortness in time—alive, a urge to crowd time full of living. It fretted me to have her act more alive than I'd ever had time to do. Spite of doing her work and mine, too, she had time left over for foolishness.

She'd run out into the dawn in her night-dress and call back to me with a lift to her voice: "I can taste the morning, Zande. It's fine to feel, to smell of. Think of it; the sun's pinking the mountain and we're alive."

I couldn't taste no morning, That kind of talk from her just give me a bitter taste, set me thinking of that outlander, that man Avery. How easy my woman talked to him…how easy he'd answered her.

But most of the time I was wondrous patient and contented, even though I was still a-bed and the days warming toward summer. The first rest-days I'd ever had in my life was forced on me and I filled out some, soon as the fever left me.

I had time to lay and make plans for my son, to wonder if he'd favor me or maybe take after Ma's side and be like the Jarvis folks. Anyway, was he a Jarvis or an Allan—even a Martin, though that thought come to me queer—he'd be a worker.

The weeks went on and my woman never said a thing. Got so them words of Ma's, "if she catches," was as mocking as the old jay-bird yelling his ya ya ya from the madrone tree. Plenty times I was minded to ask Hannah was there something wrong with her that she wasn't rounding out. I wouldn't do it.

Along the middle of June, with the work piling up and me still limping and no account and no sign my wife had any hopes of giving me a boy to count on for help, I was getting real low-down, wondering why a fellow set out his plans so careful if they all dried up on him.

One of them warm still mornings in late June Hannah run out the house soon as the eastern sky pinked.

She kept singing out, "Sunrise, Zande! Look here. Look out the door."

I was blue and low-down as a man can get, felt like, "Oh, the hell with the sunrise—"

She kept on, "Sunrise, Zande! Come see—" over and over with a voice that coaxed me to the door spite of myself.

There she was, standing halfway between the house and the madrone tree, smiling up at the pink sky and patting at that little flat she has for a belly.

When she turned and seen me standing in the door, she flashed me a smile and give a jump like a ten-year-old, calling up to me, "Look, Zande, look! If you look sharp, can't you see I'm rounding out? We going to have a new Allan yelling around here, come February."

Before she could turn her head, I saw her smile twist, her face start to work, but she picked up both sides of her night-rail and went skipping off toward the barn like she was dancing. It got me, too. I had to fight to keep from shouting out, "Hallelujah!" I was scared she'd turn round, catch me, shook clear out of myself. I says, "Well, it's about time."

She stopped skipping, dropped the white shift so it folded down again' the wet grass, and looked hard at me, her eyes hot.

When I says, "I'll get him to help me with the round-up, come next spring—" she looked at me for a moment, then she started to run up the trail to me.

She was out of breath, half-laughing, half-crying, as she come up close, looked at me like she asked me something.

I pulled her over close, grabbed the night-rail by the back and pulled so's it fit tight across her front. I looked it over, taking my time, feeling to laugh as she pinked up.

"Well," I says, "it's sunrise all right. Can see it on your face." I give her a shake and told her, "Mrs. Allan, maybe you're a rounding if you say so, but by God, I swear a fellow'd have to spit on his fingers to find it."

She tipped her head way back, took a look at me and then started chuckling. She switched her night-rail out of my fingers, went into the house and before I could hobble down to the tool shed, I heard her pulling pots along the crane, singing that song about not trusting the gentle stranger.

I got around to the back of the shed where she'd nailed up the hides like I told her. Was a good feeling as I took up a handful of salt and rubbed it well in around the paws and the thick places. I tried the hair and felt satisfied.

Mrs. Zande Allan and son could sit on that rug and he'd not be getting a mouthful of loose bear's hair to choke him up; I'd make the chair with the back to it, a better chair than Pa had.

February. That's what she said. February. Seemed a long time away from June, a weary long piece to wait for the boy I wished was already running over the hills. But February was a good time for an Allan man to come into the world. Winter's back was broke by then, the hills was green and the new calf-crop past the wobbly stage and kicking up their heels full of life.

Next February I'd show the new calves to my new son.

My son...

PART TWO

V

Haying time passed but Ma never come riding over. I'd forgot about it, what with me and Hannah riding the hills together. She was learning to ride and to work cattle, with me. I was working cattle and learning to laugh, with her. It was a short summer.

All that time the only trouble come up between us was when she said my late calves looked on the spindling side. I knowed it. I'd been going to tell her the stock was running down, that I was fixing to get new blood into the herd. It gnawed on me, having a stranger to the hills and a woman at that, pointing out there was any lack in my cattle. But I never let on she'd nettled me, let it pass by. Once I got new stock I'd tell her and maybe we'd both laugh.

Wasn't till the maples in the canyons started yellowing for fall that I remembered about Ma. I guessed Pa'd put his foot down. He'd figger she could take in the barbecue and see what sort of woman I'd found me, at the one time. My wife didn't need no one to speak up for her; my folks would see I'd did right well in my marrying.

Only thing left that worried me at all was how eager my woman was to lay hold on that trunk of hers and to get to this barbecue. As November drew closer Hannah got so she was counting the days. I hoped she wasn't going to turn out to be one of them kind that always wants to be going some place.

As time went by I got Hannah so's she could tell time of day fair enough by looking at the sun. But she said it mixed her not to know was it Tuesday or Friday, less'n she asked me. Things like that never mixed me none.

One day she borrowed my straight-edge and ruled herself out a calendar on a smooth piece of board, tacked it up on the wall by the window. She set great store by it, looked at it a whole lot and last thing before she got into bed, struck off the day as finished.

When she started in to cross off November days, there was a dance to her eyes and she went around humming herself a tune as she got our stuff ready. After she washed my buckskins and my cloth shirt, she smoothed that shirt with her fingers till a man'd swear it had a smoothing-iron run over it. She worked over them buckskins till every fringe was straight and even as new.

The early morning of Thanksgiving Day she fetched some scissors out of her satchel and wanted to trim up my hair.

"Ain't no use trying to make a dude out o' me," I growled.

My hair got trimmed. Then she laughed me into letting her part it straight down the middle and rub bear's grease on so's it lay flat.

I never give no thought to clothes before; just so I was covered. But now, after the horses was saddled and the steer I'd dressed to tote to the barbecue was quartered and sacked, all the best cuts packed in the alforjas slung over Nip's back, I kept thinking about my looks. I got into all my party-fixed clothes and went down to the spring, special, to take a good look at myself in the still water. It was all right. Even my hair looked good. Before I set down on the chopping-block to wait for Hannah to get herself fixed up, I brushed the chips off the block!

It was a nice feeling, being all clean, sitting in the early warmth of the sun, looking down my long legs at the clean cream-color of my pants with their fringes, I leaned back peaceful, looking way down the ridge to where the morning fog hung over the flats, knowing that by the time we rode down the mountain and got to the barbecue, the fog would be gone wherever fog goes and the sky would be blue as the sea.

Come to me all of a sudden that I'd been setting on the chopping-block, waiting for that wife of mine, long enough to get numb in the seat.

I stood up. The leg the bear crushed still stiffened up easy. I limped toward the cabin shouting, "What's keeping you? The day's half gone—"

I stopped and looked up when I heard Hannah's voice, sort of flustered, calling, "I'm ready. I'm coming."

There she stood in the doorway, her head high, her eyes

eager, shining bluer than her blue wrapper with the white stars.

She come hurrying toward me, but she caught my look, took a couple of slow steps, then stopped. Her voice went flat when she said, "You don't like it—?"

"Like it!" I was shaking mad at the little fool. "Like it! If I'd a knowed what you was up to in there, I swear I'd a shot you before I'd let you cut off your hair!"

She answered back, "I never cut it. I only cut bangs. I like 'em."

One hand went across her mouth, her eyes begged me as she touched the bunch of frizz with her long fingers. "My curls, Zande—they're nice. I made curling tongs out o' two nails."

I couldn't answer. I caught both her arms under mine and dragged her to the water trough. She kicked like fury, but she never uttered a sound, not even when I doused her head in the trough. I turned loose of her and said, "When you get yourself fixed like a decent woman we'll go. It's getting late."

I walked down to the tool shed and tried looking at my tools to cool off. I couldn't stop wondering why she done such a thing. Here we was, getting along all right, me feeling proud to take her down to the Coast and show my new wife, and she gets out of my sight and trims herself up like a Monterey harlot.

It was middle-morning before she come out again. She'd pulled some long hair forward so's to cover up the part she'd chopped off, unbraided the lump she'd fixed up in the back, and her hair looked like it always did. She'd put on the same black dress she'd come to the Coast in, the plain black bonnet, but no fluff of lace. There was no shine to her eyes, and she walked slow.

I felt I'd taken a strong hand to her as I come over to where she was standing alongside the saddle horses, looking meek and quiet. I was watching out though, and wouldn't a been startled if she'd took a kick at me when I lifted her into the saddle.

She never looked at me. Just spread her skirt so it flowed nice from the side-saddle and then set, holding in the mare until Ranger, with the pack animal following, was moving down the trail.

I looked back and she was following along, sitting pretty easy spite of the steepness of the trail. She'd learned a lot about riding in a little time; I'll say that for her. She picked it up quick.

She didn't seem to notice me none, kept her head down and her face had that closed look.

Her wearing her town clothes uneased me. Her wrapper hadn't got much wet or wrinkled when I put her head in the water trough. There was no call for her to change it for this other dress that didn't look so good on her, no call at all unless she was up to something. If she put the black dress on to spite me, she was wasting her time. I admit it give me a turn when she come out the house in it. I see how neat she'd patched up where I tore it the night she come here—but that was all past.

Then it come to me what she was up to. She was fixing to ride away.

By the time I figgered this out we was already down the mountain and out on the flat, I could see the smoke from the cooking fires.

I made up my mind to turn around, take her back to the cabin. The trail was wider here, the flats cut with plenty of cattle trails. Hannah give Ginger a prod and the little mare swung sidewise, leaped out ahead of Ranger and Nip.

I'd a headed her off, had it out with her, but as she passed me, she turned in her saddle, looked over and give me as nice a smile as man could ask for.

I slowed Ranger to a walk and she pulled the ginger pony one side so I could ride beside her. We was so close to the doings, I could hear the children shouting in some play game.

"We're most there," I warned her. "Say no more'n you have to. You're a stranger and they'll be watching for you to say something they can have fun over." Her jaw set and she took a firmer grip on the bridle, but she didn't answer.

As we rode up I saw it was a real, bang-up doings. All of the flat that was level enough for the party had been raked clean of cow dung. There was only a trickle of a creek across the flat, but there was a good spring, and it was cleaned out good and the fire-pits dug close by so's to be handy. I could smell the new-cut redwood even before I saw that tables'd been built. I told Hannah, "Say, this is really some fixing! Look, they gone and cut a redwood up the canyon and split out boards for them two tables, see where they drug the stuff down out o' Crooked Canyon?"

She didn't answer me. I looked around and she wasn't even looking at the tables. Her eyes was wide as a young one's is, first time you carry him close up to a steer, but what she was a gazing at was the waves breaking out on that long rock point beyond the barranca where Songer always sets up his bar. She turned her head from the sea and looked up Crooked Canyon to where the little feed shed hid behind the big boulders, and then she turned back and looked at all them folks out by the barbecue pits and damned if she didn't mutter to herself, "It's a lone country."

What could a man say to a thing like that? There was maybe twenty people, could be more, right in front of us.

I edged Ranger over to the tie-rack and Hannah followed on Ginger. Looked like every horse along the Coast was here.

Was one I couldn't make out for a minute, a black-and-white pinto with a black star and a black forelock. Then I placed him. That handsome horse was the staggery little pinto colt I'd saw down to Phil Logward's place near Piedras Blancas, more'n three years ago. This was some doings to bring folks fifty miles!

Hannah set her saddle while I tied up our three beasts where they couldn't get into a kicking match with any strange stock. I let her set there while I untied the sacks of beef I was giving to the feast and took myself a good look at what was going on. I couldn't see anybody enough to know 'em, people kept moving around so.

There was two fires, one for the meat and the other one was cooking the big iron pot of beans and a great pot of coffee. I'd better warn Hannah not to drink any coffee. We get along without it, and I wasn't going to be chipping in on the price of any kettle of coffee. Before I could warn Hannah, there was Bill Pincus and Old Songer coming right up to us, both of them grinning, ear to ear.

They stood there, edging their feet around foolish—like, and then Songer spoke up, "This the Missus, Zande? Like to say 'Howdy' to the new Mrs. Allan."

I helped Hannah down and stood between her and any hand-shaking them womenless men might be counting on, and answered as I reached for Ginger's saddle, "Yes, 'tis. Go ahead and say it."

They both sort of snickered and mumbled, "Howdy, Mrs. Allan."

Hannah bowed her head. Not a polite bow, just the start of a nod, and walked straight ahead without waiting.

I didn't mean her to be that-a-way when I told her to watch her talk. Me and Bill and Songer walked along after her.

"These are the two men I was telling you helped me when

the grizzly bear got me, Hannah."

She never let on like she heard a word or give a damn. I must a riled her worse than I knowed when I made her fix her hair right. She just didn't have the sense to know I was doing her a kindness. I'd come to like her a lot and didn't want folks along the Coast to get wrong notions from that bunch of frizz curls she'd piled up to the front of her head.

I'd thanked Bill and Songer plenty when I give them all that good meat, up there on top the ridge. Now, I had to go again' all my ways and say it again, to cover up the way she was doing.

"Yep," I said, "you and Songer did me a good turn all right, Bill."

They both looked foolish. Hannah walked along as easy as though she hadn't shamed three men with her uppishness.

I saw Ma break from the handful of women that was setting table near the barbecue pit and come forward, walking fast, her eyes searching Hannah's face. Ma's eyes could just as well been turned on a table or a redwood tree as Hannah's face. It was a blank face, with no more move or change to it than a floor.

Ma sensed something, for she almost stopped, and she looked at me in a startled way.

"This is Mrs. Allan, Ma," I said. "Her name's Hannah."

Ma was rubbing off her hand with her apron as she said, "Looks a bit peaked, Zande," and I could see she was going to get the short end from my woman.

Not Ma. She finished rubbing her hand, taking her time, and then she rolled both of 'em up in her apron.

Hannah give my own ma the same half-nod she give Bill and Songer.

I could tell Ma was upset by the way she went on: "How's

grass over your way this fall? Calf-crop up to what you looked for? Heard tell you killed a big bear, son—"

On and on she went, like no Allan on earth and all because this white-faced woman I'd married stood there, making a fool of me and my family.

"Hear more and talk less, Ma," I said. I left Hannah standing there, walked over to the pit and flung the sacks of meat on the ground. I saw there was nothing but part of a veal roasting, and veal's not fit barbecue meat, nohow. I was glad I'd butchered a prime steer and brought the best of it.

Hank Ramirez and Arvis Demas was turning the veal chunks with the sharpened ends of long willow sticks and they looked up and grinned at me. I clapped 'em both a good clout on the back like I was feeling fine and I says, "What's going on here, anyway? Never saw so much fixing. Some of you must a been working here a week, them tables and all. Oak and manzanita from way up the ridge for the fire! Good fire. Been keeping it since yesterday?"

I was running off the head bad as Ma. The boys kept their eyes down like they didn't see nothing but the meat they was turning, just nodding their heads for a "Yes" to all my talk. But when I started getting out good steaks, the back-strap, and a lot of fine meaty ribs, they looked up, grinned till you could see every tooth in their heads.

The Allans is the only family on the Coast really knows how to cut up meat.

Word went round: "The meat, Zande Allan's brought the meat." They come crowding up around the pit to watch and to smell, as the steaks slowly turned red-brown and the gold fat dripped. I was hungered as any of them to get my teeth into that meat, but I took my good time, getting them steaks cooked. Wastes meat, shrivels it, if you cook it over too hot a fire, and I was of no mind to waste something we held too near like money to eat ourselves. We was plain as possible with ourselves, but when we went to a doings, we took our share and we took our best.

The fire got a little too hot, and Hank passed me the gourd with cold water and the dousing-brush made of fresh southern-wood twigs tied together. I dipped it in the water, sprinkled the fire under the steaks to cool it down. Some of the meat was 'most done, so I nodded to Arvis and he yelled to his couple little brothers. They come over with a cut clove of garlic and rubbed the hot bark platters before they passed 'em over to me for the steaks that was ready.

The Demas family always brought them bark platters. Nacio, Mrs. Demas' old Indian mother, made 'em. God only knows what she seasoned the bark with, but I have to say she made a good job of it. Only thing I ever knowed a Indian to be any good for, but them bark platters was first rate. Nacio'd stood them on edge at the far side of the pit to heat through and they'd stay hot longer than it took to get the steaks et.

I'd been hunched over the fire so I straightened up to take the kinks out of my back. At the other fire Mrs. Ramirez was giving a stir to her big kettle of red beans cooked half-Spanish, half-Indian style. All Coast folks et these beans three times a day and nobody ever tired of 'em.

I saw Ma and Mrs. Demas was putting the salsa together. Ma brought the growing-things for the salsa: the tomatoes, the hot and the sweet peppers, the sweet purple onions and the garlic. She got all that stuff out of her fall garden. Mrs. Demas brought the oil and the vinegar, always having to hand things that had to come in on the ship, or come pack-back from Monterey or Jolon. Shows how they do, spending right and left, like that was all there was to life.

I heard Songer laughing and laughing as he and old Tony Ramirez come climbing out of the barranca south of the pit, down there where a wash from the mountain cut the flat. I knowed Songer had his stuff cached down there, for already I'd seen men and some of the big boys slapping backs, nudging each other and snickering.

Now Ramirez went to hit Songer a friendly lick on his back. He'd let liquor cloud his eye, missed Songer's back altogether and hit him a clip across the nose that set Songer staggering.

They was both laughing like fools, and then Songer's nose took to bleeding. He come up to the pit, Ramirez with him, and it was comical to see how them two looked at the blood dripping from Songer's nose.

He hung his head well over, so it dripped clear of his beard and went splat, splat, splat in the dust at the end of the barbecue pit. Everyone was laughing. Maria Demas come walking over from where she'd been helping with the table, and looked at me with them bold eyes of hers, "Better put him to the fire, Zande; cook him done. He drips."

She threw back her head to laugh. How red her mouth was, how small and white her teeth looked. Maria always started a man thinking.

I looked up from work to laugh when Maria spoke so sharp and comical about Songer and his nose-bleed. The laugh went clean out of me.

Just across the pit Hannah stood, looking for all the world like she smelled something nasty. Her hand covered her mouth and she turned away quick from the sight of a little blood, same as if she was too nice for the rest of us. But it wasn't her that wiped the laugh right off my face. I'd looked up square into the eyes of the man who'd walked over to the fire with my own wife. There he was. Blinking his sea-otter eyes, hacking out his dry little cough. Avery!

"Howj'do," he says. "How are you, Mr. Allan?" And without waiting for a answer, he turns away from the fire and walks off with my wife like it was a fit thing to do.

The thin-striped socks sagging down, his topless shoes like women's slippers; them things was part of my feelings again' him.

But more than his soft clothes, more than his wild talk, the thing that had drawed Hannah to look at him, listen to him, laugh with him, was the talk of the tunes he told her he blew out of that round black stick. Holding his handkerchief over his mouth coughing, he walked Hannah over to where some cuts of redwood log had been rolled together to make seats.

When she was sitting on the log, the little man bowed to her and said, "Could I bring you some coffee?"

My wife, the woman who wouldn't speak to my friends or to

my mother, looked right into them eyes of his and smiled as she answered, "I been longing for coffee. Ain't had none for months."

There she was, blackguarding all the Allans, getting everyone to notice she liked coffee when it was talked along the Coast that we never had it in our houses.

Avery come over to where the coffee was boiling, took a cup without even asking whose cup it was, filled it up and carried it back to my wife, set down beside her and started filling a pipe with tobacco.

Hannah, blowing on her cup of coffee, sipped it slowly, smiling as she listened to his outlandish talk as though it made sense. Then Avery pulled the flute from his pocket, first stopping to cough and wipe off his lips with the handkerchief, and the soft bubbly sound of that flute took hold on the flat, filling it all with a singing music so that, though the steaks was ready, the folks come over to the pit slow, looking back over their shoulders to watch and listen.

Nothing but plain orneriness would ever let a man break in on a meal time with music.

I went on with putting steaks on the hot platters. Only half my mind was on it, but it was my job and I done it right.

Pa give me a knowing look, turned and looked at my wife and Avery. I give him as good a steak as there was and he went off, waggling his shoulders and snickering.

I wasn't picking out no favorites; I give the thick juicy steaks to the men; the thin, better-done ones to the women and girls; and the hunks of half-charred veal to the boys who'd relish anything.

Arvis Demas was trying to set hisself as one of the men, for when I speared out a hunk of veal for him, he bobbed his head down on his shoulder, making it motion at Hannah and Avery and he says, "Beef for me, Zande; I got troubles, too!"

I whacked the top of his head with the willow stick and sent him scuttling off with the charred hunk he'd got. Every man, woman and child at the barbecue let me know they thought something was going on, but it was Mrs. Ramirez that smirked at me as she says, "Your wife gets acquainted awful easy, don't she?"

I had it on the tip of my tongue to lie, to tell her, "Mister Avery's a old friend to both us." It stuck in my throat.

I let on like I didn't hear her. Ma was standing next in line to Mrs. Ramirez and I says to Ma, "Here's one for you, Ma."

When I give her a fine steak with plenty of good fat to it, she nudges Mrs. Ramirez with her elbow, whispering real loud, "Ha, it's something lucky to have a new-married son. He can't keep his mind on the barbecue meat."

Ma tolled Mrs. Ramirez away from the pit; the two of them whispering together and giggling just as Maria come up, twitching the fringes on her leather skirt, making a face and sticking out her tongue as she calls out, loud enough to hear up to Cone Peak:

"Meat for me, Zande! Say—wouldn't you like to know what I know?" I saw them that was still hunting places to sit, stop and look around, start laughing.

I looked slow over the meat that was left on the cooking bars, picked out a fair piece and before I put it on the bark platter for Maria, I answered her, loud, "Guess if I knowed all you know, wouldn't weight my head down none."

Took her a minute to figger it out and then she laughed loud as the rest of 'em, kicked some of the loose dirt back at me with her moccasin, twitched up the back of her skirt a mite and went off to the bean kettle to get her gourd full of the beans.

The point of my willow stick had found meat for everyone's plate but mine, Hannah's and Avery's.

Avery was still playing away as though it was all the business he had in the world, not even stopping when I come over with a plate for myself and one for Hannah. When I pushed the platter into Hannah's hands and said, "Here," he stopped playing and looked up at me.

"Nice to see you again, Mr. Allan," he says, smooth and smiling. "That looks a good steak. I must go get one. I just remember I must be hungry."

"I'm giving out the meat," I said. "I brought it and I give it out."

Hannah smiled as if everything was just to her taste, hands her platter over and says, "Take this one, Mr. Avery. Zande will get me another."

There was a sharp bark behind me. It was Pa laughing. He

expected me to break the platter over the little man's head and then break him in two. I couldn't do it. If he was a woman, I could a fetched him a slap and took the plate away from him and no one'd thought the worse of me. But he wasn't a woman. Even if he weighed only one hundred and ten pounds, even if he was no thicker through than the blade of a ax, he was still a man and had to be treated like he was one. If I was to knock a little man like him flat, every man, woman and child along the Coast would be down on me, and they'd have reason.

I could see that Avery wasn't easy in his mind, and that made me feel better. He had a foolish look to his face, as if he didn't know just what the proper thing was, and he stood there fidgeting with my wife's platter of steak in his hands.

My clean buckskins, my new-washed shirt was fine. I made a better figger of a man than he done.

Easy as *he* could, I said, "You take this one, Hannah; I'll get myself some more."

The bars that had closed Hannah's face tight let down slow, and a smile started from deep in her eyes. As far as she went, I'd did the right thing.

I turned around and saw Pa's face looking like I'd just stepped on his corn, and I felt sure I done right. Ma had been forgetting to eat, and letting all that good yellow fat turn cold and stiff. Now she set her teeth into it, and I could see a laugh to her face while she took bites up and down that rib like it was a mouth harp she was getting a tune from.

Feeling better with myself I got to the pit. There was naught left on the gratings over the coals but a couple of shriveled scraps of veal. Again I thought quick. I fished down in the sack, took out a piece of meat I'd been saving for the evening barbecue and threw a good steak on the coals for me to eat a little later. Then I picked up one of the bark platters and went over to the bean kettle and put a couple good gourds full on the plate, helped myself to salsa and tortillas. I'd show people nothing put me out. I took the bean dipper, lifted it out of the beans and washed the sauce from it in the spring overflow. Then I dipped deep into the coffee and got myself a big gourd-ful. Coffee is a good drink all right.

I drank that measure and then I filled it again, walked over to Mrs. Demas and told her, "Here's your four bits, ma'am, to help keep the coffee going. I had some, and my wife had some, too."

I talked good and loud. Let Avery know that Zande Allan paid for what his family used. I was hoping that Avery didn't have a nickel in them striped pants of his. He'd feel a fool, having drunk his coffee, if he couldn't pay for it.

Mrs. Demas gathered her rebosa closer to her chin, pulling it across the lower half of her face, her eyes for all the world like Maria's, as she urged, *"No, no, Zande, no. Tu portes mucho carne, cafe es nada."*

I put the fifty cents down in front of her and says, "Take it and think nothing of it. Meat I raise, but coffee you have to send out for."

She shook her head, but she picked up the silver and was slowly turning it over and over in her hand as I left her and went walking over to Hannah.

She was setting on the log, eating hearty at the fine rare steak I'd counted on eating, and there he was, leaning again' the log, his legs stretched out on the ground, nibbling on the good meat I'd picked out for my wife.

I made up my mind I'd took all I had to from Avery and I was fixing to tell him there was a few words I wanted to say to Mrs. Allan, private.

He got ahead of me. "I was just saying to your wife, Mr.

Allan, that I'd like to ride up to your place before I go back to Monterey and take a ship out to the Islands. I've given up the idea of taking land—I may not come this way again." Seemed like his eyes got a queer, hunted shine to 'em for a second, but he says, real bright, "Before I go, I want to furnish my mind with little mountain homes to take away with me."

Whatever he was talking about, he wasn't going to furnish his mind with my little mountain home, not by a damn sight. Long as he was leaving I did wish he was the sort of fellow I could a asked about that there scrip he'd told us about first day we'd met him on the trail; I wouldn't give him a chance to be telling me nothing, though. I looked square at him when I said, "We won't be there for a time. We're fixing to go for a visit with my folks."

Hannah raised her head, her eyes wide, and I heard a sharp laugh behind me. Maria'd come sneaking along soft-footed as that Indian grandmother of hers, laughing mean as she asked me, "I bet that's first your wife heard it. Ain't it, huh?"

Hannah looked troubled, but Avery's teeth showed white, smiling as he said, "Then I'll be sure to see you both again. I promised your brother Mel I'd be up to tell him something about my music before I leave the Coast. Your brother's a very keen lad, Mr. Allan."

Maria's laugh mocked a meadow lark that run a song up and down the flat.

She reached out and grabbed Hannah's hand as though they was friends, and she says, leaning close to Hannah, "Oh, Mrs. Allan, you remember you asked me where is my man? I'll tell *you* special, what's the big surprise to this party."

Hannah didn't say anything, but I noticed there was a bit of a smile about her mouth, and her eyes looked at Maria as though she wanted to hear the surprise.

"The surprise is—" Maria stopped, looked all around— that was her way, to make a big story out of anything she told. "The big surprise is—I'm getting married tonight, here, at the party."

I could see that even Maria believed Hannah when she said, "Well, that's a surprise! I hope you'll be very happy."

Maria looked straight at Hannah for a second, then lifted her shoulder and answered, "I'll look out for myself, all right."

Avery put in, "Who is the lucky chap?"

Maria was all smiles for him. Any man could get a smile and bright look from that Maria. She leaned over so close that it looked as though she was about to kiss him, and she sounded like purring, "Tony Gallo, it is. Owns half Rancho Seco, and he's riding over with the priest from Soledad Mission and a cousin of Tony's that plays the accordion. Tonight we'll dance and be married. Tomorrow I'll be Mrs. Gallo and ride over to the Salinas Plain with my husband."

She turned toward me, sounding like when she was a little girl with braids down her back, "What *you* think of that, Zande?"

"I don't think nothing, I guess," I answered. "Seems like that's your business."

Maria turned her back on me and says, "I'm going up to the grain shed and get fixed for the dancing. I got all new; dress, and shoes, too. I been a ride to town since I see you. The ajunemiento of Monterey, he throwed a letter to Tony for me. Tony'll be here."

Maria come over to her slow when Hannah asked, "Would you mind taking my hat and jacket along, and putting them up there out of the way, please? The hat hurts my head and I feel so warm."

Maria says, "You'll feel better or worse, a few months from now." She held out her hand for the things and Hannah, her face pinked up a bit, handed them to her. As she walked away, she give me the strangest look I'd ever see from her, and then she stopped walking slow, started to run across the field and up Crooked Canyon to where the little hay and grain barn stood. All the folks that was planning to stay the night and hadn't made camp yet had pitched their stuff in there to be out of the way of the children running over it.

Marrying Tony Gallo, was she? She might be fooling herself but she wasn't fooling me none. She wasn't happy. I kept thinking about the look she give me and that maybe I'd never again come riding along the Coast trail, meet Maria and be tormented by her.

Things was changing, just as Hannah said. This very night a man she'd poked fun at, to me, would know all of Maria I could of had ten years ago. There was something between me and Maria, something that made it seem like I'd have to have a word with her before she was busy with dancing, with a party that would finish with her wedding.

I looked at the meat for the night's barbecue standing in the sun, and flies buzzing around the sack. The best thing to do with it was take it up Crooked Canyon and hang it inside the shed. Happen Maria was there changing her clothes I could call to her and hand in the sack for her to hang up in the shade.

There was good shade under the big sycamore that leaned over the spring. I saw heads turn when I picked up the meat sack. No matter who looked, or what they thought, I'd pack that meat up to the shed.

Maria had looked at me and my feet was carrying me up the draw beside the little cress-choked creek.

I come alongside the door to the shed, and it was pushed open a crack. I looked around. Not a soul in sight and the children's voices, cricket-thin, seeming to come up the bar-ranca from a long way off. I couldn't hear a sound inside the shed. I felt like the biggest fool in the world. Everyone at the barbecue would damn well know I wasn't thinking only of beef when I packed that meat away from the pit.

I'd be a fool to pack it down again after I'd come up with it and found Maria gone.

Feeling cheated as much as ever I'd felt in my life, I pushed at the door, opened it and stepped into the cave-dim shed. I was feeling for a nail or a peg to hang the sack on when I heard Maria's voice:

"Zande! No—go away!"

My eyes had got used to the half-dark by now and as my head turned I could see her bend to the floor and from a box at her feet snatch up a wide white petticoat and hold it before her. I started to back out of the door, feeling as out of place as if I'd walked into a strange outhouse and found my mother setting on the board.

My hand was reaching to shut the door when she said, "What you doing here?"

She wasn't trying too hard to cover herself. She was a brown young thing, her breast swelling smooth and round; the red of her soft mouth pulling at me.

I didn't want her. I didn't want her at all. She was trying to break me down, get the best of me.

But I walked inside and hung the meat up careful on a wood peg, as I answered, "I'm hanging the meat where the flies won't get to it. Thought you'd gone or I wouldn't a come in."

She come flying toward me, the petticoat trailing over the dirt floor, dropped clear to the floor as she wound both arms around me. "That's a big lie, Zande. I called you and you come. I died, Zande; I died when you took that old homely woman. I don't want Tony; only you. Always, only you—"

"What you want is a good clout," I told her, taking hold of her shoulder and shaking her. The touch of her was soft brown fire, but I had a holt of myself. "What you'll get is a black eye to get married in if you don't turn loose of me and behave yourself." I felt proud and sure of myself when I told her, "I wish you good luck, and Tony, too. I got a wife of my own—"

"What *you* got—"

Maria's scorn lashed up the anger I'd felt all day. "What you got! A hoe-handle of a woman, making you a fool to the whole Coast with her high and mighty way to your own mother while she sits smirking at that old goat! What you think she wants from him, you fool? Music?"

I shook like I was palsied, half rage at Hannah, half the power on me, the pull to the brown youngness of Maria.

She softened again' me and whispered, "Don't be a fool, Zande; not always. Tony'll never know. Tonight I'll be married, tomorrow I'll be gone, I'll be gone."

Her arms tightened around me, pulled my head down to her mouth...

VI

The voices was 'most at the shed door before I heard them. Maria heard them, too.

As I jumped from the pile of coats and blankets we was laying on, I heard her whisper, "Holy mother!" I saw her reach for the wide white petticoat and pull it over herself. I crossed the floor of the shed in two jumps, pulling up my buckskins with one hand, feeling with the other for the catch on the wooden shutter at the end of the stall. I'd seen it often enough, shoveled dung through it many a time. I knowed it was wide enough for me to slip out through if I could only find the cursed catch.

"Miss Demas hung it in here, I think."

The voice was right outside the shed door. It was Hannah—looking for her coat.

Even then it come to me what a fool I'd been, what a fool!

I found the shutter-catch. I pulled the trap door open. I was shoving my head and shoulders through as the shed door started to creak open. Snake-swift and quiet, I flowed through that dirty little opening, all out but one leg, when I hear Hannah's voice again. "I didn't know it was so far up here. I should have sent my husband for my coat; climbing isn't good for your cough."

I heard Avery trying to cough. As if I didn't have enough trouble on my mind without that two-for-a-cent gentleman walking my wife away from the gathering, getting her talked about from one end of the Coast to the other. I thought I had more trouble than I knowed what to do with. Then I found a fringe of my pants leg was caught on a nail sticking out near the floor.

I didn't dare tear it loose; might leave a piece of the fringe behind. If I did that, it was like writing the Coast a note. "Alexander Allan was here with Maria Demas." My wife'd find out if I tore them buckskins, and when the tale come to her, she'd remember right enough.

I had need to get free and do it gentle, but I worked my leg like a kicking steer being in the awkwardest place ever a man found hisself. I got so I almost hoped the door would open, she'd see me and it would be over.

Then I felt the buckskin give. I was free. I slid my leg out through the trap door and shut it down quiet. I felt my two feet on the ground and I crouched again' the wall of the shed, fair holding my breath. Was no chance for me to crawl away through the thick, dry brush. I'd be heard if I tried. I stayed quiet.

I heard Hannah say, "So dark in here, I can't see a thing."

My hope jumped high. I remembered how dark the shed seemed to me, how I'd been feeling for a peg or a nail when Maria startled me. If only my wife would find her cursed coat and hat and go away quick.

Then a real fear hit me. That heap of blankets and coats. God!

I wished that black Spanish wench in the bottom of hell.

I had no hankering after any more of Maria. I'd already had too much. Even while I crouched down there in the dung-heap, sweating like a spent horse, I could see clear as light how lucky it was for me I'd not took up with Maria them years she hunted me.

First time it ever come to me so sharp, how white and fine my own woman was. If I'd a had no woman before her to match Maria again', I'd maybe thought myself well suited with her. Tony Gallo was welcome to her, far as I went.

I quit thinking about Tony, or Maria, too, when I heard Hannah saying in a quick, light sort of way, "I've found my things. They was right here on top this heap."

The door creaked shut, and I heard their two voices fade away down the trail. I had to get gone before Maria judged it safe to call to me. Seemed like I'd kill her if she said one word. Soft as I could, I eased my way beyond the brush that grew thick on both sides of the stream, out into the clear hill-land.

Then my feet was a grass fire, running before the wind, to get me mixed into some bunch of men before Hannah and Avery got back.

Two of the Ramirez boys and Arvis Demas was walking over

to the pitching ground they'd made, and I seen they was all carrying muleshoes or horseshoes.

I was walking along with them before they got to the place where they was going to pitch.

"Got an extra shoe, Arvis?" I asked. "I wouldn't mind beating you at this stuff." "Got some money that says that's a true brag?" Arvis' eyes had that same nasty look to them Maria's eyes get when she's sneering at a man, but I just laughed, short-like, and says, "You know I never bet."

"No money, no game—" Arvis' voice was as flat and set as his words. I looked up the trail and I couldn't see a thing of Avery or my wife.

That woman of mine needed to be wrapped around a tree, gallivanting off like that with a stranger, an outlander man.

Arvis turned to Tao Ramirez and prodded him, "You're a good sport, Tao. Got a peso that says you better as me?"

Tao was stepping up sort of foolish but he didn't pick up the shoes. I took another look up the trail and went cold all over. Hannah was ahead, Avery following close after. Running down the trail after them was Maria in her leather skirt. She put her hand on Hannah's arm, leaned close to her. Hannah seemed to motion Avery to go on ahead and then I saw both women step off the trail and around some big boulders, out of sight.

My head was swimming, my tongue thick, but I got the words out, "My dollar says your peso's in the wrong pocket."

Arvis jumped around like a banty rooster, crowing, "That's your tell! You try what five throws each says! I throw first."

Maria and Hannah was still hid out behind the rocks but Avery was stepping along brisk, almost down to the flat.

Like talking in my sleep, I says, "However you say is all right with me."

I pulled the dollar out of my pocket, handed it over to Songer, who was going to hold the stakes.

Arvis started throwing slow and careful. My mind was so took up with what Maria could be telling Hannah that I scarce noted he throwed four ringers, one right after the other. The crowd got cheering for him, he got too eager and the last shoe missed.

As I picked up the other five shoes I see one of them was a muleshoe, lighter than the others. Any other time I'd a stood up for my rights. Now I could only think that Avery was smiling from the edge of the crowd, that now I could see Hannah's black bonnet bobbing down the trail and Maria nowhere in sight.

I wanted to throw the shoes away, tell Arvis he could have the dollar. I wanted to do anything but stand there and throw them shoes like it mattered.

But I did my best. I made myself take my time, throw careful. The four throws rings the peg. One more throw and I'd win. There was only the muleshoe left to throw and then I'd be free to face Hannah, find out what I had to face.

What I couldn't do, no matter what, was do less than my best. That's the Allan of it.

I heard the clink of metal and I told myself I'd made the five throws all good. Then I heard the high laughing of the women, the coyote laughing of the men, and I see the shoes rolling away from the peg. The mule-shoe had hit a mite low, bounced off the peg and pulled the two top shoes along with it.

It was none of my doings, but anyway Arvis had won and I was free. I spoke to Arvis like he was a man, the short-sounding joking way men use to men along the Coast. "I couldn't catch you at it but I know well you knocked my elbow," I said. "That's a good dollar you got from me; take care of it."

Arvis was spluttering with laughter, biting on the silver dollar I'd put up, waving it around, shouting, "It bites good but I bet ya if Zande turns it loose, there's something wrong. That Zande!"

I didn't mind the laughing. Most times it would a got me fighting mad. Not now.

I seen Hannah standing on the edge of the crowd, Mrs. Demas and Ma right to one side of her, Mr. Avery on the other. Ma and Mrs. Demas was acting as if Hannah wasn't there at all. Avery was talking, talking, and Hannah saying nothing. Listening.

I watched her. She wasn't listening to Mr. Avery. He was wasting all his fine-sounding words. Hannah was listening to her own thoughts.

Then it was like I felt the cold nose of a mountain lion touched my naked back. What if she was thinking about seeing me and Maria up to the shed?

She couldn't be. It's again' all nature that my wife should *know* I'd been laying-up with Maria. If she did know it, she wouldn't be standing there quiet, her shoulders straight and proud. She'd be on a hunt to pick Maria's eyes out.

My thoughts going round and round like that made it hard for me to keep my mind on all I held again' Hannah.

I turned away from the pitching ground and started over to Hannah and Avery. "Happen I'd like a few words with my wife, myself, Mr. Avery," I said, and I give him a look that should a warned him. "Guess I'll have to take her home to get them."

He never blinked an eye. Gives me a smile and a bow and answers, "Oh, quite, Mr. Allan; right you are. Your wife shouldn't be so charming."

"That's one thing you're damned right about." I took a holt of Hannah's arm and she knowed I meant business when I said, "I'm saddling up, right now."

Her face didn't change color, not a muscle of it moved, though beside her a mare nickered and it was Ma; right behind her an ass brayed, and it was Songer.

Hannah walked light beside me, as if of her own choosing, and there was no more snickering from any of the crowd. I took the first deep breath I'd drawed since I heard Hannah's voice coming up the creek to the shed, when a regular tornado blowed up in front of us. It was Maria.

Here she was, ribbons in her hair, ribbons to her shoes, a regular fog-bank of white skirt held up in both hands so she could show all them lace-edged petticoats as she ran. She had a laughing mouth that her eyes give the lie to, as she stopped, skirts wide spread to halt us.

My legs said, "Run," but reason told me that if I didn't stop, right on the tip of Maria's tongue was the will to shout to the whole crowd all that had happened between us.

I took one look at Hannah's face and seemed like there was nothing left to my bones but the glue. Hannah's mouth held that little smile and I saw now, plain, that there was something cruel to it. Her eyes was narrowed down more than I'd ever seen them, and the look in them was a match for the look in Maria's eyes.

There was a brittleness to Hannah's voice as she said, "Oh, how dressed up you look now, Miss Demas."

The hair crawled along the back of my neck. Had she brought that word "now" out to stand before the rest of her words, or did I only think it? Was it just my own guilt that read into simple words all this trampled sign?

Maria answered, cool as you please, "My wedding dress! You know; me, my madre and all my sisters, we sewed ourselves blind. Four petticoats, all insertions and ruffles and edging, beside all the tucks to the dress, and only two months to do it. But nice, yes?"

She turned slow before us as though she hadn't a thought in the world but ruffles and edgings, whatever in hell they were. But I knowed that one.

Every man, woman and child in the crowd was ringed around us now, a swarm of bees buzzing at Maria's fine dress but sensing something stewing up. Only Avery, he seemed to see nothing out of usual. Might happen he was extra schooled in hiding hisself from outside eyes, but I don't think that was it. He had put in too much of his life in cities to be as alive to things happening around him as our Coast people was. I figger it's all wrong and again' nature for humans to spend their time looking at city streets; it blinds their eyes to real things all around.

I stood first on one foot, then on t'other while women chattered about how many yards of lace, how many spools of thread and truck went into her get-up. I noticed Hannah didn't touch the dress, feel of the lace.

I waited. How soon could I get Hannah started toward the horses? Could we get away quiet, without Maria making trouble?

I thought now it was just one of her little picky meannesses, nothing of any real account. She'd drawed all that crowd around and they'd spread so thick across the trail, it was like we was held prisoner. I'd either have to shove a way through the crowd to get my wife over to the tie-rack, or give Maria a chance for a laugh at me and Hannah picking our way through the bull-thistles that was waist-high over this end of the flat.

I made up my mind to let her laugh. We'd go.

Maria must of knowed what I was wanting to do. She suddenly twitched her ruffles out of Granny Ramirez' hand and looked at me. Her voice was loud enough to get everyone looking. "Don't let on like you're leaving before the wedding, Zande. I won't let you. I'm going to dance with all my old beaux till Tony gets here, so you ain't going." All the black Indian in Maria put hell in her eyes. Before I could think of a thing to answer, my wife put in, "Don't worry, Miss Demas," she said. "Zande'll be here. I wouldn't leave till I wish your husband luck."

Hannah spoke so easy, her voice half-laughing, I felt sure she hadn't an idea of how things stood between me and Maria. What had seemed to me a hair-trigger waiting under a double charge of powder, faded into nothing. I wasn't even mad at Hannah for saying she wouldn't think of leaving before the wedding. I felt sure now that Maria'd turn loose of me easy. All she wanted was to be sure I'd be standing by suffering while the marriage words was said over her. If she'd a knowed how I hoped I'd never see her handsome face again, she might of lost that smile.

I saw Hannah walk over to my mother. I couldn't hear what was said, but I saw Ma give Hannah the stony look. Hannah didn't back away from it. She went on talking, and pretty soon I saw Ma's face crack in a smile, then I heard her laugh right out and Hannah's laugh mix with hers. Ma called Mrs. Demas over and Mrs. Demas held out her hand, and I saw her shaking hands with Hannah real genteel. I doubt Mrs. Demas knowed there'd been any trouble going on.

I saw Mel and Avery out on the long rocky point that reaches into the sea just north of the flat, two black shadow-men moving slow into the hurrying darkness. The swell wasn't heavy, but the rocks out beyond the point always make water-talk sounds, and over them I could hear the sad music of Avery's flute.

Hannah heard it, too. I seen her stop and listen as the first notes blowed in with a sound of sea-sadness. Her head was turned to better catch the call of the tune and then she went on, moving back and forth in the twilight right along with the rest of the Coast women.

Arvis was prancing around teasing Maria and I heard her warn him, "You tell and I'll take the cleaver to the top of your head." She swung a slap toward him, but he dodged under her hand and run for the edge of the flat too fast for her, weighed down with all her fine petticoats and ruffles, to catch him.

Arvis jumped off the trail and out into the thistles and then he shouted to the crowd, "Make place for the cake! Is a big cake with honey and raisins in, and white sugar to the top! She's to cut after the wedding and you should see it. Anyone get married for that cake!"

Maria roared with laughing, just like the rest of the crowd, and Old Songer run his beard again' his shirt sleeve and yelled, "Bring on the music and let's get to that cake. Hell, anyone can get married, but it's ten years since I et cake!"

Men and boys turned to clearing the levelest spot, picking up sticks and rocks. Then they fetched the pitchpine torches, lashing them to posts drove in to mark off the dancing space, rolling forward cuts of logs for them that wasn't dancing to sit nice and easy while they watched.

Before them logs was fairly rolled in place, they was covered with women and girls, their teeth shining white in the torchlight, their toes tapping and their heads nodding to some tune they heard in their heads. First tweak of Bill's fiddle they'd all dropped their work and come stampeding up to the dance place squealing and laughing.

Avery and Mel come strolling in from the Point chewing on jerky cool as you please.

Mel was acting biggety as he told Avery, "No, not 'los ojitos'—that's saying 'the little eyes.' What you want to say is 'los *ositos,'* when you mean 'the little bears.'"

Avery laughed good-natured and said after Mel, *"Ojitos—ositos*—eyes, bears. Not much difference to the sound but a lot of difference to the way you'd dance it."

He laughed, munching away on the last string of jerky as Mel urged, "You'll play the *Dance of the Little Bears* tonight, won't you, Mr. Avery?"

Avery swallowed his jerky and answered, "Of course. I'll play it if you'll dance it."

Mel's face burned red under his straw-colored hair. He slouched over to sit on a log and muttered, "I don't do no dancing."

There was no stopping Avery when he got a notion. "Then I'll dance it myself and play it, too."

He whipped his flute out of his pocket and flung one of his smiles around the crowd, hunched his shoulders up, his head down and started playing.

Clear around the marked-off space he shuffled, playing the callingest tune ever I'd heard, and then he stopped, smack in the center and called out, "This dance is for the little ones. Come on, children, fall in and we'll have the *Dance of the Little Bears*. Try growling while you dance."

I never thought to see it. Coast children was shy with strange folks, but not with Avery. He started that tune again and the little ones come tumbling after him, heads pulled down, growling, laughing, shuffling their feet like bears to the flute music. The last one to fall in was Old Nacio. Not that she didn't belong there. Bunching herself up like au old she-bear, Nacio wasn't any bigger than the children, at that.

It was bold of Hannah to start the clapping, and she a stranger, but her boldness was catching. First one woman, then two, then ten took up the clapping, keeping time to the tune and throwing back their heads and laughing. Even the men took it up and shouted, "Good! Fine! Go to it, bears!" to the top of their lungs.

Avery pranced and played, played his tune and pranced, till everyone but him and Old Nacio started slowing up. One by one the little fellows dropped out of the dance and leaned back again' their mother's skirts, puffing and laughing. Round and round went Nacio and Avery, two bears if ever I see them. Everyone had the tune now, humming it, hands clapping softer in the torchlight, and the tune was more than the dancing.

Avery broke off playing, put his hands, still clutching the flute, hard again' his chest and started coughing. He made out to get one hand off his chest and reached into his pocket for that white handkerchief of his.

He put it across his mouth, stumbling out of the light. Nacio looked around, her bear-head weaving to the music that no longer sounded, then shuffled away as the crowd laughed. I see the red spreading across the white cloth held to Avery's mouth. I see the slow way it spread. It was no polite put-on, that little huff of a cough he was always covering up. Lung fever, and that's a hard slow death.

He come back in a few minutes, smiling, waving the flute.

"Mountain people are too much for a plainsman," he called out, sounding gay as a colt. "I couldn't dance you down. I'll sit and play, leave the dancing to my youngsters."

He more fell than sat on the nearest log, and I see Hannah's long fingers go quick across her mouth. She half made to get up from the log. Her head give a little shake, and she settled back again, let her eyelids come almost shut and sat very still.

Avery—and my wife. A plainsman, he'd called himself. Well, my wife was from the Kansas plain. Maybe he come out to the Coast because she was coming, all this acting like they'd never saw each other before was only to hide what they had between them.

Maria come running into the center of the dancing place, Arvis Demas along with her, and him dressed in all the style of the Spanish gentry. 'Twas comical to see Arvis, decked out in tight cloth pants with silver buttons, a bright silk shirt and a long serape around his waist, a silver cord to his flat black hat.

Bill had tucked his fiddle under his chin and said he was going to play the *Coast Waltz*. I held up my hand to stop him, stepped out where everyone could see me.

I felt pretty good, talking so easy when I said, "Neighbors, what you think if we make this a change-around dance? Change partners when another man taps your shoulder, and don't none of you fellows get a stone to your fist and tap heads by mistake!"

I waited for the laughing, taking in the big grin on Ma's face. Knowing she was proud, seeing me lead like that, I let words out like band-tailed pigeons streak acrost autumn.

"There's two almost-brides here," I says. "Mrs. Allan to say howdy to, Mrs. Tony Gallo to tell good-by and good luck. I'm leading off with Mrs. Allan."

There was clapping as Bill and Avery struck into the *Coast Waltz* and I went straight over to Hannah, bowed and held out my elbow to her like if I'd a been a courting man instead of a husband.

She looked hard at me for a second. Then stood up, laid her hand on my arm. I didn't have no notion in this world if my wife could dance or not.

Along the Coast some won't work, but they all can dance, and it was a thing come natural to the Allans. Out of the tail of my eye, I could see Pa getting ready to go whirling off with Ma. I'd look a fool if my wife turned out to be one of them women with no spring to her step when she put it to a tune. She walked light, I knowed that—but did they maybe have some outlandish way of dancing where she come from.

Bill had the time set good to the tune, but I stood there, holding back long enough to let Hannah get the feel to the music and see how smooth other couples could swing out over a dirt floor when waltz music was played.

There was nothing showy about Hannah. Her face looked thin and tired, her black dress showed dusty from sitting around on the logs, and I could feel her hand tremble on my shoulder as she rested the tips of her fingers there.

She couldn't be much of a dancer if it got her shaking-scared, but I told myself I had to do my best with her. I could see Maria whirling off with Phil Logward, the fellow with the small ranch on the Coast near Piedras Blancas. Maria hopped too much for my taste in waltzing, but she was a lively dancer and good at following.

"Shall we start?" Hannah asked, looking up at me as though it was my place to start right off, without giving her a chance to see how we did our dancing. Seeing it was plain waste of time to try to do her a favor, I stepped off.

Hannah could dance! She made Maria look coarse and bouncy, made me see the dust to the edges of all them flowing ruffles. Hannah danced cool and quiet, easy as pouring water out of a jug.

I was the only man on the Coast except Pa who could dance a waltz and reverse on his turns. I thought I'd tell Hannah that I was going to do this next time we turned, and then I looked at her face and changed my mind.

There she was, floating along not watching where we was going. She wasn't even thinking that she was waltzing with her husband for the first time. She couldn't be thinking about me and looking over to Avery with sorry eyes and smiling mouth.

I didn't care if she tripped or what. I swung her round the other way from every turn we'd made, and round she come, neat as if she'd done it all her life.

Every uneasy feeling I'd had about my wife come rushing back to me.

She'd told a story of hard work and a hard life, but she'd found time to learn dancing better than anyone else at this party. That meant someone to dance with. Avery? A feeling like pain hit me. I knowed what it was. I'd felt a tug of it when one of my brothers made a better shot than I did, or got more brush cleaned in a day. It was the same pain then, but never like this.

A hand tapped me. It was Bill Pincus, waiting for a whirl with Hannah. I turned loose of her, glad it was Bill and not one of the younger men.

I thought I'd tap Pa and take a turn with Ma, but I looked around and caught Hannah's glance coming to rest on Avery and his flute.

My mind never told my feet to go over to Avery. I was over there, bending down to say to him, "Soon as Bill comes back to fiddle the tune, my wife would like to have a turn with you."

"Very kind of you, Mr. Allan. I'll go rescue her from the old fellow."

I looked up and saw Bill already coming back, picking a trail through the dancers so as not to throw them off their step. Old Songer had got hold of Hannah. He was a regular mule on the dance floor, braying and hee-hawing, knocking into couples and holding onto his partner like she was trying to break away from him.

Hannah was sailing along so easy, she almost made it look like he could dance.

Avery knocked the wet out of his flute, laid it careful on the

133

log, got close to Songer and tapped him to change partners.

Songer'd forgot what was up. I'd told how it was, but he hadn't paid no mind to my words. Now he let go of Hannah and made to fight with Avery.

Hannah picked at his sleeve, told him again what I'd already told him.

Nothing went right at this damned party. Not even the littlest thing. A misery like I'd et twice too much beans blowed up inside me and still I couldn't hardly wait to see Avery dance off with Hannah.

Songer had got the idea into his sheep's-head by now, and was over swinging down a heavy fist on Pa's shoulder.

Avery and Hannah stood where Songer left them, talking, not dancing. Hannah's lifted face looked straight into his, her fingers rested on his sleeve. She was saying something in a voice too low for me to make out.

Every motion of her hands, her lips, told me she was pleading with him, begging him to do—or not to do— something.

He listened in that polite way and then he shook his head, put his hand to my wife's back and swung off, waltzing.

That was what I waited to see with my own eyes. It took me less than a minute to see where she'd learned to reverse like that.

I stood there until I was sure it was no chance that he'd happened onto that step. He did it again, Hannah following like she was part of the tune.

With a feeling for smashing something, anything, a log or a rock, I run out of the reach of the torchlight before I let go myself and shook the life plumb out of Avery.

I could see Maria bouncing from one partner to t'other, and I run back to the dance floor, grabbed her from Tao Ramirez and whirled her off in the fastest gallop I'd ever done to a waltz tune.

I put both arms around Maria and hugged her up close. Maria let her head fall back, looked up at me with her black eyes shining soft, lips parted, to show the points of her little white teeth. It made no difference to me. The soft feel of the woman again' me was no more than if I'd a been holding a sheep to shear. All I wanted was to make a show of myself with Maria, hope Hannah would see it, feel the same ache that was shaking me.

She didn't seem to pay me any heed. She was dancing smooth and quiet, her face showing nothing, floating along cool in the dusk, her black dress setting her out from the rest of the women.

Songer tapped Avery and he turned loose of Hannah, easy as if she didn't mean a thing. I felt a new knife pain. Sly. That's what they was. I had no doubt they had it all fixed up to meet some place along the trail.

My wife took a few steps with Songer, said something to him and he started laughing that silly laugh of his. But he stopped dancing and steered her back to the log she'd been sitting on when I asked her to dance.

I was watching Hannah and soon as she was sitting down and looking around, I started loving up Maria.

The tighter I held Maria, letting my hand slide down her back to press her closer, the more pleased she looked.

Plenty of people was nudging and whispering and I caught Old Nacio's black lizard-eyes staring unblinking at me. Hannah sat, her hands loose and easy in her lap, smiling and shaking her head "no" at the men who come to try for a dance with her.

I was coming to my senses. I got to wishing that some man, any man, would tap my shoulder and take Maria off my hands.

Her hand worked soft along my arm, she made little sounds

like dove-courtings. She whispered, "I didn't know what to do, Zande. I didn't want no marrying. I only wanted to make you hurt, like me. I won't marry Tony—" Not till then did it strike me what Maria was thinking.

I could a cursed myself. Every time I tried to think anything out I figgered wrong. All my plans to spite Hannah got buzzard claws to 'em, flew right back to tear at me.

Maria hung to me, still waiting for me to answer. Hannah sat quiet as though I wasn't making a public show of myself. I had to say something. Maria give my arm a shake, "I won't bother you, Zande. I'll wait. You'll come. Whenever you come—"

I couldn't bring out a word. I couldn't even think of the fix I'd be in if she didn't marry Tony. All I could think of was how Ma broke cats of chicken-killing by tying a dead chicken to the cat's neck.

She leaned closer to me and sighed, "You're right, Zande. With the accordion, the cake—the priest coming clear over here. I guess I got to."

I'd kept still because I couldn't say a word and she'd give herself a answer. She looked sad at me. "You think I got to; all them people here, huh?"

"Seems like," I told her. "The priest coming and all." She smiled at the people watching us, said low, as she broke away, "I'll come back for a visit, that's what."

VII

The stars come out. Supper'd been et and the women started unrolling lion or coyote pelts from their bed-bundles and tucking up the littlest children safe and warm on the ground behind the logs that faced the dance place.

The music seemed to be growing softer and thinner, almost fading away, and I seen Bill nod to Avery. Bill lowered his fiddle and Avery come in strong with his flute. Bill was going to get him a dance.

Bill got fat little Alice Ramirez by the hand and started dancing with her over to one comer, showing her the steps and she, turning the full-moon of her face to shine all over anyone who looked at her.

Then she screamed, and her mother and father run for Bill, their faces ugly with the fear he'd put a feeling hand on the fat little goose. Seemed like even a Ramirez should a thought better of Bill Pincus than that.

Alice went on screaming, Bill looking puzzled. "It's the big music! I saw it! It's coming!"

Everyone was so worked up that no one seen any sense to what she said. It looked bad for Bill till Hannah come and took Alice by the hand, "Tell us what you saw, Alice, what scared you and made you scream?"

"Who said I was scared?" Alice's lip hung down and she kicked at the dust with her bare toes. "I said I saw the music, and I did, too. Someone up the mountain made a light, maybe for his cigarro. I could see something shine way up the trail. Maria said the music would come in a box with silver and gold and diamonds all over it, she did so."

Maria ran through the crowd calling, "Accordion! Mamma! The dulces! Bring the cake! Make a place to set it out. Clear off, all of you, quick! Tony and the padre, the accordion. They're coming! Hear the horses!"

By the time the dogs was rounded up, Arvis come running forward with the cake. One of the short logs had been roiled into the center, stood on end, and the Demas young ones was putting out green feather redwood tips to make a cover for the top.

Hannah, her lips soft, eyes bright, put out one finger to touch the new green twigs, whispering, "A real wedding cake."

If she thought to make me feel bad that she hadn't had a wedding cake, she'd picked the wrong time for it.

Maria was charging round, screaming for more lights, telling everyone to stand back, to go and set down so as to have the cake show good when the wedding party come riding up.

They was near enough now that we could hear the horses real good, and it struck me that Tony Gallo was taking his time riding up to his wedding. Would have looked better if he come in at a good clip, but maybe he wasn't as eager as Maria thought. Then I saw the rider on the first horse and knowed from the robe it was one of the Mission fathers riding in front. That struck me all of a heap. The man behind the priest looked sharp-featured and stern, the light picking up just the lines to his face.

Maria run over to the priest and asked, "Where's the accordion?"

The priest didn't answer. He was mumbling something to

himself, all the time making the sign with the flat of his thumb across his mouth. Then he stopped his crossing, looked up and the torchlight showed red again' his glasses in their steel frames. Then round owl-eyes first swung the whole circle of lifted faces and then he spoke right out, "Bless you, my children."

Maria run over to the priest as he stood up, grabbed hold his shoulder, urging, "Where's Tony? Where is he?"

The priest cocked his head one side and give a knowing smile. "He'll be here. A looking glass would show you why."

Whatever he was getting at made Maria show all her teeth and her head lifted proud as she looked around at her mother's worried face.

Then her hands went to her heart and she says, in a put-on sort of way, "Oh, listen—"

She held up her hand for quiet and we all heard it—horses coming like a runaway.

At the last second the two riders pulled up and the paint-horse and the sorrel stood tall on their hind legs for an instant, then swung, with the mean Spanish bits pulling at their mouths, till they faced the tie-rack and their riders dropped reins and swung to the ground.

I caught the look on Maria's face as she took in Tony Gallo in all his wedding finery; the spank-new buckskins, silver buttons, a bright red neckerchief and a woodpeckers red feather stuck in his wide black sombrero. The look she sent him seemed to say "I want you" plain as if she'd put it into words. That's how she looked, but what she done next was step back of her mother and stand looking down, like modest and shy, as Tony and his groomsman come forward.

The stern-faced fellow that rode in with the priest had took the priest's horse and his own chestnut mare over to the tie-rack, had been busy unsaddling and rubbing the beasts down but now he come forward with the other two travelers and they was all busy, bowing and naming theirselves. I listened and caught on to the fellow on the showy paint-horse being Tony's cousin, name Henry Close. The dark, set-faced one was Frank Gallo, older brother to Tony, and the priest was called Father Montara.

Tony was standing first on one foot, then on t'other, looking at Maria over the priest's shoulder and making signs for her to come over to him but she was too smart to make a show of herself.

She turned to Henry Close, smiled right into his eyes as she touched the back of his hand with her fingertips, coaxing, "Come, Cousin Henry, get the silver box off the horse and make a tune from it, huh?"

Henry run with her, smiling like she had the right to give orders, but Tony stayed by Mrs. Demas, his head bent respectful while he listened to his bride's mother.

By the time the accordion was off the saddle and out of its buckskin wrappings, everyone come running up to get a good look.

I had to admit it was worth a look. Not only was it shiny white and trimmed up with silver but it had glittering stones set into one side of it that spelled out ACCORDION. But the thing that set all the young ones to jumping and laughing was its long mouthful of buttons like black and white teeth. When the children seen how Henry only had to touch them teeth and the thing howled like a wolf, the bold ones doubled laughing, but the shy ones scattered for the brush and hid.

Songer was whispering to Tony and Frank Gallo, to Henry and even to the priest. The priest seemed like he looked sort of sad as he shook his head to Songer's urging, but Henry put the accordion down on a log and the three men followed Songer, all heading for the barranca.

Tony called back, "The first dance is for me and Maria!"

Maria didn't answer him. Her eyes narrowed and got one of them scheming looks. She waited till the men was out of sight and then she calls, soft but clear, "The first dance is for me all alone. I dance good-by for the Coast first. After the wedding I make dance with Tony."

She walked over to where Avery was standing with Ma and Mel, and she started talking to Avery at a great rate.

I looked around for Hannah and it didn't please me none to find she'd walked back to the post where the wedding cake was sitting in its green bough nest. Her face had that sad, faraway look; and though she raised a hand now and again to shoo off the big moths that come blundering into the torchlight, I got a feeling that she wasn't thinking about the moths at all.

I soon caught on that I wasn't the only one noticing Hannah, and it got me hot under the collar to have my new wife making a long face in a place like this. I'd a gone over to her right then, drawed her off to sit quiet on a log, but that I happened to hear the crackle of paper. Avery was standing with a bunch of papers in his hand. He passed one paper over to Maria. She folded it around a smooth stick and give it to Arvis, who put it in his leather pouch, listening careful to what Maria told him.

They both give me a look and there was a mean grin to both their faces. Ma and Mel had wandered off and was gawping at the accordion with the rest of the crowd, so there was no way for me to find out what they was up to unless I asked Avery or Maria. I wouldn't ask either of them and I turned it in my mind, trying not to feel bothered, but I was. Sudden I thought it could be the wedding paper. Might be Avery had been in town and got it. Must be. Arvis was like head of the family, being the oldest boy, so it would be fit and proper for him to carry it, bring it out at the right time. But why should they look at me like that?

I give it up and went over to Hannah and touched her on the arm, saying, "I want for you to come set with me a spell."

She turned her head, looked at me like she'd never saw me before and she asks me, "Why?"

That stopped me. I'd give her a reason; I'd told her I'd like for her to do it. What more reason could a woman want?

But she didn't make no move to follow me, just stood there waiting. I hung onto my temper and answered her civil, "'Twould look better."

"How things look don't matter much. It's how they are that counts with me."

That's what she said. It didn't make sense any way you think

142

about it so I told her, slow and careful, "How things look is how they are. Everyone knows that."

Hannah lifted her shoulder, let it drop and she said, "Everyone?"

How she spoke it made a question out of it, but I let it go. She moved along at my side and sat quiet on the log beside me, saying nothing, scarce seeming to take note of anything going on. Tony and his crowd was coming up out of the barranca capering like colts. Maria had got holt of Avery and was acting the fool in the middle of the cleared place; talking quick at him, making slow steps all around him, then stopping to talk some more.

Then I heard Avery say, "The *Dance of the Little Bears,* but about pavana tempo, I think you mean." He picked up the big music box, slung the strap across his peaked shoulder, hurried over to where we had fixed a place for the music players.

I took a quick look at my wife. I'd got my wish that something would take her mind off her brooding.

She was leaning forward, her eyes taking in Avery, turning to follow Maria as she run over to her grandmother. They was gurgling together in Nacio's Indian talk and I couldn't follow a word of it. Finally Nacio clawed the black rebosa off her own head, hung it over Maria's hair and give the girl a little push toward the dance place.

As her grandchild walked into the center of the cleared space, Nacio went around and re-lit the four torches closest to Maria and then scuttled over to a place by the edge of the barbecue pit. Maria stood quiet, her hands clasped in front of her, her head bowed until her grandmother slid down to a seat on her own heels, fixed her old brown hands to cover all her face but the lizard-eyes.

Slow and sorry-like, Maria lifted her head, took the old

worn rebosa off her hair and slid it down to rest on her shoulders. The music started. Maria, keeping her hands folded in front of her like she was praying, let her head drop down lower and lower. Then her shoulders started tracing the time of the tune, she keeping her feet close together, only following the tune with weaving shoulders.

Avery was playing the *Dance of the Little Bears* but only for it being the same tune, it didn't sound anything like the music he'd played to get the children dancing.

Now the gay tune sounded sad; singing slow in the dark night. Maria's thick black hair, spite of the oil she always rubbed on to shine it, hung in heavy hanks like black, wood hair. It never stirred to the music, though it hung down across her shoulders. It was like dead hair.

Then, with a quick fling her head come up high, she stretching her neck up long as she could get it. Her breasts come up to stand out firm and round as she lifted her whole body up from the waist. It seemed like she growed a foot taller.

Then she stepped out. Long steps. Slow. Her arms come up and her lip pulled back in more a threat than a smile. She started a sharp tossing of her head. With them jerks, the long black snakes of her hair come alive, and followed her tossing head as her steps quickened.

Her dance-feet drew a circle clear around the flat space. Then she started again in the slow, long-stepped walk she'd started out with. It was like she drawed a square, north, south, east and west, the square-points just touching the edge of the circle she'd made.

Watching her, I could feel a pulse-beat hammering hard under my ear, and I seen this strange dance was plucking at everyone. The women was watching, following every step with wide eyes. I took a quick look at the men close by and their

144

hands was tight clenched, their mouths slack. Even little Alice had her fat neck stretched up long as she could get it.

Finishing drawing her square, Maria let go all the tall she'd drawed into herself. Her shoulders slumped, and her snake hair went back into lank hunks as she walked to the strict center of the square she'd drawed inside the circle.

Avery was near to the end of the tune again as Maria made herself rock-still for a few seconds. Then she stretched out her arms like to make a cross of herself, and turned slow, bowing deep down, first to the east, then north, south, and finished off with two deep bows to the west.

Like it was all over, the accordion jewels stopped winking in the torchlight, and the creepy music stopped.

But Maria wasn't done yet. She took two steps in toward the log I was sitting on with Hannah, gives a deep bow and blows a kiss off her cupped hand straight at me. I heard Hannah catch her breath but I never moved. I couldn't. Cat-quick, Maria swung half around, done the same kiss-throwing to Phil Logward, to Tao Ramirez, to other men that was sitting by their own wives.

I looked for Tony to shake the teeth out of her but he was laughing, clapping Henry on the shoulder like it was a joke, and when Maria picked up her skirts and run over to hide her face in Nacio's leather apron, Tony went running right after.

"*Amapolo rojo,*" he says, pulling her to her feet and holding her with his arm around her waist, "I got to get ring on you so you know which fellow belongs along with you. Look here what I got for you." Tony took a piece of buckskin out of his pocket, unfolded it and handed her something. Quick as a trout Maria grabbed the bright bait and run with it, first holding it above her head and then trying to get it on her finger as she screamed out, "Come quick! Look! See what I got!"

She poked her hand with the ring on it right into Mrs. Ramirez' face, her voice shaking as she said, "It's mine. Tony give it!"

Mrs. Ramirez' jaw dropped, her eyes bugged out as she whispered, "Holy Mother, a diamond!"

Tony's big mouthful of square white teeth showed but still he sounded sheepish as he followed along after Maria and said, "Is a garnet stone; good garnet, the peddler told me so."

Maria clasped her hands together, keeping the ring up so's it would show good, and run over to the priest who was holding his coat spread open before the coals of the barbecue fire and looking sleepy.

Maria started coaxing him like he was any man, not a priest. "Padre," she sings out, "would you make the marriage words right away? Then I could have wedding dance with Tony. We cut the cake, too."

The priest let go his coat tails and clasped his hands to the front of hisself, looking sort of doubtful till Tony come over and says in a low voice, "Maria was never baptized, Father Montara, like I told you. You marry us now and, like I said, we get married in the church all over again when she's Christianed."

"Tsk tsk," the priest clicked his tongue like scolding, but he was smiling as he said, "Too bad, but these trails make it a long way to church. We just have to do the best we can." He sighed, shook his head but said, "Well, call your witnesses. I'll get my Book."

He went over toward his saddle-bag and Maria started whispering to Tony. Whatever she said was too low for anyone to hear but Tony spoke right out, "Witnesses, someone to stand up with us. Henry's going to stand up with me. You pick whoever you want."

Maria's eyes searched the crowd and she went over to

Hannah, who was talking to Mrs. Ramirez.

Maria's back was to me but I heard Hannah's clear voice, "I'd rather not, thank you. Not now."

Maria must a urged her, anyway, for Hannah come back with, "No, really, I'm such a stranger here. I'd rather you asked some old friend of yours."

There was nothing backwards about Mrs. Ramirez. She stepped right up, asking Maria, "How about me? I'd like to. Next best to being bride, is what I think."

Maria sounded grudging, "Well, if you want to." She started back to join Tony and the priest, Mrs. Ramirez following, seeming not a bit put out by the short way Maria took her offer.

Halfway over, Mrs. Ramirez turned and hurried back to Hannah, put in her two bits' worth of woman talk.

"Poor thing!" She give Hannah a wise look and patted her hand as she told her, "I remember how it was. I don't forget, no, I don't. You're lonesome now, but you wait. You'll have the nino soon, then some more and some more. No time for lonesome then."

Hannah answered her, "Thank you, Mrs. Ramirez," cool as always, but she walked clear out of the circle of torchlight and when she come back I see her stuffing a wet little wad of handkerchief into her pocket.

My strange woman was crying at a barbecue, a dance, and a wedding all rolled into one. And crying because she was lonesome when she was right smack in the middle of all the folks on the Coast. Looked like I never would get the right of her.

I seen the priest was getting ready to start the marrying. The crowd moved closer so's to hear real good and I stood shoulder to shoulder with Hannah as she come forward with the rest. Soon as the wedding was over, the cake cut, we could go home. Hannah wasn't lonesome in her own house any more, leastwise she never let on to it, and I was mightily of a mind to try to ease my mind of my own sin by being better talking-company for Hannah once I got her promise that there was nothing between her and Mr. Avery.

The wedding words didn't take long to say. I heard Tony's "I do" and that Maria answered when Mrs. Ramirez punched her but then the priest went into some long speech in talk I didn't know at all, and I forgot the wedding and got to wondering if it wouldn't be a fine plan to cure them calf hides soft and fine and make Hannah a good riding skirt. I'd even tell Hannah about the fixing of it.

Even as I made up my mind to it, I knowed I couldn't. What if the leather went tough or spotty? If I rubbed in too little brains, if I used too much ashes, if every one of a dozen things wasn't just right, the leather might never come soft and fine like I wanted for Hannah.

No. I couldn't ever tell her I was fixing to do something for her. It would have to be all done and done right before I could say, "Here, Hannah, this is yours."

I heard the clapping and the cheering, looked up to see the kissing and hand-shaking going on and I saw the wedding was done. I'd missed seeing if the paper Arvis had was Maria's wedding lines.

I says, low, to Hannah, "Let's tell them we wish good luck to them, eat cake if it goes around, and then ride for home." Hannah come with me. I hung to the idea that everything would pass off smooth, we'd soon be away from all this crowd. Maria would take a new trail, start a new life. And one thing sure—I'd got clear rid of my hankering for Maria Demas and that was a load I was glad to put down.

VIII

Getting away wasn't as quick as I'd counted on. Every last man, woman and child wanted a share in the big doings, and one at a time they filed by, shaking hands, wishing happiness. The men was full of rough jokes; the women windy with wise words and fine wishes for big family, happiness and money; the children, even Alice, just gawking and mumbling.

Through it all Maria hung to Tony's arm, smiling, bobbing, showing to everyone that she was tickled to be the whole show.

Hannah had to do a little different from the rest when her turn in front of the bridal pair come. She stood back a little way, didn't offer to shake hands with either of them, but she bowed nice and spoke like she meant it when she said, "I hope you'll be very happy, Mrs. Gallo, and the same to you, Mr. Gallo."

I went out of my way to be hearty, after Hannah's coolness, clapping Tony on the shoulder as I told him he was lucky, laughing to Maria, "No leaky roofs or cross-eyed young ones for you, Mrs. Gallo, with the husband you got."

Maria colored up and snooted her nose at me. I felt Hannah stiffen and she edged her shoulder away from my touch. But the crowd laughed and thought it was good and before anyone said anything to the Gallos or to me, Songer broke in. He was the last in line and finished it all off with a good laugh as he asked, "What you holding out on that cake for? I thought the reason you got married was so's you could cut the cake."

Quick as a flash, Maria puts in, "If you think cake is what ladies marry to get, no wonder you old bach all your life!"

Beside me I felt Hannah shake and I see she was turning her head away to hide her laugh. The other women all give Maria the long-faced look but, scared as I was they'd catch onto Hannah, I couldn't keep from laughing with her and the men. Tony's laugh bust into a fine spray and he was rubbing off the back of his hands on his new buckskins as he urged, "Take my knife, Mrs. Gallo. You want cake, I'll see you get it."

Mrs. Demas leaned over and said something to Maria, shaking her head and looking at the priest. The girl give a impudent toss to her head but she said, in a wifely kind of way, "Mrs. Tony Gallo likes first the one dance with husband. Then for everyone, one big dance and after, the cake. Save for end of party, huh?"

That seemed to suit everyone but Songer and the youngsters. They didn't count. Bill got his fiddle, Avery took his place and tweedled his flute while Henry come over with the accordion looking proud and sure of himself as he calls out, "The jota, Maria?"

Tony and Maria grabbed hands and run to the center as Henry turns to the other players and says, *Seville Lady,* that's the best tune."

It was something to see, something to hear, when that accordion turned loose on a dance tune. It made so much music a fellow had to listen careful to hear the fiddle and even the sharp flute couldn't come out to top it. The dance matched the music. I'd never saw Maria so light-footed, seen her teeth shine so steady as they did while the whole Coast watched her and her new husband do brand-new steps to the old jota. Tony tore off his red neckerchief and stomped around Maria, waving it like them bullfighters the Spanish like to tell tales of.

Maria circled him like a fox circles a trap, but her face, her hands, all of her, coaxed him to catch her. Even while I was looking at it I was thinking I'd still see, still hear this music and dancing when I was old as Pa. I forgot I wanted to go up to my own place. I forgot to feel like them two was making a bold show of themselves. When Maria slowed down, come closer, Tony caught her, swung her clear off her feet, held her up with his arms straight above his head for a second. Then he set her down and they both started bowing as the music stopped.

No one wanted them to stop. The hands slapping together drownded out the slap of the sea again' the cliffs and here and there was shouts of "Morel More!"

Then Bill Pincus, his big hand tight around the slim neck of his fiddle, stepped in front of me, stopped me while he whispered, "Don't let on, Zande, but the *Sierra Nevada* is coming, sure as shooting. I just happened to catch her light as she pulled into Tan Bark Creek before the Point hid her so she could be here in another hour. Be a good joke to keep 'em all so busy dancing no one would know she was here till she hoots."

"The *Sierra Nevada?*" I asked him. "You sure of that, Bill? Never knowed her to land here in the middle of the night before."

Bill says, "I'm sure. It's her all right. Must be she broke down some place."

If Bill was sure, he was sure. No getting around that.

I thought it over quick. It'd be the funniest thing ever happened on the Coast if we could do it. Most folks held the boat coming was a bigger thing than even a barbecue and once she was sighted all hell broke loose. Men left their branding irons sticking in the fire, left their plow in the furrow, and headed for the Landing. Women let go washboards and young ones dropped their weeding or whatever and ever' last soul of 'em run like mad or rode hell-for-leather, all pouring down mountain like cloud-burst creeks. Tonight everyone on the Coast was already here pleasuring themselves with food and dancing. Would be a laugh for twenty years if the boat sneaked in and told of it with that wolf-howl whistle.

"I'll get 'em, Bill," I told him. "One of them change-around waltzes will get all the men's eyes on the bride and all the women watching and wishing for Tony to tap 'em. If your arm holds out with the fiddle, we'll make it!"

Bill never cracked a smile as he went back to his place on the log, but he made out to sneeze and so covered up his laugh as I yelled like I was driving pigs and told the crowd a change-waltz was starting.

Dancing was what they wanted and they all turned to and it come out just as I'd figgered, only that Hannah run Maria a close second for which changed partners most. The waltz went on and on and I watched close. Soon as the changing partners started to slow down a bit, I got behind Henry and poked him

152

in the ribs, calling loud in his ear, "Start that polka you was telling Maria about, the new one, *Chicken in the Pea Patch*. That'll wake things up."

Henry nodded his head and when he come to the end of the waltz next time, he swung right into a good lively polka and I yelled at the top of my lungs, "Same dance! Change partners and keep it going!"

You'd think someone'd switched their legs with nettles, the way them tired waltzers started prancing and bucking into that polka. I was taking a short sashay with Hannah and I worked her over to the edge of the dancers so I could manage to make out if the boat was close.

I jumped bad as the rest when, even before I got where I could see past the torchlight, the old *Sierra Nevada* let out a howl like she'd been kicked in the paddle-wheel.

Hannah's hands was clutching me and she said, shaky, "What's that?"

Like it hadn't jumped me a bit, I answered, "That, my girl, is the boat with your trunk on it."

I shouldn't a done it. I never got the chance to go up and laugh with Bill. Hannah clung to me, clear broke down, her face working as she says over and over, "My little trunk, my little trunk…"

I had to stand there patting her back, asking her, "What's wrong? I thought you'd be glad to get your trunk."

There wasn't a word in her but, "My little trunk."

I give her a couple of breaths' time and then I spoke up, rough enough to get her over it, "Hurry up! Someone else'll get it if you ain't there."

She lifted her head, give me a shaky smile as she said, "Of course, let's hurry!"

We run together and we got there near as fast as the rest of the crowd. Maria was out in front, wailing, "My white mantilla, she's right there and I'm here, married already."

Tony was telling her, sensible, "You'll need it all new, when we get church-married," but I could see he was already finding her out. When she wouldn't quit being sorry and watch what was going on, he went off to help build a big fire right on the cliff, to see by.

Even the littlest ones, the ones that got so scared they run and hid when the whistle blowed, was coming chirping out of cover by now. They crowded close to the cliff and had to be dragged back to keep the place around the cable clear so the freight could come ashore on the double cable.

I left Hannah standing with Ma and Mrs. Demas and run over to give a hand with the windlass, although I knowed the boat wasn't tied up yet, much less ready to start the freight to shore. Every able-bodied man in the crowd was there already.

Bill Pincus was first in the line, his hand firm on the crank that would start the cable moving, his face set and ready, like the rest of him. But when he seen me he loosened up, started grinning and then laughed right out.

"We done it, Zande," he calls out.

Timateo Ramirez was next to Bill and he asked, "Done what?"

That was what Bill was a fishing for, to get someone to ask what we was up to. Bill was usual a regular old sobersides, but he laughed till he plumb rolled over the crank, trying to get stopped long enough to tell the joke. He had to give up. He was sitting on the ground, tired with whooping, when he managed to say, "You tell 'em, Zande."

I pulled up one of the blue-curl was growing there by the rocks and stood roiling it in my fingers to smell the strong, late autumn smell of it, as I answered, mild and easy, "'Twas nothing much. Bill, he spotted the boat more'n a hour ago, and we figgered it fun to keep you all dancing while the boat sneaked up."

That crowd turned into a bunch of hornets. Most of the laughing come from the men, and they doubled up bad as Bill done. The hooting come from the women who was all for pulling our hair. All the heavy groceries and any sort of kickshaws they was to get for most of a year was on the boat and seemed like they all thought the stuff would be better if they'd been hanging over the cliff, watching the boat for hours. The youngsters sided with the women and started gathering up clumps of wire-grass, flinging 'em, roots and all, at us. Things was right lively till Benjy flung a cow chip that wasn't none too dry and then the women turned on the children and put a stop to the fun.

The yellow man in the boat's kitchen flung open one of them little round windows about the size of his head and shut off most of the candlelight behind him while he was trying to make out what was going on. Maybe he thought we was a crazy lot, but I could of told him what I thought of a man that had his hair braided and wrapped around his head like a woman.

There was a plenty long time of waiting and watching before the fellow on the boat yelled up, "Ready, here!"

That was what we was waiting for. Bill loosed the load-hook so's it could slide down the cable and the boat crew got the first sling of goods hooked on tight. I got gooseflesh, my own self, when a voice on the boat sung out, "Let 'er go!"

Bill and three helpers humped their backs, bore down on the big crank till, slow and creaking, it got to turning. I held my breath, same as when I was a tad, when that first load started out over the dark water, just missing the slap of waves breaking on the big black rocks between where the boat was tied to the landing cable and the cliff that was the shore.

We landed it safe, never wet or lost a thing. The men that couldn't get their hands on the windlass crank got their chance to work when the sling landed. Eight of us jumped at the load, dragged it far enough back from the cliff so the women could get around it safe. We rolled off the barrels of flour, big stuff like that, and dumped the rest so we could send the sling back for the next load.

The children followed every barrel and bag, smelling 'em, patting the stuff, then making a wild run back to their mothers so's not to miss anything. As Arvis drug the empty sling back to Bill and his crew I threw some small brush and some grease-wood roots on the fire so as to make a bright blaze. It flamed up good and all the women but Hannah tore into the small stuff, holding it to the light so's to see what name was marked on.

Hannah looked like she'd lost her last friend and was trying hard to bear up, so I circled around the crowd to her. She seen me and come slow to meet me. Her voice was dead flat, as she said, "My trunk. They never fetched it."

I knowed it could be. Times was when they forget to set stuff out for the boat in Monterey. But I told her, "Hold your horses till the last load's in. What's took you? You ain't the give-up kind."

She give me a watery smile. Her head come up and she says, "Thank you," like I'd done her a favor and she looked real bright when I told her there was maybe eight, ten loads still to come off the boat; that there was anyway forty barrels of flour to come, for one thing.

Her eyes widened, brightened, but her voice come low as she asked me, "Any flour for us?"

"One barrel," I told her, firm. "I never figger on but enough to hold the corn meal together."

Just as firm she comes back at me, "There'll be cake for

Christmas, and no corn meal in it either."

I fooled her. Mild as milk I says to her, "Well, you're the cook, Mrs. Allan," and I walked back to the windlass ere she could as much as say "scat."

What with Hannah's trunk coming off on the next-to-last load, Maria shrieking around and waving her new mantilla in everyone's face and Mrs. Ramirez shaking the teeth plumb out of Benjy for sneaking out a pinch of raisins from someone's sack, bedlam roared around the unloading. Mrs. Ramirez was moaning, "Little pig-child, you et someone's Christmas and we got no raisins to pay back."

Hannah was wild because she left her trunk key in her reticule up to our place and kept telling Mrs. Demas there was a picture of a nice old man with a wheelbarrow full of flowers and fruit pasted inside of the lid of her trunk. "It's like looking at an old friend's face," she kept saying. We only lacked one real crazy thing to make it like boat landing always is. Maria fixed that.

She run back to the dancing place, snatched up the cake and come tearing back with it, bound to send some cake over to the men on the side-wheeler so they could have a share in her wedding.

Maria come up to Tony, saying, "Your knife, Tony! Give quick!"

Like she was wearing the pants instead of him, Tony give her the knife, didn't even ask what she wanted with it. Biggety as the tax collector, Maria whangs right through the middle of the cake, takes the half of it and wraps it up in the paper her mantilla had come in and drops the whole business in the sling. Then she turns around, hands what was left of the cake, and the knife, over to her mother, "You cut, madre. Make him go round for taste to everyone."

Maybe she thought that was easy, maybe she didn't give a damn. Anyway, she grabbed hold of Tony and the two of them stood there, bowing and waving as the good-luck wishes come back across the water. The boat crew licked the cake off their fingers and then, while part of 'em took care of getting up the riding anchor, the others got the boat loose from where it was tied to the cable. The paddle-wheel started churning up white water, the whistle give a long hoot, and the *Sierra Nevada* bobbled off like a fat old woman.

Everyone stood right where they was, not talking or moving. 'Twould be a year before the boat come back again with freight, and all eyes followed the ship, watching till she bobbed around the Point and her lights was gone.

Mrs. Demas had hacked up the cake till there was a bite all around, though some didn't have none of the white sugar top part. Maria was helping her mother pass it around. I see her coming, so I quick grabbed up a piece from the old woman's dish and made off after Frank Gallo.

Frank had took his cake and started over to the tie-rack. He was tightening the cinch when I got there and he started in talking.

"Well," he said, "Tony gets a wife and a new house and I hope he does good for himself. Me, I lose my partner and get a empty house to ride back to."

I eased myself down on my heels and didn't say anything, being busy with thinking that now, just a few more minutes, and I'd be clear shed of Maria. It went off better than I had any right to hope and I got a feeling that in time I could get the whole business out of my mind, like it never happened.

I looked around in the fast-growing light and seen Henry was strapping up his accordion, that families was getting their share of the freight gathered in heaps to pack. Hannah was sitting on her trunk talking to Avery.

I stood up. I'd get her off that trunk, get the trunk packed on Nip, get my wife back to myself and away from that fellow.

Frank stopped fussing with the horses as I stood up. He looked at me across the back of Henry's paint-horse and he says, "Mr. Allan, you fixed to buy some cattle?"

Of course, I was thinking to buy, but I answers him, "I got about all my range will carry. But if they're cheap enough, drive 'em over and I'll look at 'em.'"

"A hundred head, white-faced," he says, short as you please. "A few strays of late calves, but I'll call it an even hundred. I'm clearing out, just made up my mind."

My way is to figger, for a long time before I buy anything. I was thinking about it; maybe this was the chance I'd hoped for. Frank wouldn't wait, he spoke up again, "Ten dollars a head I'll make it, if you take delivery on my place. There's the offer. Take it or leave it."

My last ten head cost forty, each one of 'em. I couldn't turn my back on such a chance. There was Hannah to think about. Had to go easy with her, she was carrying. It was a hard trip across the mountain and she no great shakes yet as a rider.

"I'll ride over and look at 'em," I told him. "I can fix things to come tomorrow."

"I'll sell to someone and be on my way to the city by tomorrow," he says, flat as his black hat.

I seen he meant it.

I couldn't take Hannah. I couldn't leave her; not with Avery fooling around the country not six miles from my place.

"Be with you in ten minutes," I said. "I got to saddle." I went down the rack to where my horses was munching barley hay, throwed Ranger's saddle onto him.

By now the rest of the crowd was rounding up their families, cramming saddle-bags with stuff the boat brought in, getting the children mounted. Out of the tail of my eye I see Pa leading out his saddle and pack horses.

I felt a load lift when I heard Henry Close sing out to the priest that he'd stay at the Demases' place, ride back with him when the baptizings was over. If the accordion was staying, Maria'd make Tony stay, too. I wouldn't have to worry over having her riding along with me.

I found Mel was still sitting on the cliff, his face turned to the Point where the steamer went out of sight. I rode over to him and he looked around quick when I said, "Mel."

"Wipe them cake crumbs off your chin," I told him, laughing to see how quick he run his hand across his mouth. I leaned down and told him, quiet, "Mel, I want for you to pack my wife's trunk on Nip, see that it gets up to my place."

He asked no questions, just said, "Sure," and I pulled Ranger around, knowing the trunk was as good as up to the house.

Beyond the barbecue pit Ma was making for the string of horses Pa was bringing up, and I cut across to her.

"Ma," I told her, "go on and ride over to my place with Hannah, stay with her till I get back. Just a couple days."

I give Ma no time to tell me she couldn't and I rode by Hannah without seeming to look at her. I wasn't such a fool as to tell, in front of Avery, I'd be gone for two days. I'd do no talking to her till I got her alone and she'd be glad enough to see me when I come back driving a new herd of prime cattle.

Tony's brother was holding in the chestnut he was riding and I said, "Let's get going."

I was in a hell of a hurry now to get out far on the trail. I touched Ranger with the spur and he took out in a easy lope, Frank's chestnut picking up speed to stay with Ranger.

Below us on the flat, horses was nickering to each other, voices shouting as pack loads was tied on but I didn't look back till we got where the Jolon Valley trail branched off, headed for the big pine timber high up. To the north the trail that led to my cabin was in sight for about half a mile along the Coast before it dipped out of sight into a canyon. The stretch of trail I could see was empty and I hoped Ma and Hannah was already deep into the canyon on their way home.

Behind me I heard Frank pulling up the chestnut mare and then I heard the fast clatter of hoofs. Both laughing, both riding at a gallop, here come Maria and Tony tearing along the trail after us.

Maria was leading and she called out, her voice gay, "You riding home with us, Zande?"

On my tongue was, "I'd see you in hell first," but I clamped tight on my teeth and made like I'd not heard her. It's a waste of time to try to put Maria Demas off a notion she's got in her head. She pulled out of the trail into the lilac brush, rode past Frank and up so close to me I could feel the palomino's breath.

Maria was still smiling, but her voice had no smile to it as she tossed her head and said, "Your woman was looking funny when she watch you down this trail. She never waved hand to you, neither."

That was all right with me. I wasn't the waving sort. I wasn't telling my business to Maria either.

She just laughed, loud and mean, says, "Cat got your tongue, huh?" She waited a minute and then she let loose her temper and her words come spite-sharp: "Well, never got your wife's tongue. I heard her talk plenty when she walked off with the funny little man."

Maria laughed so hard that Tony called across the racket of hoofs, "Tell the joke, we want a laugh, too."

I kept my wits enough to call back, "Guess Maria got ticks dropped on her when she brushed the lilac and they're tickling her."

By God, it tickled me! Never made a joke before in my life without I studied on it for a long time and this one come poppin' out by itself just when I needed it bad.

I didn't have to let on I was laughing. I laughed till I doubled over and the rest of them laughed along, forgetting whatever it was started the laugh.

By the time the joke was called back and forth from one to the other, the horses was setting their haunches to the five-thousand-foot climb and the grind of loose rock under foot covered any chance of talk.

It give me a misery, chewing on the notion of Hannah walking off with Avery. I'd told Ma to stay with Hannah. She'd never let Avery ride up to the house with them.

Or would she?

Queer, where words of comfort come from. I thought of the long-gone day when I heard Demas tell a bunch of men that was sitting whittling and talking women: "No use to try to watch a woman. All you can do is trust 'em.

PART THREE

IX

Ranger walked out, well ahead of the chestnut mare, and I let him take his own gait. He was a good climber and I was glad to see Maria couldn't keep up.

Most that bothered me was knowing another hundred head would be over-grazing my range. On the other hand, white-faced cattle from a new strain would go a long way to building up my in-bred young stock. I'd get more land.

There was fenced land along the Coast for sale, cheap, too. But I wouldn't pay for what them Spanish called fences. I had money. Ever since I'd started with a bag of salt and my bare hands, I'd laid by part of every dollar I got hold of. My sons wasn't going to start bare-handed. The money laid by was for them.

How was I to get new range? Maybe Hannah had land rights, too. I'd heard women could take land though I never knowed any that done it. Seemed like I'd heard a married woman had to be a widow to get free land.

See-saw, back and forth, trying to keep my mind on land and cattle, I'd get wondering if Ma'd took Hannah to the old homeplace. If Avery went up to Pa's place with Mel—right this minute maybe Hannah was setting out a plate of victuals for him. Hannah could be sitting on the log near the myrtle, half-smiling, her eyes bluer than the blue-myrtle. Her hands would lay quiet in her lap, her head be bent sidewise, while she listened to the call of Avery's flute.

Mustn't think about Avery; land, think about land, that's it. There was pre-emption. I'd heard that if a fellow'd used his homestead right, he had to buy school-scrip and then turn it in on the land he wanted. I should of got Avery to talk about that scrip he said he had.

It was a fair warm morning when we'd left the Coast, more like summer than like late November, and it got hotter as we climbed. I'd thought it was hot when we topped the divide, but when we hit the floor of Jolon Valley, the heat was plain hell. The oak leaves hung limp, the trail writhed and danced in a blue whirl of heat-devils.

We crossed a dry fork of the San Antonio River, but it was cooler and there was shade from big sycamores and cottonwoods. That made me think of the dark cool redwoods of home, and I could of cried out. I had thought of what to do about more land!

About the same time as my folks come into the Big Sur, a half-breed named Juan Duro located a piece that cornered my upper pasture, give out that he was homesteading. He never done a tick of work. What he was up to was getting a squatter's right, thinking to pick up a easy fifty or even a hundred for his squat. After a time, he give up, drifted off.

I growed up thinking of that land as Juan Duro's. But it was anyone's land. It was going to be mine. After the business about Gallo's cattle was done, I'd ride over to the Jolon stage-station, post a letter up to the San Francisco land office. A family man has to keep an eye out for times to come.

I'd get me a fraction on the Coast, too, build a boat-landing of my own. I'd make big money on Gallo's cattle if they was any good at all, make it quick and easy. With that money I'd buy the land Ramirez wanted to sell; that three hundred-twenty laid

between Juan Duro's old place and the Coast. Then I'd have a place.

Me and Hannah and the boys could look from the highest top of the Santa Lucias down to where the sea beat again' the black rocks, and every valley, hill, tree and creek we looked at we could say: "Them's ours. This is our homeplace."

I come back to the heat and the hot Jolon trail when I heard both the Gallos calling to me. There was a fork to the trail where I was and through the heat shimmers I could see what was left of the Jolon Mission about eight miles off to the northeast.

Behind me both Gallos had pulled up and I see Frank leaning over from his saddle, talking to Tony, shaking hands with him. I swung Ranger around, eased my feet while I waited to see what was up.

Maria must of dropped behind a ways back but now she

come forward, patting at her face with the bandanna she fished out her riding-skirt pocket. She looked too hot, too tired, and not very pretty. For some reason that made me feel softer about her. I wanted to make her feel good.

"This your turn-off, Mrs. Gallo?" I asked her. Her lip got a sorry pucker to it and I hurried up to say, "Hear tell your new house's got three rooms and three glass windows."

She brightened up. "'Dobe house, too, not like them old redwood boards."

She turned her head quick, but I heard what she'd whispered, "I'm scared. I want to go home."

If she was scared, I was stiff with fright. If she wanted to go home I wouldn't of put it past her to do it. I edged Ranger over close to the men's horses and called out, hearty as I could, to Tony, "It's no good trying to hold up a man on his way to a honeymoon, so I'll wish you both good-by and good luck. Henry was telling what a fine new place you had to start in with."

Without giving Tony time to get a word in I called, "Come on, Mr. Gallo, lead off."

Frank tightened his reins, touched his sombrero with his fingers and the chestnut mare stepped out on the trail following the foothills. Behind me I could hear Maria's voice, "We'll see you on the Coast, Zande." Frank Gallo didn't have a word to say, to Maria or to me, though our horses was close together. Neither of us looked back.

We turned due north after a time, missing the Mission by a good eight miles, and started climbing again. Three ranges of foothills we had to cross before we come to the dry Arroyo Seco, and it struck me any man would be a fool to settle in this brick-oven country. We plodded along slow in the heat and I got so sleepy I lost track of everything.

Ranger's stopping jolted me awake. I see the chestnut mare

was already tied to a hitching rack out in front of a sun-bleached adobe. Halfway to the house, Gallo was standing over a Indian fellow about sixteen, gabbling Spanish gun-shot fast and loud.

I come wide awake as Gallo knocked the boy down and shouted, "You're lying. You low-down thieving dog, I'll kill you. Your uncle run that stock off and you helped him."

He grabbed the boy by the neck, pulled him to his feet, started shaking him till I thought the boy's head would pop right off, start rolling across the flat-land like a gourd loose from its stem.

"The truth! Tell the truth!" He kept yelling. "Where's my cattle?"

It's not good sense to put into another man's fight, but seemed like if Gallo wasn't stopped, he'd have a dead Indian on his hands. It's hard enough job to get truth out of a live Indian.

Climbing out of my saddle, I walked over close, but Gallo didn't seem to see me. The limp Indian's bare toes was dragging back and forth in the dust with every shake, his head lolling. I thought he was a goner.

"Let him get his breath!" I put my hand on Gallo's arm and told him, "He'll talk. Let him loose."

Gallo looked around at me and I almost jumped back. If ever I see a crazy man, I was looking at one. I looked into this fellow's crazy eyes and for the first time in my life I didn't feel proud of the way I was so free to let go my temper.

Fact was, I felt sorry for the Indian boy; he was no match for Gallo's weight and strength. He'd quit shaking the Indian, but he still had both hands tight around his neck. Beside, if he choked the boy, I'd likely never find out what become of them cattle and I'd come over a lot of mountains for a look at 'em.

I put my hand on Gallo's shoulder and I says, "Turn loose

of the boy! He'll talk now."

Gallo's hands loosened. As the Indian dropped in the dust, Gallo pulled back his leg, give the boy a kick that turned him face down in the dirt. He stood looking down at the boy for a second, his jaw-stubble looking blue again' the tallow of his face. He looked up, his eyes meeting mine like he saw me for the first time.

His face was still working, and his voice none too steady as he said, "I shouldn't a lost my temper till I got the truth out of him. I'll throw some water on him—" He stopped, and a crafty look come to his face.

He fished in his pocket for a block of sulphur matches and broke one off, struck it on his spur and held it to the boy's bare foot.

The Indian sat up, giving a scream like a eagle, and tried to crawl away. Gallo grabbed him by his long greasy hair and dragged him to his feet, held him up as the fellow's legs started to buckle under him.

"Tell the truth, and if you don't—you tell what you done with them cattle or I'll hang you dead."

The boy's voice was thick and his words come slow. "Curly-dog, he come in with his guts hanging out, crawling he come. I put them ten feeders in the barn, quick I done it. Then I went, bareback and so fast, I went to the range. Three men, it was, masked like bandits. They shoot at me. I jumped, but they killed the horse. Go, señor, look, for God's sake! Them bandits they drove the cattle off. By the Virgin I swear—"

Gallo's hand smacked the boy's face, and his other hand still held him up. My back crawled. I believed that Indian spoke the truth, but he was Gallo's Indian and if he was set to hang the boy it was his business, not mine.

I spoke to Gallo again. "Let's ride out to where the boy says his horse was shot. If there was three riders running off the cattle, we'll find their tracks."

"There'll be a dead horse, a dead dog and plenty of horse tracks." Gallo sounded short and sour. "This fellow's got a mess of thieving renegade relatives. Course he fixed it up with them to run the stock off while me and Tony and Father Montara was out of the country. Hell I'm sick of the country. Sick of the cattle and God-damned sick of Indians."

He turned loose of the boy, who scuttled around the house and out of sight, as Gallo yelled at him, "Get food, pronto, or I'll put a bullet through your back if it's the last thing I do!"

Without looking to see if the boy stopped, Gallo walked fast toward a big barn at the top of a small wash about a hundred yards from the gate. "There won't be no ten head shut up in the barn," he called over his shoulder. "You'll see. That's just more lies."

He stepped over the body of a curly black dog that was lying across the trail to the barn. Sure enough, his guts was hanging out, withering like strings of jerky hanging in the sun. A cloud of blue-bottle flies come up around our heads as we went close by the dead dog, but Gallo never looked up. He jerked the door to the barn open, and then he looked sort of foolish.

I stepped up close behind him and looked in. There was ten head shut up. I could see the shine to their fat red sides, and as some of them turned to look back at the light from the door, I could see the clean white faces, a long white blaze down the middle of each wide head. The thought of having a hundred head of such stock fair made me itch.

I turned to Gallo and said, "If all the stock is like this bunch, I'm going after 'em soon as I grab a bite to eat."

He looked at me, his eyes dull, and kicked at a coil of hair rope laying alongside the door, "The hell with 'em. Indians steal you blind. Was bad with Tony here, but without him—" He shrugged his shoulders, leaned again' the door frame and studied the tip of his boot. Then he looked up, "You want to pay me ten dollars a head for these, they're yours. Make it worth your trip. You want to hunt the rest—that's up to you. You'll never find 'em. Happen you should—they're yours."

"Thanks," I said, "but us Allans pay for what we get. I'll give you a writing; ten dollars a head for any I get back and I'll pay it soon as I've got the stock on my own range. And I'll settle in cash for these ten in the barn right now, if you'll make out a bill of sale."

"Come up to the house," he says, walking off. "I'll write it out while you eat, providing Iowana's got something ready."

We no sooner stepped into the adobe, than the Indian come out of a lean-to in the back with two heaped platters of chili-beans, fried eggs and sliced green peppers. He put the dishes down on a littered table and went back into the comeda.

Gallo felt around among the square nails, the bits of rope, bridles, spilled tobacco and crumpled papers, with a hard look to his face, the look he'd had when he rode onto the flat with the priest. Finally he found a piece of pencil, tore the edge off one of the printed papers, and working slow, he made me out a bill of sale.

I read it over, pulled my money pouch out of my buckskins and took out five twenties. The gold felt good in my hand, but I didn't mind letting go it; not for them cattle.

Gallo'd only et a couple spoonsful of beans; when I handed him the money he took it, stood up and held out his hand like he was aiming to shake hands.

That was what he was up to. "Well, I wish you luck finding them cattle, Mr. Allan," he says. "My advice is let 'em go. Indians got plenty ways of killing a man so it looks an accident. I'm off for San Francisco, and maybe I'll drift up into the gold country."

"When you aiming to start?" I asked him, just letting his words about going after the stock slide by.

"I've started," he says. "I'll ride the chestnut back to Jolon. Fellow there'll buy the horses and mules and I'll catch the first stage out for the city."

He walked off, his long legs swinging out on the trail to the gate.

I picked up a platter and stood in the doorway watching him and his horse gradually trimming down in size until the heat devils and hot blowing dust hid them clear away.

I felt so wore out I wasn't even hungry. I couldn't finish up my plate of food. I took both plates and walked into the little lean-to with them, thinking I'd ask the Indian boy, Iowana, to ride out with me to where he said the bandits run the cattle off.

The kitchen was empty, the fire dying down in the stove. I knowed that thing was a stove. I'd heard talk of stoves but I'd never saw one in a house before. I looked it over good, lifting up lids, opening a door to the side of it and finding it must be the oven. It was still hot, though there was little fire in the fire-box. Struck me it was a handy sort of thing, though I'd not trade a good fireplace and Dutch oven for it, myself. But I was too sleepy to look at it long.

No sight or sound of the Indian boy anywhere.

My head was buzzing like a fly on a window and I made my way over to a bunk back in the other room, thinking to rest for a half-hour.

I thought I'd only slept a minute, but I woke to find the sun just topping the mountains.

Never felt so much a fool as when I went over to Ranger,

took his saddle off, and led him down to the barn for water and feed. If I'd a caught a ten-year-old treating his horse that-a-way, I'd sure batted down his ears. I give Ranger a good rub after he'd filled with water and was chewing away on the barley.

Gallo had been right about the Indian helping to run off the stock, else why did he skin out like that?

I lit a fire, warmed up the beans and then I slung the saddle on Ranger soon as he'd finished eating. Struck me would be a good idea to ride in a wide circle across the plain, keeping the shack to the center. By the time I was half around I'd picked up the tracks. The bunch was easy to trail, even across a plain cut with cattle trails. This trail was fresh and the stock had been moving fast. I followed a couple of hours, I reckoned, and then the trail started spreading out, drifting more toward the mountains.

The heat pressed on me till it seemed bad as trying to follow a ground squirrel track. I done my best to find where the cattle I was following had bunched up again, but for a long time it was beyond me.

I'd back-track till the prints was plain again and for a time I'd be all right. Sooner or later—I'd find myself right back where the herd spread out, and every trail I took from there petered out in some blind canyon so blocked with rock a goat couldn't of scrambled out, much less a herd of white-faces.

I most lost track of time. Three days of riding that plain, seeing the baked red earth so dry it laid open like long red knife-cuts, and I knowed I'd have to find them cattle quick or they'd be dry and starved as the land itself. No wonder Gallo was willing to sell cheap.

Third night I rode in tuckered out and close to discouraged, the Indian boy, Iowana, was in the kitchen. He come out, set food on the table, just like the day I come.

I could tell he was bothered. He come in and out of that hot little comeda, his feet not making a sound, his eyes looking to the floor when I looked at him but I knowed he was looking at me when I bent my head to eat. Finally he stood close by me shuffling his feet and then he blurted out, "Mr. Allan, you go now. Hay getting short. You take ten head, drive back to Coast."

Way down in the bottom of me I knowed I wanted to do just that. Hannah and what she was up to pulled so hard on me that I was fighting that itch hard as I was fighting not to give up a thing I'd started. If I could of, I'd a let the whole thing pass by, but I couldn't.

I looked the Indian square in the eye, "Gallo had the straight of it. Your uncles did drive off that stock." I seen his mouth go tight, watched his hand close over that lead cross he was always fingering, but he wouldn't give in. He never said a word. Soon as I'd finished eating he cleaned up the table, went out with the plates and shut the door.

Thinking he'd went off for good this time, I set there feeling mad as hell at myself. I should of been like Gallo: grabbed him and knocked the truth out of him while I had the chance.

I was trying hard to tell myself I'd give up, take the ten and start the drive home at dawn, knowing all the time I wouldn't do no such thing, when I felt the thick air stir.

The kitchen door opened slow and Iowana popped back into the room, grinning.

"Them Gallo boys," he said. He stopped to shuffle his bare brown toes on the dirt floor, grinning sheepishly, "Them's cousins with me. We got the same no-good uncles."

He slammed the door shut and was gone before it come to me what he'd said. Then I got it.

"I'll be damned." That's what I, told myself, feeling plumb disgusted with the whole bunch. That's how they are, them mixed breeds. Frank Gallo'd made a proper fool of me with all that put-on about Iowana's uncles and knocking the boy around, near to kill him. Sudden it struck me funnier than hell. I chuckled, thought about it for a second more and then I whooped laughing till you could of heard me half way up the mountain.

Soon as I laughed, the door come open again and Iowana was peering around it. His voice was sort of stiff when he said, "Not so funny; them uncles plenty bad, got guns, too."

He stood nervous, twisting on the leather thong that hung the lead cross around his neck. He acted like he wanted to talk and couldn't bring himself to. I waited.

"You go back along Coast, Mr. Allan. Ten good fine cows is better as dead man."

I give a snort. "I ain't dead, not yet. And I don't go one damn step without I catch them renegades, turn 'em over to the sheriff."

Iowana's face got like ashes, his hand clutching the cross looked so tight clenched the skin could pop open. "No one was steal your stock. Them fellows, it was Gallo's stuff they run off. Don't cost you. You go home safe now."

It was plain to me he meant good even if he didn't have the sense to see right and wrong. Patient as I knowed how, I told him, "Now look here, boy, stealing is bad. It works bad for anyone does it; I found out that's God's truth. If a fellow knows thieving's going on, he can't turn his back to save his own hide. He just can't do it. You see?"

Iowana shook his head. Like a sulky mule, he says, "Three bad men. Three bad guns. You, just one gun, no chance for you catch 'em."

He turned away, walked out to the kitchen, slamming the door behind him. I heard the outside door open, shut with a crash. Iowana was gone.

I set by the open window a few minutes looking out but not seeming to see the miles of flat baked plain, hot in the moonlight. I was trying to look across the mountains, see Hannah waiting for me, smiling.

Next morning I got Ranger saddled first thing and was fixing to ride. I'd give up ever seeing hide or hair of the Indian again, but he had me fooled. Iowana come out of a little shed near the barn. He had a short stick to his hand. He give a shrug to his shoulders, his dark face took a comical twist as he says, showing me the little cross on the leather string, "Little Jesu's Madre, the Lady God, she like I go along, help with you, boss."

I had to study on this a minute before I figgered he was talking about Mary, the Mother of Jesus. I had my doubts about her paying any special heed to cattle-thieving, but I was glad Iowana felt to do the right thing. I didn't want him along, but it would help if he'd talk now. I knowed he was holding something back.

"My horse won't carry double," I told him, "and I see the Jolon fellow Gallo sold to must of come for the horses and mules. You tell me where them rustlers hide out and that'll be all the help I'll need."

He quirked up one eyebrow and rubbed the back of his hand across his nose. Then he says, real smooth, "You think so?" He stood his stick careful again' the rails of the fence and then run back of the shed he'd come out of, calling, "Wait now, boss. I come."

He'd been up before me and got all ready, I could see that, and I liked him for it. But I had a job to keep my face straight when he come in sight hauling on the lead-rope of the swaybackest, jug-headest nag of a horse I'd ever set eye on. The damned horse looked all head and ribs, a sorry beast not worth shooting. But seemed like Iowana was of no mind to find fault of his animal. He sounded proud enough when he told me, "Lady God think maybe all right, so I borrow horse."

"Who the hell did you borrow that from?"

He give me a sort of hot look when he caught the tone of my voice, but he answered civil, "From them same uncles. I didn't ask 'em, just took away."

Thinking they couldn't be such tough hombres if this young one could go steal a horse from them without their knowing it, I called to him, real hearty, "Get set, boy. We'll go get 'em."

He took the stick up from where he'd leaned it against the fence, swung hisself onto old Jughead's saddle and we started.

I thought to favor him by holding Ranger back to a slow walk, but Iowana's mount was better than his looks. That scrawny crowbait with never a measure of oats to his starved gut had strength to him and plenty of speed.

I let Ranger take his head and the jug-horse kept even. I give Ranger a sly touch with the spur and old Jug joggled right along side. I glanced down and found Iowana grinning up at me. "I lead," he says, "I show you cache camino. Is good hid-away-road, all right. You go by him dozen times, I bet. I show you."

I felt he was sort of over-stepping his place as well as running down my horse, but I paid his brag no mind, just waved him to go on ahead, I'd follow.

The cache camino was named right: hidden road. Iowana was right too. I'd been passing by the opening, never guessed it was there. No cattle tracks led into the narrow opening. It was only wide enough to squeeze in single file; a rocky ledge that come out from the rest of the rock cliff like a half-letter S, the opening into it low enough so I had to tuck down my head not to scrape rock overhead. It was solid rock trail for a short way, the ledge of rock running out flat and the dust of the plain covering it on the valley side.

Soon as we was both inside the narrow valley, Iowana pulled up, waited for me to come alongside, and motioned me to ride out in front. I pulled Ranger in as I got even with the boy and waited while he says real low, "Bad place. Old people, they got medicine cave hid in here. Is ghost people place. Cave is for bury witch mans. All painted inside with ghost hands. I seen 'em." He give a shiver.

"Forget ghosts, Iowana. We got plenty to worry about from live outlaws. Looks like three men with guns could hold off a dozen sheriffs in a place like this."

"Is like I said. We go home now?"

"For God's sake," I said. "You go home. You showed me the place, that's all I wanted. I'll come back with the thieves and the stock safe enough, so you go on back."

"You go, I go."

Well, I'd give him his chance once so I said no more.

A short way up, the valley started showing a bit of green here and there and after the trail made a sharp bend where one of them broken ridges turned contrary to the rest of the bare ridges, we come to a damp stream course with here and there a pot-hole full of brown water. I see we was climbing fairly fast and when we rounded a lot of big granite boulders that was tumbled into the stream course, we come to a lazy stream mosying along under willows and crooked sycamores.

Somewhere ahead I thought I heard a woodpecker rapping, but behind me I heard Iowana's hissing, "They telling we come. Look out!"

We pulled to a stop while we was still hid by the tangle of branches overhead. I studied the country ahead. The valley had flatted out to a pocket most of half a mile wide and nearly a mile deep before the rock cliffs that ringed it stood straight up and much as a hundred feet high. Right in the center of the back cliff was a fine pile-up of limestone rocks, each rock looking big as a good-sized barn.

There was no fight in Iowana's voice, and 'twas a shaking finger that he pointed to the big rocks. "Medicine cave hid down in big rock. Them rocks is hollow, I seen one time. Plenty bad scare I tell you."

I was studying on how this sort of place could help the outlaws, not forgetting to study how I could turn it so's to make it be a help to me. It looked bad. Fellow never had ought to fight his way up-hill, but looked to be no other way to get back of them rocks. There was a scant scatter of sage and black-brush, but even a snake crawling from one to t'other of them would be in plain sight from up on the rocks.

The sound of a woodpecker rapping come again and right behind me I heard a clatter. I took a quick look over my shoulder and seen that the loose leather on Iowana's saddle was rattling from the shake of his knees. The saddle was a sight, must of been laying out in the weather for years till it looked more like a old bird's nest than a fit thing to put on a horse.

"You wait here, Iowana," I told him. "I'm going to make a run for the face of that cliff." "Don't do! Them fellow, they hid in rocks. Got guns."

"You said that twice already. I got to chance it. See, that spot right in the middle's got a bit of overhang, got a shadow there on the right. I'll get behind that outcrop."

Iowana's face was sour as his voice, "Not so good. You ride like hell, get there, jump for shadow. All right. Three Indian in that shadow maybe. Then what?"

There was no answer to make him. I squinched up my eyes,

tried to see into that shadow, figger if it would give cover to me and to Ranger. I hated risking my horse but looked like the time had come when I'd have to.

Iowana whispered, "No cows here, boss. We go back, try tomorrow again."

I heard a pop like the sound of a shot far off and right after it the bawl of a steer, far off, too.

"Stay here, boy," I shouted and dug Ranger with my spurs. He lit out at a fine clip and the valley floor seemed to spin past. I was more than half across and there wasn't a sound or move from the cliff ahead. I felt some of a fool to be making such a dash at nothing. I was thinking to pull Ranger in when all hell broke loose. Hot lead screamed past my head. Bullets plowed ground half a jump before me, one flatted on the saddle horn and like to twisted Ranger out his course.

He didn't need no spurs. I knowed he was going his best and that's not slow; him long-legged, long-barreled and liking to run. But seemed like that cliff was running back, getting farther off 'stead of me catching up to it. I'd never rode through no lead hailstorm before and, by God, I didn't like it none.

I couldn't see no one to shoot at. I couldn't of shot straight, rate we was going anyhow. All I could do was ride. I swung my weight, side to side, and he zig-zagged, making it harder to hit me. That tight feeling I got made me keep spurring Ranger, though I knowed he was doing his level best.

The cliff was seeming to come to meet me, by now, and I half took a breath. It looked a safe place to get, with all the shooting them varmints was letting loose. I didn't hear so many shots but the whine of them bullets made me feel they must a had guns stacked up like wood and all loaded ready. That lead sung mean.

I flatted myself on Ranger's back and just as I ducked down

I felt a ball fan past my ear. I didn't feel it hit. There was a salt taste of blood in my mouth but no pain. I shook my head and then I seen blood spatter, hit the reins, strike my hand that was holding them. Right behind me I heard a shout, then words. "*Caramba!* Son of guns them cattle!" The jug-head, Iowana hanging to him, was thundering along right behind me. As I turned my head, seen him, Iowana laid out almost ahead of his nag, screaming, "Watch him, boss! Them bastards stampede cows at us!"

I looked. I seen 'em coming!

From both sides that rock mad-scared cattle was pouring, piling up atop each other, crazy with fright.

They blocked any way to the shelter I'd rode for. Might as well ride into a bandsaw as into that mess of dashing horns and hoofs.

There wasn't but one thing to do.

"Turn back, go back!" I yelled at Iowana as I dug the spurs to Ranger.

I got my gun free, got it at the ready and still I made myself hold back the fire. It was hard not to pull the trigger.

Three more jumps and Ranger'd be in the middle of that crazy wild stampede.

I shot.

I see the fine big steer leap toward me, see him give one last jump and then come crashing to the ground.

The sound of the shot, so close, the smell of hot blood, still closer, started a stampede back again the crazy cattle pushing to the center from both sides. I pulled up on the reins like I'd lift him and Ranger cleared the rolling body of the dying steer. My stirrup caught on the horns of another wild galoot, I felt my pants leg rip, and then the cliff was right there.

Ranger stopped so fast that as I swung off I 'most lost my

footing but I made the leap clear, my empty gun still to my hand.

As I hit the ground, the jug-head slammed into the rock wall, grunted, and Iowana lit right behind me, his stick tight in his hand.

"The rock ledge," I yelled. "Duck behind it!"

We both raced for that much shelter, made it, and ran smack-dab into two Indians. Their guns swung over their heads like clubs.

Both of 'em jumped me. There was no time to even swing my gun for a club. I doubled up, my head a battering ram aimed at the belly of the pock-marked one that was a step in front of the one-eyed fellow.

My head hit him so hard it rocked me back on my heels and I heard a hollow woof as his belly buckled. As I fought for footing I had one thought: boost him over my head, knock old one-eye over with his fighting partner.

I heard Iowana yell. Blood was in my eyes. My blood. I couldn't see the boy. I couldn't take time to wipe away the blood. I raised up under the Indian I'd winded, felt the press of his weight as I heaved and over-ended him, clear of me. He laid there.

I run my sleeve across my eyes, cleared 'em and looked for Iowana. The one-eyed galoot had him, one hand lifting the boy by his hair, the other hand twisting Iowana's arm, trying to make him drop the stick. Iowana was spitting words hard as rocks: "Devil you! I kill you!"

The fellow felt like iron as I leaped on his back, tried to drag him down. He let go the boy, swung a fist under my chin that like to took all the fight out of me, but I kept my head. I slid down, low as I could, upped with my knee and felt him gasp, turn limp.

"We got 'em, boy," I gloated. I turned to catch a look of blind terror on Iowana's face. "The gun!" he said, like his tongue had went thick. "Boss, watch him gun! Shoot him!"

Puzzled, I looked at both guns them Indians had. They was laying in the dust same as mine was. It didn't seem there was aught to any of them guns to put fear on the boy. I looked at the two fellows I'd knocked out of any itch to fight. Both of 'em looked broke and empty as the guns but as I looked I see the second fellow give a twitch and try to double hisself up, so I started over to Ranger, drawing my knife. I'd cut me a couple proper lengths of rope, truss them varmints up so they'd make no more trouble.

By the time I'd made the turn to face Ranger I heard the eagle-scream of Iowana as both his hands, gripping that stick, raised it full length above his head. Then I swung clear around like a snake'd bit me.

It was too late. The third one of them thieves had come dropping from some place. His finger was on the trigger and his gun-barrel almost grazed my chest. I seen Iowana bring his stick down on the back of this third man's neck just as I heard the shot. I was froze, like in a nightmare. I heard the shot, felt the hot pain, smelt the black powder and scorched leather. It didn't seem like it was happening to me. I knowed I got that charge right in the chest. I had to, I was standing almost again' the gun when he shot. How was it that I could still stand, still think?

I stood there watching the man with the gun buckle up slow, tumble face forward, fall atop his gun.

I stared at Iowana as he run over to me, the stick still tight in his hand. "Did he kill you, boss?"

I thought it over for a second, muttered, "Guess not."

Iowana was like a crazy man then. He jumped, he smacked

the rock ledge with his stick, yelling just like a Indian!

I made out his war whoop was something like, "We got the bad mans, we got the cows back, we ain't dead killed."

I wanted to whoop, too. But I was too growed up to be acting like a tad; beside, I couldn't seem to move foot or hand. Iowana come laughing over to me, then he bent forward, peered at me.

His voice snapped like he was driving mules, "Boss, you get on horse, make quick!"

I listened to him, but seemed like I couldn't argue, I couldn't move. Something hot and wet, a lot of it, was smearing up my side, but I wasn't honing to feel of it, find out what.

My head started clearing and I tried to figger what all happened, but I couldn't. I could see the fellow I'd laid out with a knock of my knee in the right spot was still twitching and I remembered what I wanted. Rope. To tie them outlaws up so's to get 'em safe to the sheriff's lock-up in Jolon.

Seemed my mouth let go them words slow, dropped 'em heavy, as I told Iowana, "Rope, boy. Tie 'em up. Get rope."

Iowana was leading Ranger alongside me though Ranger didn't like it none, kept snorting. There was a queer hum going on inside my head, I knowed I didn't want to try even one step forward.

I don't remember just when it was he got his shoulder under my good arm, just how he set me into the saddle. He did. He took my lass' rope off the saddle, tied my feet into the stirrups and then together under Ranger's belly, passed the stout rope around the bullet-scarred saddle horn, and I was safe from falling off.

I found out I was none too safe at that. It was a job to hang onto my sense, not just slump and let that hum get the best of my head. But I give Iowana a look and said, "Get them three tied together, hands back of 'em and bring 'em along. We take those men with us."

Then the haze come up over my eyes.

"I want water."

That thin voice was me talking. I was in the bunk. There was candles lit and a fat man was shutting up a black bag. He snapped it shut, come over to the bunk.

"Water?" I see Iowana come in from the comeda, a gourd dipper in his hand. The fat man took the dipper from the boy, slid his arm under me and raised me up. That was like Hannah done when the bear clawed up my back.

"Hannah?" I says.

But the fat fellow paid no heed. "Drink this," he says. "Water is good for a man that's lost so much blood."

Lost blood. Yes, I guess I must of. Seemed like the water hurt, after I'd swallowed it. I didn't much care. "You the sheriff?" I asked.

He sort of laughed as he said, "No, not me. I'm just ol' Doc Henry."

I'd heard tell of him; good doctor, folks said. Could do anything, pull teeth, set bones, heal a sick horse.

"Where's the sheriff?"

The doctor eased me down flat on the bunk as he told me, "He's been here. It's all right. He's got your prisoners over to the lock-up. You got to rest now."

"I can't; not just now. I got some stock I'm taking over to the Coast."

I see him beckon to Iowana and the two of 'em walked outside together and I could hear the voices for a time. Then I didn't hear them no more.

I hadn't got that charge square in my chest. Iowana and his

rabbit stick had swung in time to save me. All wrong with me was a flesh wound to my arm and a few splinters of bone off it, and seemed the ball cut through a rib or two. Wasn't what you'd call a bad wound, ordinary, but that doctor fellow said 'twas the cloth, some dirty wadding and the black powder drove in from being so close that got the wound so full of pus and fever.

I had to lay there. No matter how strong the pull on me to go on home. Doctor Henry come and went, pulled off dressings, scraped at what he called gangrene and slapped on more bandages. It made me sick all right, even if 'twas a small wound, Half the time I didn't have my sense, didn't notice if 'twas day or night.

The day Iowana drove in what was left of the rustled cattle I had to get the words set steady in my mind before I could say, sensible, "How many head, Iowana?"

I didn't hear him answer, couldn't keep hold my head that long. I'd lost all track of time.

By the time I was fit to sit up in the bunk for a hour I asked what day it was.

"Friday," says the doctor. "My last visit, I guess. Now you take care of yourself for a week and you'll be ready to start home if you take it in easy stages."

I didn't let on to him that I was starting home tomorrow and going fast as I could haze that herd along.

"Friday what?" I asks the doctor, remembering it was Friday after Thanksgiving when I come over here. I was scared he'd say I'd been two, maybe even three Fridays in this place.

The doctor rubbed his head, laughed. "I lose track, myself. It's about the middle of January, one day or so don't matter much. About the fifteenth, I'd say."

It was a good thing I couldn't answer. I might of said

something would a scared him. Middle of January! I had to hold myself not to jump out of that bunk, but I knowed that was no way to get rid of him. I laid still, my hands tight together even if it did hurt them sore ribs.

The doctor put his stuff all back in his bag, held out his hand and said, "You can be proud of yourself, Mr. Allan. If you hadn't been tough as mutton you'd be a goner."

I blinked at him and he cleared his throat, sort of flustered as he said, "The bill's all settled, you remember? I told you the Monterey cattle men that posted the reward wanted to take care of the medical bill, too."

I didn't know what he was up to. I just told him, "I settle my own bills, always have."

He picked up his hat and his satchel, give my hand a pat like I was a baby and made no mention of what I'd just said.

"I'll tell the sheriff you're well enough to see him now. And remember, take it easy. You can sit up, out of bed, for a short time, say—tomorrow. A couple of days and you'll be walking. In a week you can travel."

I wanted to tell him he fixed me up good, spite of how long it took, but I felt my face go red and all I could say was, "Well, Doc, well, I—"

He says, "That's all right, Mr. Allan. Good luck and a good trip home."

He shut the door and he was gone. I waited till he'd have time to get a mile or so off, then I slid over to the edge of the bunk, tried my feet on the floor. They was full of pins and needles, wouldn't hold me up. I tried 'em a couple of times more and then I was glad to lay down. Seemed I didn't have no strength left. I'd have to work up to walking, go easy at it.

With working at the standing up, wiping the sweat off my face, easing back to bed and wondering what the doctor was getting at about cattle men paying my doctor for me, the afternoon went. It was getting on to chore time and I heard Iowana ride in. I'd ask him what he was holding back soon as he come in. He didn't come near the house and I was fixing to call him when the sound of hoofs come to me. I leaned over to where I could look out the window and I see some fellow in a short-tailed coat getting off a big roan. There was a metal badge pinned to the coat so I reckoned this fellow'd be the sheriff.

He was. And he was in a hell of a hurry, seemed he'd got word of a murder, down in Priest Valley, he said it was a fight over a line fence. He was the talkingest man I'd ever run up again'. Most I could get was some jabber about how he nearly didn't pay any mind when Iowana come in his office all wild and out a breath talking about cattle thieves and Gallo's ranch and bring a doc. Time he was talking, he had the pencil ready, and he ended up saying, "Sign right here."

Before I knowed what was up he'd shoved three fat money pouches into my hand and says, "That's my receipt; shows I turned the reward over to you. You did the county a good turn, Mr. Allan. Proud to know you."

He was out of the door and larruping his horse across the valley floor before I'd half took in what he said.

I picked up one pouch, hefted it. I pulled the draw-string and took a look. It was no dream.

"Fifteen hundred dollars" reward. Five hundred dollars each for them varmints. Posted by the Monterey county cattle men."

That's what he told me. Must be so. That's what the doctor was getting at.

I raised up, yelled, "Iowana!"

He come a running, asking, "What wrong, boss? What's now?"

189

I showed him the money, asked, "You know anything about this?"

"Sure. I tell you. Old doc man, he tell you, couple times. I hear him."

I shook my head.

"Half this money belongs to you, Iowana."

He shook his head, his mouth set, "Won't have. Don't want."

That riled me. "Look here," I said. "I don't care whether you want it or not. You're taking it. There's no call for you to turn over your money to me."

He started turning that cross of his, his eyes not looking at me as he muttered, "I got no money. You got." His head didn't raise, but he shot me a quick look out them black eyes, "Lady God sent you here along Frank Gallo. Him kill me dead that time if you no here. All money belong with you."

I laughed at him. "Bad Indian, he kill me that time, you no swing rabbit stick. Evens that up—so—half the money is yours."

He tried to go along with me, started to grin, but a quick shake run all over him. He shook his head. "Blood money," he muttered. "Them fellows no your uncles, Mr. Allan. All right for you to take. Not for me."

He walked off, his bare feet hitting the dirt floor in a way that sounded stubborn and set, and shut the door behind him.

I didn't see him no more till he come in with food for both of us. I was hungry and we fell to, eating with no talk till the plates was scraped clean.

"I'm starting for the Coast Sunday," I said.

"*Buena.*"

That's all he said. "Good." Not another word. I'd sort of hoped he'd ask if he couldn't go along, but he didn't. Must be he meant it was good to be shed of all the trouble I'd been. I'd been good for nothing.

By Saturday night I was walking around some, but it still looked a hell of a way over to Gallo's barn. I was soft as a baby's backside, I had to admit it. I grudged the extra day, but it was Monday before I'd got up enough of my old gumption to rightly stay on my feet.

It was bitter, finding out that Iowana could only gather up thirty of that fine herd. He looked like he'd et something bad when he told me he'd had to finish off them that broke their legs stampeding down the rocks.

There must of been some more of 'em scattered out behind the rocks and on the mountain slopes but it's a tough job to gather in stock from that sort of country. I give in. I wasn't able to make the try.

But in the dawn of early Monday I felt pretty good when I seen the forty head together. Iowana'd been throwing Gallo's feed into that half-starved thirty and even them wasn't in such bad shape.

He come out with me and he was hanging to that rabbit stick of his. He was a big help in getting the drive started.

"I run turn 'em, boss, I fix."

The boy was good as his word. He was everywhere, running fast and strong as I wanted to but couldn't. Not yet.

The cattle was all out of the corrals, headed for the unfenced plain and I see some of them was bound to head back for that little valley where the caves and the water was.

I swung Ranger to head that lot in with the rest and as I made the turn, here come Iowana, atop old Jughead. He was circling the other side, keeping the stuff bunched by taking a poke at 'em with his stick.

Working together that way, we got 'em settled down and moving slow across the hot plain. I could handle the drive

191

alone now but I called a order to Iowana now and again to keep him working.

I was loath to see him turn back. I'd got right used to having him around.

Night come and we was fixing to bed down the cattle where they'd get water. The San Antonio River still held a few deep holes that hadn't clear dried up; there was some live brush the bunch could browse on, too. And I couldn't go no further. About twelve miles we'd made and I was dead beat.

Iowana was coming over to the Coast with me. He never said so and I didn't ask him. But he made the fire, rustled up grub, and the way he called me boss and looked after my stuff made me sure.

Iowana took the first watch that night. I should a been getting some sleep but I set by the dying camp fire, poking at the few red coals and feeling mighty good.

I'd had plenty troubles. It was a hard trail ahead, but I'd get the stock safe home, even the wild and run-down bunch of thirty. I was run-down and skinnier than any of the cattle. That wild steer had gored the same leg the bear'd help stiffen up. My sores was still none too healed and I had near a two months' beard on my chin.

I could still look for trouble with Hannah when I got back. Still I felt good. I'd started out to get some good cattle cheap. I was a fellow got what he set out for. I'd tell Hannah that. And when things was smooth between us, I'd tell her about the reward. I reached behind me and felt my bedroll. The gold was safe.

X

Worse than I wanted to keep meat on my stock I wanted to get home. We hazed 'em along fast, splitting the night watches so's each of us got some sleep. By doing that, we made the top of the Santa Lucias in three days.

When we topped the ridge and I seen the great wrinkled ocean swaying deep-blue clear out to the faded blue sky-edge, I felt like bawling. Still looked a long way down to where my ranch was only a speck in all that folded-up golden country. Still, it was a lot closer than when I laid over at Gallo's, thinking maybe I'd seen my hills for the last time.

When he seen the ocean, Iowana's eyes looked scared and he started fingering the lead cross he wore. It was just a cross hammered out of a spent lead ball he'd found some place, but the Indian thought a lot of that trinket.

I had to laugh. The boy glanced at me, shrugged his shoulders and looked at the ocean.

"*Agua grande.*"

"Yep, lots of it," I told him. "But it's salty."

I could tell by his face he didn't believe me. Well, he'd told me true things I hadn't believed. The only real lie he'd told was to save face for Gallo much as for himself and he'd owned up, after Gallo had went.

I thought things out a lot, going along the trail home, Iowana showing himself a worker that no one could complain of.

It had been my plan to take the cattle down where the trail divides and turn there, take them into the high pasture where I'd killed the grizzly. I couldn't bring myself to do it; it was out of our way home.

I told Iowana there was too much risk to putting strange cattle so far from the house.

"I'll sleep with them cows," he told me.

"You'll do what you're told," I answered him, short.

The cattle would be safe with someone to watch them, but home was pulling me like the cable pulls the bucket over to the limekiln. Ranger felt it, too. His head come up and he started lengthening out, keeping right on the cattle's tails.

They was bawling fit to be tied. Before long Hannah'd hear them if she was at the homeplace, and by the time I come in sight, I hoped to see her crossing the dooryard to the open gate.

If she'd be there, waiting, seemed like I wouldn't want anything else. My heart liked to suffocate me, thinking of the soft feel of her hair, the clean smell of it. I'd been so long away.

By now every tree, every bush, every stone in the trail was an old friend. This was my own country. Once we'd dropped down into Clay creek and climbed out of its canyon, made the turn where the twin pines are, I'd sight the house.

Them damned cattle took to milling around just before they started up Clay canyon. We must of lost most of an hour trying to get them started up the trail, and day would be about done before I hazed them into the corral back of the home-barn.

As the stock climbed the dry clay hillside, the dust went up in such clouds that me and Iowana both was coughing and cursing. I couldn't see the length of my arm. But the dust

didn't last long. Soon as we passed the twin pines, the pine needles underfoot made a clean passing, and I stood in my stirrups and craned my neck.

All I seen at first was just my own roof, but it was enough. I had to keep hold of myself as I pointed it out to Iowana. "That's my place. Down by that bunch of trees. See the barn? The tool shed's there by that madrone."

Iowana said, "Lot' green tree country. Looks a long way."

"Half an hour."

That's all I said, but seemed like my toes had a life to themselves. I could feel them twitch and wiggle. I was dog-tired, but happy. All I needed was some yarb to clean my blood, and I'd heal off them sores quick.

As we got nearer to the house I could see green around it. Even on the Coast the rains was late and the country was still gold as dry feed could make it. Hannah must a been throwing out a lot of wash water to keep such a big piece green.

Struck me she must a turned the spring overflow out so's it would come around the house. Women ain't got no business doing things like that without they ask their man. She needn't be in such a hurry to take things to herself. The green looked good but I made up my mind I'd turn the overflow back where it always had been.

The trail was high-grown with sage and cascara, with wild cucumber and morning glory, and I couldn't get a clear look at the place till we rode out into the open just above the barn. I felt I'd come to the wrong place. She'd turned the water all right, got it ditched, proper too. But that wasn't half of what she'd been up to. There was young trees set out. There was a truck patch. I seen the hen yard, but 'twasn't till I seen the staked-out cow that I blowed up.

My fingers tangled up in my beard, pulling till my lip sagged down. Iowana backed out of reach when I muttered, "That woman! She's turned my ranch into a town lot!"

There was a woman coming across the dooryard. I had a bad moment of thinking Hannah must a took in some stranger. Then I had a worse moment.

This was Hannah.

Feeling her way careful toward the gate was what had been my light-stepping wife. Seemed like she'd tried to cover her size by hanging a apron on a yoke from her shoulders and putting a ruffle to the bottom of the yoke. It didn't help none. I felt the tingle run out of my toes. I'd been thinking of her as well rounded out, not like this.

She walked up quite close, kind of smiling. Her color was bad, there was lines to her face, and her eyes had bad-looking blue smudges under them.

Then I seen her hands. Them was Hannah's same hands.

The rest of her had turned mis-shaped.

I set there on Ranger, fighting not to feel more lost and sick than when I'd been near dying.

She come forward slow, her eyes getting wide and startled. I see her lip quiver, and she put out one hand in front of her. I heard her say dry-like, "That horse? That's Ranger!"

I never thought of me having a beard and being so thin, as well as long gone. Seemed like she'd gone clean crazy. My stomach went back on me, and the grease from what I'd et at lunch come up and stood burning in my throat.

"My God, Hannah," I said. "What's come over you, anyway?"

She grabbed at the gate, put both hands to the top rail and hung on, her eyes brightening as they searched my face.

Then she started to laugh. She laughed till the tears run down her face, and that big belly of hers shook.

"Zande," she gasped at last. "Zande! With a beard!"

She picked up the tail of her checked apron and dabbed at her eyes, shaking with her laughter.

Then, like she remembered, her voice went stiff, as she asked, "Does Mrs. Gallo like that red, white and black beard?"

I didn't know what she was driving at. Mrs. Gallo? Maria, she meant. This was no time to be talking about Maria.

Her eyebrows come up when I said, "Stand away from the gate, I'm bringing the cattle through."

There was a snap to her eyes and to her voice as she lashed out, "Not through my garden, you're not!"

Ranger was standing there, paying no heed to the gate he knowed how to open. I pulled him to one side, half turned him, and reached for the catch.

"Get out of the way," I warned my woman. "The stock will run over you."

"Let them try!"

She pushed again' the gate so it wouldn't swing open. I couldn't turn back now. I'd said I was bringing the cattle through and she heard me. There was more between us here than whether my stock should go over her patch of green stuff; it was a test of which of us was boss.

I kept hold of myself, said again, "Look out for yourself; the stock has to come through."

She fair screamed at me, "They don't! You take the corral fence down."

"This is the stock gate." I put my hand on the gate and sent Ranger forward. The gate give slow, but it was opening. I didn't want to hurt her, only to show her I meant business, and that a wife can't go again' what her husband wants.

As the gate pushed again' her she slid back, her feet still braced.

The stock come pouring through and made straight for the young rows of stuff. I was hot-mad and I didn't hurry too much about turning them back.

Hannah did.

She run over that loose ground, cow-heavy, but heifer-fast, and fair throwed herself at a big steer that was out front, his mouth dangling the pea vines he'd grabbed.

He paid no more heed to her than if she'd a been a fly.

Iowana come running in through the gate after the last of the stock, cut across the garden patch and started to head them down the trail toward the corral. I was circling Ranger to get around the other side.

All of a sudden Hannah stooped down and picked up the biggest rocks she could lay her hand to, started heaving them at my white-faces as wild as if them cattle was raccoons.

She stampeded the stock, and they started milling around

like crazy. It's a wonder Hannah wasn't knocked down before she was. I saw the steer roll her, but before I could even jump off Ranger, she was up and spotted the steer with a big rock right between the eyes.

"You get out of this! Get back to the house where you belong," I yelled at her.

She was more a grizzly than a woman as she jumped for me, her fingers clawed. I was set to hold her off, try to reason with her but sudden-like she doubled over, clutching her belly.

Iowana come running up, his face anxious.

"Your woman put out boy damn-quick, maybe so?" Iowana was pulling at the fringe on my buckskins, his face screwed up, trying to get me to answer him.

"Not till the short month," I tells him. "Not time yet."

"Bad time. Can slunk boy easy now. Missus pretty bad, I think."

She was doubled up on the ground, biting her lip and making a bad sound. I couldn't get a word of sense out of her.

I got all mixed up. There was the cattle tromping down her green stuff, pulling it up and milling around breaking down what they wasn't eating. But if I took the time to get the stock out they'd maybe tromp her.

If I carried Hannah up to the house first the cattle would finish the garden but—

"Take her feet, Iowana. I'll get her shoulders. Easy, now,

She didn't make it easy. Hannah had a misery, but she had strength left. She kicked and struggled and screamed, "My garden from home! They're killing it. Let go! Let me go!"

We got Hannah into the house and laid her down on the bed, her grabbing the covers, starting to tear at them like a woman with no sense at all. I stood, wondering what to do.

I told Iowana to start a fire; seemed like I heard tell that hot water was good for sick women. "Better stay here," I told him. "I can get the stock corralled by myself."

I was sorry the stock had ripped up her garden and I whacked that last runty heifer a cut with my quirt, sent her scampering and bawling down to the corral after the rest of the new cattle.

I shoveled in the feed, grudging nothing. At least I was home to my own barn and feeding out my own hay and grain to good stock I'd got cheap. Forty head; all good stuff. Eleven of 'em heifers, too. By the time the boy was crawling around a corral, this new stock would mean something pretty solid.

I watched the smoke curl out of the chimney for a while, thinking how different I'd pictured it all from how it really was when I got home. Not this way, not like this. The woman who bent over me in the shadows of my fever was slim and round, gay and loving. My soft-voiced Hannah. I'd got to be pretty terrible in love with her, like I dreamed her, them bad weeks.

I slid off the fence and made my way up the trail. Iowana was coming for me, plenty scared.

"She say, "Maria." All the time she say so."

"Maria?" I said. I went in and asked her, loud and close to her ear, "What in hell you want of *that* wench, Hannah?" She never took any notice.

"I'll saddle the mare and go after my mother, Iowana. You stay here. Watch she doesn't come to any harm, understand?"

"I catch 'em."

There was no sense to his words, but I'd got used to the boy, and I felt a lot easier leaving him with Hannah than I would of felt leaving her alone.

She was muttering, "Maria," over and over.

I shut the door hard after myself, thinking I'd see Maria in hell before I'd ever let her step foot on my ranch.

There was a lot I wondered about as I urged Ginger fast toward Pa's place. I wondered how come Hannah'd be calling for Maria? I wouldn't let myself wonder where Mr. Avery had got himself to. I'd settled in my mind a while back that long ago he'd gone away to them islands he was talking about.

There was no light showing as I run up to Pa's place and damned if I didn't knock on the door, polite as a stranger. I heard the scrape of Pa's gun, as he drawed it across the split floor, and the hammer click before he yelled, "Who's there?"

"It's me, Pa," I answered, as I lifted the latch and stepped in.

"Who's there?"

Pa sounded so sharp that I answered him quick, "Zande. It's me, Zande. Where's Ma?"

Pa's voice had a quaver to it like he was scared. "The hell

you say. Zande? My son Zande? He's run off; or dead."

I felt along the shelf, found the block of sulphur matches, struck one and had the candle lit by the time Pa come out of the other room, pulling up his pants.

He rested the gun in front of him and peered at me, shaking his head. "By God, I don't believe it."

"Where's Ma?" I said. "My woman's sick and I want Ma to come over to the place—"

He give me one of them looks of his, and he says, "Oh, you do, do you? Well, well. If you ain't dead you can look out for your own woman. I got work for mine to do here." There I stood in the middle of the night, thirty-five years old, and a beard streaked with gray falling across my chest, and still feeling for all the world just like I did when I was ten. There's something about Pa takes the wind out of a fellow quicker'n any man I ever see.

We was standing within three feet of each other, both our necks craned forward, trying to stare each other down, when Ma come out the room. Big woman as she is I never heard her bare feet on the floor, and I jumped when I heard her voice right behind me.

"I got some meat soup, son, take just a minute to heat it up. Better have some 'fore we start."

I looked around and felt a warm feeling all over me as I seen Ma, still buttoning up her wrapper, squat down in front of the fireplace and reach for the big hunting knife. She whacked off some splinters of fat pine and blowed on the coals, swung the big pot over the new blaze, and stood up to face me almost before I could catch my breath.

"Hannah took bad?"

"Steer rolled her, and she's all doubled up—"

Ma's voice was anxious. "Tearing her clothes, is she?"

Pa sat down heavy, like he was tired, but there was a sharp snap to him as he said, "You're not going over there. I got the seed cut for that 'tater patch."

Ma's face looked waiting for my answer, and I could feel myself ease as I told her, "She was a-tearing at the quilts—"

Ma's mouth firmed up. She give a half-nod to her head as she went back to the room they slept in, saying, "I'll get some things. Keep that fire going."

Pa shuffled his toes together, reached for his gun, twiddled it around on the point of its stock, and leaned it back again' the wall before he said, complaining-like, "It's a hell of a time of the night to be waking a man up. By God, we give you up for dead. Where'd you run to?"

Instead of throwing the pine stick in my hand at the old fool's head, I put it to the fire and answered him decent, "I never run no place. Indian renegades shot me. I got a sickness."

Pa's nettle voice said, "My Lord A'mighty! Indians. A son o' mine."

He got up, blowed out the candle and stomped across the floor, shaking all the loose boards, went into the other room and slammed the door shut. Well, the fire felt warmer and the soup smelled better in a room rid of Pa. I squatted down on my heels in front of the fire, held my bony hands to the blaze and shivered. There was something gone from the room, but I couldn't think what it was.

Ma come out, went over and lit the candle in spite of the light from the fire. She had her shawl on, and her little satchel in her hand. That satchel turned me colder. It held all Ma's yarbs and sick stuff, some of it even from town, and she never brought it out lessen a woman was took bad.

"Never mind the soup," I said.

"You drink your soup." Ma picked up a gourd, poured it full of the hot stuff and handed it to me, and I took it, trying to smile at her as I lifted it up. She gave me a little push and said, real businesslike, "I'll get a sack for some of the meat Pa shot. A real fat buck, 'twas, and the broth will strengthen the both of you. That wife of yours is skinny as you are. Saddle up when you finish that."

Ma laid her satchel down by the hearth and went out to the meat safe at the back. I finished my broth. I saddled Dapple for Ma, still puzzling over what she could of meant by saying Hannah was skinny as me.

By the time I had Ginger and Dapple out by the gate, Ma come along, the Satchel to her hand, and acrost her shoulder the sack of meat. I tied them both onto the saddle for her, and then got Dapple turned by the mounting block.

Once Ma got her toe in the stirrup she swung on spry as a boy. She was puffing as she settled herself, but she was good for a ride clear to Monterey if she had to make it.

We didn't have no chance to talk on the long ride over to my place. I let Ginger step out good as she could, sorry I wasn't on Ranger. Dapple couldn't do any better than Ginger, and all I could do was try to haze 'em along.

We was topping Alder Hill when Ma called to me, "I smell new smoke. She must be able to build a fire."

I shouted back, "I brought a Indian boy back from the valley with me. He's tending fire."

I heard one of them *tisk* sounds Ma makes. There was no use yelling how come I had Iowana along with me. I looked at the sky and saw it was going to be daybreak by the time we was to the house.

Iowana heard us coming and was out to open the last gate when we got there. I turned the horses over to him and followed Ma into the cabin.

The fire felt good. There was no sound from the bed where I'd left Hannah moaning, and I was fearful to walk over and look. There was a bad feel to the room, the same sort that Gallo's place had when I was trying to come to my senses in it.

Ma, she put the satchel down, leaned the meat sack up again' the table leg, walked over and stood looking down at Hannah. I watched her peel the quilts down. My wife's shoulders showed scratched through her ripped dress, and I heard Ma making that damned *tisk, tisk* sound again.

Sweat was dropping off me, cold and fear was shaking at my bones, and I didn't dare ask Ma a thing.

Might be I should of took the corral fence down. But I had to be boss; that was right. Pa told Ma to stay where she was. She never even answered him, just come along with me, and I could see that was good. But still I'd heard *Ma* say a home wasn't worth a hoot lessen the man run it.

I kept telling myself that Ma fought cattle and Pa to get her green stuff, was how come she set such store by it. It was hers because she'd fought for it and won. I'd tell Hannah she could have her a garden. Seemed like it would be a treat to tell her.

My back was turned to the bed corner, my forehead resting again' the rock of the fireplace. Ma said not a word, only clicked her tongue again' the roof of her mouth in a way that said everything and nothing.

I turned quick when I heard her coming over to the fire, my face asking what my voice couldn't say.

Ma sounded hard, and yet gentle, as she told me, "You find something to do outside and keep that boy along with you. This is no place for you now."

I still stood there. She give me a push and said, "Go on. Get along with you."

She bent over her satchel of stuff, started rummaging inside it, her back to me.

My feet dragged across the floor, but I went. I couldn't help looking back as I shut the door. There was no sound, no move from the dark heap in the bed. I must a looked all the misery I felt, for Ma said, "I'll call you if I need you."

She shut the door after me, and I was outside in the dawn.

Iowana come walking up from the madrone tree, asking, "What old woman say?"

I told him, "Nothing. She wants us to stay outside."

The Indian shrugged his shoulders, let a grin split his dark face, and says, "*Bueno.* I caught a pail milk from Missus' little cow. Drink milk, go sleep in barn. Good, huh?" He started toward the spring.

Pretty soon he come back with a bucket of milk. He handed the gourd for me and held up the pail.

We stood there, dipping in the gourd, first one of us, then t'other, drinking till the pail was empty.

Ma must a give the animal to my wife. I'd not make Ma take the cow back. Hannah could keep it. I'd just grumble when I felt called on to chide her.

As I walked up to the house there wasn't a sound. No stirring inside; nothing. I walked close to the door and called, soft, "She all right, Ma?"

Ma squeaked the door open and whispered back: "Go away. Go on off somewhere and don't be bothering around here."

The door shut, but I didn't feel so shut out as I done before I et. I went down the trail noticing how much work Hannah'd got done around the place, and found Iowana squatting on his heels by the madrone tree, half asleep. There was a heap of work to be done for both of us, but for once I made up my mind to let the work go.

"The hay's deep in the loft," I told him. "I bet we could fall asleep in it if we tried hard."

He grinned as he rubbed his knuckles again' his eyes. "I try hard, boss," he says. "Maybe so I catch 'em."

I smelled the soft dusty smell of the hay, felt its warmth, and heard the little crackle it give as I burrowed into it.

That was the last thing I heard. I was so deep asleep that it took the banging of a stick again' a pan to wake me.

Whistling the old boy-whistle I used to answer Ma with, I come running up to the house and burst into the room. I got a mean look from Ma.

"Get the hay outa your hair, Zande Allan. Wash your face, and don't come tromping in like you was a herd of cattle."

The firelight was throwing over on the bed, and I could see that Hannah was still laying there. She wasn't making a sound.

"She all right?"

"No thanks to you," says Ma with a sniff, and raised her voice. "Get that hay shook outa your hair and call the boy if you're going to eat tonight."

My heart got warm and quick. Ma was acting like things was going all right with Hannah. I went high-stepping out of the house, whistled for Iowana, and we come in spattered with water, hair slicked down like two dudes making for a shindig.

First time I ever et a meal like that in my cabin. There was threads of young carrots and onions swimming in milk gravy alongside chunks of venison. We fair wolfed it down, and it wasn't till I got the edge off my hunger that it come to me where the taste of them onions and the milk to the gravy come from.

I pushed away from the table and walked over to the bed and says, real soft, "Hannah?"

There was no move, no stir, no answer.

I looked around and there was Ma, grinning at me as mean as ever Pa done in all his life.

"Save your breath," Ma says. "You just pushed your wife one mite too far, Zande Allan. She's through."

My throat closed too tight to get a sound out of; I had to swallow before I could ask, "Is she dead?"

"Go finish your victuals," Ma snapped. "It's no thanks to you she ain't."

I didn't know what to make of it. "She don't answer me; she don't move," I said.

Ma said, "Huh!" Then she walked over to the table, started picking up the plates, making a great clatter of putting the food away. Me and Iowana had to pull back again' the wall to keep out of the way. Never see Ma act so blamed uppity in all my life. I had to nerve myself to ask her a question.

"What's the matter with her?" was what I finally said.

Ma let the spoon she was holding fall with a bang; she put her hands to her hips, and she stuck out her chin.

Every hammer-word she swung at me hit me square between the eyes. "She's just good and God-damn sick of you, that's what's the matter with her. She's through with you, and I'm standing up for her. You! Littering the Coast with your get, and riding off across the mountains like God A'mighty. Huh!"

Ma bent down and picked up the spoon, wiped it off on her skirt and turned her back on me.

I stood shifting my weight from one foot to t'other, feeling my scalp prick and them nasty little pluckings in the small of my back.

I could see Ma wasn't going t'say no more. Hannah must a heard me call her name, but she wouldn't answer.

Iowana followed me out of the room down past the madrone tree and up into the hay barn. No fox could a been quieter, slipping along, swifter burrowing into the hay, or better company. He could a said, "Old woman damn mad." That would a been human and natural enough. He said nothing, got out of sight quick. He wasn't Indian; he was a true man, a friend.

Sleep was long coming to me. I turned it all over and over. Ma was glad to see me when I come to Pa's house. When I first brought her to Hannah, even when she sent me outside, she was still all right. While I slept in the hay, Hannah must a told Ma whatever it was that got both of 'em so terrible mad. "Littering the Coast with my get—"

My God, a man had a right to get a child from his own wife. *"Littering."*

There was no chance she was talking about Maria. Was there? Had Maria been around telling I'd laid her?

I turned again, flinging myself over hard. I'd turned a

thousand time, and no rest for my mind or my body.

If Maria talked, told anyone, before she left, my ma wouldn't a had to come over to Hannah to find it out. That sort of tale would run by itself from one peak to t'other, all the length of the Santa Lucias.

I picked up a head of barley, hulled out the grains with my teeth, and pushed the beards out with my tongue. I chewed that barley like a cud, but there wasn't any comfort for me anywhere.

"The hell with it."

That was the best I could come to and that, such as it was, brought me sleep.

When I sat up, there was light coming down through the cracks in the shake roof, blue fingers of light across the dust that come up from the hay. Iowana's head poked out of his burrow, and I told him, "Get jerky out of the meat-safe. We'll saddle up, and take the new stock to the high pasture."

I come down the ladder and looked up at my house. The door was shut. I was shut out.

I shrugged the hay off my shoulders, run my fingers through my hair and beard, and went over to the shed where Iowana was saddling up.

Once we got the stock out on the trail and moving up the mountain to the pasture, I could feel the sun warming me clear through. The blue iris was showing here and there, them thin white footprints-of-spring was covering big patches of ground, smelling good. I seen how golden-green the new alder leaves swung in the sun, and I felt warm inside, too. There is a sap that rises in everything, everyone, come spring. Spring comes to the high hills in the Sur country with the turn of the year, when the new green blades start pushing away the folded-down gold of the last year's grass, and the sorriest man feels hopeful.

Me and Iowana would get this bunch of cattle safe in pasture, take the day to ride fences, and if rails or pickets was missing, we'd put 'em back. A day's fence-fixing in the early spring is hard work in rough country, but it's work that shows, makes a man feel he's got something solid done.

There's a deer trail leads cross-corner of the hundred-sixty acres I was fixing to locate. Juan Duro's old land would have to wait unclaimed now till next fall. When I drove stock to market, I'd find out the law on getting this piece of land.

When the deer trail was close ahead, I called to Iowana, "Help turn the herd onto this trail, and I'll show you some new land I'm after."

I pulled Ranger up and turned to watch how nice Jughead flowed down-hill, sway-backed, but no stiff knees to that beast. Iowana could ride, too. He was down and circled the strays, bunched them and had them headed right almost before you could tell it.

I waited till he was about even with me, and then we moved the white-faces forward, easy. They was milling around, turning back on us, trying to jump over each other before I even seen the fence we'd run them into.

That fence jumped at me like a grizzly. What was a fence doing there?

This leaning, bastardly fence was the work of a lazy man. I knowed it.

Not even when I seen Arvis Demas run forward, gun raised, did I get any idea of what was going on. He had the gun to his shoulder, and it looked for all the world like the idiot was pointing it at me. I remembered my beard, that Iowana was a stranger, and was fixing to call out to him, when he spoke to me. It was comic to see him stick out his chest, though his voice cracked. I 'most fell off Ranger when he said, "I'm here to protect this place and I'm a-going to do it."

"Well, for God's sake, Arvis," I said.

Right over again, like it was a lesson from the Book he'd learned, and had to tell it, he says again, "I'm here to protect this place and I'm going to do it."

I bust out laughing. "For God's sake, Arvis, don't you know me? It's Zande Allan. What you fixing to protect?"

Then he seen who I was, and his face brightened up and he says, "Them white-faces, Zande, where you get, huh? Them cattle Gallo's stuff?"

"Yep, sure. I bought 'em from Tony's brother. Who fenced off this trail, Arvis?"

I was ready for most anything but the answer he made me, his lip pulled back in the wolf-grin of a mean Indian:

"We did. Your woman helped. That Mrs. Hannah Allan. This here's Maria's land now. She got it with that school-scrip Mr. Avery give her."

'Twas like somebody hit me in the stomach. I couldn't of said a word if I'd tried. Now, at last, I knowed what the paper Avery give Maria was. The land-scrip. And she'd filed on the land I was aiming to take and set Arvis up to hold it for her. Now she had an excuse to come back.

And Hannah'd helped.

When I could, I says, "Open the gate, Arvis. I'm bringing the cattle through to my upper fields."

Dragging his gun along by holding onto the end of the barrel, he hurried over to the crazy slat gate and let it down.

"Pull it back!" I yelled at him as I turned Ranger. "You think I want my stock breaking their legs, getting caught in that fool gate?"

I didn't look around to see whether he pulled the gate out from acrost the trail. I knowed he would.

We hustled the cattle through the opening in the fence, Arvis helping. The work of getting the cattle together, getting them started along the trail above the canyon edge without scaring them, kept my mind busy. I followed Iowana and the cattle around the turn that led down to Pine Spring, the little creek where my stock come down for water when they was put to graze in the upper pasture, and I got the next jolt.

My own fence had been moved up the mountain, put on the real survey line. My cattle was cut off from Pine Spring.

Small things make a man fight, give way to his temper. Was how I always done. But when his whole planned world cracks wide open, when it seems hell's right where he's standing, he don't do nothing.

I felt dead-quiet inside as I turned to Iowana and said,

213

"Take down a section of fence, let the critters through. After they've drunk I'll put the fence back."

Iowana looked at me, that blank Indian look. "I catch 'em, boss."

I said over and over, inside myself, "Jesus God, what next?"

I h'isted myself onto Ranger's back like a old spent man and give him a jog with my heel.

I would a rode through, never remembered the fence at all if it hadn't been for my horse. What's a fence when a man's struck numb?

I held Ranger in, spite of his snorting and trying to bolt, till I'd got him well past the fence, and then I dropped the lines over his head so's he'd stand. I went back and propped up rails. I went down into the creek bottom and got stuff to brace up the shaky rotten fence like I had a interest in keeping my own cattle from their nearest water.

I'd said I'd put my fence back. I put it back, good as I could without no tools.

Riding up the trail after Iowana, the thought that Maria'd stole my land was like a tooth that's aching. Hannah, helping Avery and Maria cut the ground right from under me, while I was off working, almost dying, for her. It was beyond me.

When I got to the pasture Iowana was circling the herd, slow and easy. They'd settled down good, and I could see the boy had the right feel for cattle.

"Round up some of the old stock," I called to him, turning Ranger so's to draw in the old black muley-cow with the bell. "The new ones will go with the others. There's a spring over that high ridge, and we'll drive 'em over to it."

I could a killed that two-faced Demas girl. She'd done me out of a good spring along with beating me out of needed range.

We got old muley out to the front, and soon as she settled down and headed for Bear-Kill-Two-Calves Spring, the rest of the cattle followed along.

Soon as we saw some of the new bunch drinking, I told Iowana we'd hit back to my place.

Iowana was nobody's fool. Soon as we got into the door-yard, he says, "I catch 'em camp back of shed, boss. Sleep a little, catch meat, and go back to new cows. Bear bad up there; old woman bad down here. I watch bear."

"You got it easy."

That's what I told him. I meant it. I rubbed down Ranger, done my share of the feeding, hung up saddles and blankets, decided my money was as safe in my bedroll as anywhere else, and fooled around till there wasn't one thing left to do.

I picked up the little bucket of milk Iowana had pulled from the tan cow, and I took my first good look at the cow. I never saw a cow like that one before. Not much bigger than a good-sized deer, light tan on her back and her hindparts, and dark around her head and fore-quarters. Spite of all the trouble that was waiting for me inside my own house, I took time to study that cow, wonder how Hannah got her. I seen now this cow was none of Ma's doings.

A snail on a cold morning could beat my gait as I went up the trail to my cabin. Smoke was pouring out the chimney; inside I could hear such a clatter as Ma makes when she's redding up a place. No sound of talking.

Seemed like I was so down at losing that land, I felt to throw a saddle on Ranger, ride away. There was free land down in Texas, over to Arizona. Cows was cheap south of the Rio Grande, and the place was big. Man could get all the land he needed down there.

I opened the door and walked in.

I set the pail down on a shelf by the window, passing right close to Ma to put it there. She went on shaking up the straw pillows like that was all in the whole world.

I joggled the bail again' the bucket, but she never turned her head or looked up.

"Here's the milk, Ma," I said. "Pail's most bigger than the cow. Never seen that breed before. What kinda mixture is it?"

"Ain't Spanish and Indian and Allan." Ma give me a look that dared me to make her out a liar.

I felt the hot of anger spread through me.

"I've had all that sort of talk I want."

Ma give a nasty laugh and says, "Tell that to Maria, why don't you? 'Tain't what you want, but what you get, that makes you fat—iffen you're a woman and there's a Allan man running loose."

I took just one step forward with my hand lifted when behind me I heard, cool as a gourdful of spring-water, "That's enough of that, Mr. Allan."

I took a quick look at the bed comer and saw Hannah sitting up, her back straight as a young redwood for all the great bulge to her front.

Her face was white, but I could see the steadiness of the Mariana-blue eyes, the firm set of her chin, the tidy look of her hair, and it was like I was sitting across the table from her in the Pacific Ocean House once again, both of us unbroke colts trotting out to try life's trail together.

I stood there, dumb, looking at her.

"Sit down, Zande, we got to talk, but I can't—not yet."

Hannah laid down, slow and careful, pulled the blanket so's to cover all but her eyes. If she was fighting tears she never give in to them.

I set down on the stone ledge to the front of the fireplace, started throwing little chips in.

I looked over to the bed when Hannah said, her mouth still under the covers, "If you could tell Ma you're sorry you went to hit her?"

It was a question, and I considered it. If I could do this it would please Hannah.

I could see Ma's face redden up. The new chips cracked loud in the silence. Hannah waited. My voice stuck in my throat; I could feel Hannah, waiting.

"I ain't sorry."

That was all I could say. Hannah made no answer. She got quieter, waiting.

All of a sudden words come pouring out from me. "If Ma'd scandaled only me I'd a still should of smacked her. "Tain't right to answer like she done. But it wasn't only me. She made a stud-horse out of every Allan man with her loose talk. She's talking bad again' herself when she says them things."

Ma put in, her eyes hot, "I'm no Allan. I'm a Jarvis, and no one ever lived could say the Jarvises was out bringing woods-colts to their home range."

I looked hard at Ma, but held my voice down, as I said, "You lie. You're Allan from the minute you said the marriage lines—"

Hannah broke in: "We're Allans, all of us. Far as I can see now, that's nothing to be set up about. But we ain't through yet."

Ma nodded her head like she thought Hannah spoke truth, and hurried over to the bed corner as Hannah tried to settle herself with her back turned to the room. Ma could swing a ax along with most any man on the Coast, but her hands went mighty gentle as she helped Hannah down, pulled the cover up over her shoulder.

I could hear my wife's voice, just a whisper, slow and tired-sounding, "I'm so tired. Make him go way."

"I'll look out for things," said Ma. "Don't you fret, just go to sleep."

Hannah's shoulder give a shudder; I heard her sigh.

Ma beckoned me, and I followed her outside the house, down the trail to what was left of the garden. She looked at the tramped-on crop, then out over the redwoods to the far-away sea. At last she turned and looked straight at me. "You been with Maria?"

I felt all my muscles tighten, my mouth go dry, but I shook my head. "I ain't seen her since the barbecue."

Ma sat right where she was, though the ground was none too dry, and motioned me to sit near her. I sat on a redwood stump and watched Ma's thumb going back and forth, back and forth, across her mouth. We set there till the little black bats started clicking their crooked trail across the pink sky. Ma tucked her apron up across her hair like a fascinator and I said, like always, "Them things won't hurt no one, Ma."

Ma said, same as always, "They get in your hair, that's what they do."

Seemed like the bat was a help to both of us, for Ma spoke natural and easy, "Nobody along the Coast knows about you and the Demas girl; not even her mother."

I made myself ask, "Knows what?"

"I didn't know a thing till it come out last night. Your wife, she's real close-mouthed. I found that out."

A feeling of shame, a feeling of anger, let out, "Not closed enough, seems like, to keep her from lying about Maria."

I know the taste of gall from breaking it when I was cleaning a quail when I was just a lad. Seemed like I tasted a whole cup of it when Ma answered, tired-sounding, "She'd a never

218

said a word in her right senses. She'd want to do the best she could for you. It's not your fault you ain't got the death of your wife and child to answer for, Alexander Allan."

It was 'most pitch dark before I could say, "I told her I was going to open it. Was nothing else I could do but open the gate. I never went to hurt her; I told her to stand away."

All Ma said was, "Men." But how she said it made me feel I had no eyes, had a head both ends of me, and crawled through the ground. After a minute she said, "You'd better start worrying what to tell your wife."

She didn't say no more. I couldn't ask her the thing all of me wanted to ask every second. What did Hannah say? What could she say? How'd she know what was only between me and Maria?

I was glad it was dark so Ma couldn't see how I took this. If ever I needed to be crafty, it was now. I told Ma, "Well, my wife should be proud of herself, dirtying up her own nest. What give her the crazy notion about Maria?"

I held my breath while I waited. I could of shouted when I heard Ma say, doubtful, "Well, she was fever-talking, I know that, but she said Maria let her know."

Maria's word wasn't worth a tinker's damn to any one on the Coast, for she'd told lies since she was creeping. What passed up there was between me and Maria. There was no witnesses.

"Well, if you had a penny for every lie Maria Demas said, you'd have a stack of coppers. What's the matter with your good sense, Ma? Or Maria's? She ought to know better than pick a new-married man to lay blame on if she's been fooling around."

I could hear the edge of hope in Ma's eager, "Zande, son, you mean you never?"

I'd set on to lie and I made a good job of it. I told her, "I mean every word of it and I'm sorry I shoved Hannah with the gate. I didn't go to hurt her; but that's all the hurt she's got to hold again' me."

Ma was fairly chirping in the dark: "Hannah never even said a word that you'd did that. You ought to be horsewhipped shoving her around at such a time. But never mind, women has ways—she'll get even for it. I would. I'll never forget what I done when your Pa—Oh, well, that's between your pa and me—"

Ma set there in the dark for a long time, thinking about something; maybe Pa. Anyway, she startled me when she groaned. She was getting to her feet, stiff with the long sit in the damp, I guess. Short sounding, she says to me, "Your Pa would a done better if he'd kept outa my sight for a while."

Walking alongside Ma up the trail to the door, I was getting to feel lighter than I'd thought to feel again. Now I could think. Seemed I could see my way clear of all this. I'd have to lie to Hannah, firm as I'd had to lie to Ma. I'd have to do it, but I'd never again do nothing she could tie onto and get her back up at me. Hannah would have this boy, and another, and another, till we had a houseful.

Hope spread through me like the new balm-of-Gilead buds spread sweet gum in springtime. Maria'd find the land done her no good. After a time she'd tire of pestering me. I'd buy my land back from her, go on, same as my plan.

"Where'd Hannah get the little cow, Ma?"

Ma's answer wilted most of the new starch from my step.

"That Mr. Avery Mel went trailing after to Los Angeles, he sent it up when the boat come back a couple weeks ago."

Avery. That man! Every time I thought I was rid of him, he come butting into my affairs. I'd angered beyond bearing when

I saw that milk cow tied up in the homeyard; cows was beef. But if Hannah'd milk and take care of it, I'd been thinking that with a child growing up, it might even be some good. But Avery. No gift of his to *my* wife was going to stand around eating up pasture on my place.

So Avery had tolled Mel off to Los Angeles. That was what was wrong in the room at Pa's place. Mel wasn't sleeping in his corner of the big room.

Ma broke in on my thoughts. "Mr. Avery looked bad when he left, coughing all the time." She sounded hopeful when she went on, "Maybe when he dies, Mel'll come back. Seems like I've lost him, though." Ma sighed a long deep breath, and let it out slow. "Him and Mel and Arvis and Hannah, they all put in the garden. Hannah had garden seed in her trunk, and Mrs. Demas let her have the little fruit trees. 'Twas Avery give Maria the scrip for taking up Juan Duro's old place where Arvis is living at, so Hannah tells me."

Was like a hot fire started in my head. I was blazing mad with the thought of me laying over on that Salinas plain, racked with sores, dying, while Avery and Hannah and Maria stoled the ranch I was fixing to get—and Hannah helped fence my cattle away from Pine Camp Spring, too—

Ma was blabbing on: Avery this, Avery that. I didn't half listen. In my own mind I was burning up Arvis's shack, tearing down the fence, burning up my own shack, and telling them all to go to hell.

My breath stopped dead still on me as Ma said slow, "Most thoughfullest thing ever man done, though, all them pins and flannel and stuff for the baby—"

I fought my voice steady. "For Hannah's baby, did he? Where is it?"

Ma got all chipper. "Hannah's got the bundle. She's going

to cut it up and fix things right, soon as she feels better. No child on this Coast ever had such stuff, I'll tell you. You want I should show you?'"

Ma took my silence for a answer, and went tiptoe to the door, pulled it open soft, and looked in. She come back and whispered, "She's sleeping. I'll get it. Might make her mad if she knowed. She's pretty set in her mad at you, Zande, but she'll be all right, once she knows you never went chasing off after Maria, knows Maria'd tell a lie on her own mother to make a story."

Hell with Maria. She was nothing. Avery was at the bottom of all my troubles. Him and my wife, spreading talk about me to cover theirselves.

I was close to murder. I stood outside while Ma blowed up the fire for light, waited while she took a sizeable bundle from under the bed and come sneaking to the door with it.

I reached out my hands for the bundle, took hold of it. Feeling like my legs was about to fold up under me, I run around to the back.

I was back in front of the door again, heard Ma's whisper: "What you done, Zande? What you done?"

Shaking all over, a red-craziness blinding me, I yelled, "If that slut I married wants any more babies, she can get 'em from Mr. Avery. If I ever lay eyes on him, I'll throw him down the same dirty hole I throwed his God-damned flannel. I've a mind to throw her after it right now!"

XI

My arm was flying up and down like a windmill turning. It ached. I didn't wonder where I was. I didn't care what my arm was doing. Let it ache.

Then I heard the breathing sound. It was bad. I wanted to get away from that hard, coughing gasp. I was moving. I was going along fast. That ugly breathing sound went right along with me.

I jolted forward so hard that some of the red-blindness lifted from my head. The breathing stopped. I was on Ranger. That bad breathing stopped when he stopped.

I could hear someone shouting, "Go back on me too, would you, Ranger? My own horse goes back on me!"

I kept hearing the words. Sudden it come to me that it was my voice. I was the one that was yelling like crazy. I was on Ranger. I'd run him most to death.

It was like I'd stepped into Big Creek in dead winter. My crazy head come cold sober and I jumped to the ground. Spent as he was, Ranger tried to pull away from me when I run to his head.

Every rattling breath he took hurt me. Seemed like I was fighting for breath, too, as I squatted down by his head, too froze-dumb to even curse myself.

I was afraid to look around.

I didn't want to remember. I couldn't hold it off though. I

tried to swallow and my throat was dry as sand.

I'd finished things now.

I couldn't do nothing for myself. But there was Ranger, there was things I could do for him. His head still hung most to the ground. His rasped breaths stabbed at me.

I steadied my voice, "Stand, boy. Whoa now, it's all right!"

Careful I loosed the saddle cinch, lifted the weight of it from him, took the blanket and rubbed him. Easy at first, and then stronger as he started coming out of his terror, stopped fighting for every breath.

I was working on his chest when he moved his head, nosed my shoulder. I never come closer to being clear broke down in my life. I buttoned my lip, held on to the hurt. I had it coming. Fighting humans could talk back, fight—or run if they wanted to. Any man who'd larrup a willing horse was pretty small and low.

I felt smaller than anything I could lay name to. I had to study out where I was, what I'd do next. Hannah had too much again' me now for me to try to ask her to overlook it. I'd been all right if only I'd not let hate of Avery push me too far. Ma'd said Hannah would get over her mad about the garden in time, take her own way to pay me off for that. If I'd held straight to my tale that there was naught between me and Maria, that would of passed off with no more than Hannah having small use for the girl.

Avery, he was the one to blame. Uneased as I'd been, hurting Hannah with that gate, finding she had suspicion of the truth of me and the Demas girl, being so overwrought at Maria stealing away my land; all that had been more than I knowed how to handle. But finding Avery pushing into my place, sending a cow for my woman, buying cloth for my son like I couldn't take care of my family by myself; that's the thing set me crazy.

There I'd been, over in that cursed hot country, looking after my business, making a good buy of the needed cattle, coming close to death just to build up a fine place for my family. I'd got no thanks for it. No, sir. I come home with reward money, honest-earned; never got the chance to even tell of it. All I hear is Avery this, Avery that— To hell with it.

I saddled Ranger, picked up the reins and told him, "Come on, fellow." I'd walk a piece, not ask him to carry me.

Walking slow in the dark, I pushed ahead on the trail I'd been traveling. Even if Hannah'd overlook my doings, I'd be damned if I'd swallow her and Avery. She could have him. Let her find out just how far fine words and silly bowing and scraping went when it come to fighting mountains for a living.

Thinking that way, getting hot-mad all over again, I stepped out good, 'spite of the dark. I'd walked quite a while before I seen the big glimmer of high white rock. Then I knowed where

225

I was at. Marble Peak was right ahead. I must a run Ranger up-hill and along the ridge-top for most of an hour. No wonder he was so blowed and spent. He was still wore out, but by now I knowed he'd be all right. I hadn't wind-broke him.

From Marble Peak there was a old Indian trail that was still kept up some by use as a trail to drive cattle out from the back country. I could follow that trail down to the Big Sur trail. I wasn't turning back to my house when I got there, neither. More I thought about going back, trying to humble myself on account of Avery putting into my affairs, the hotter mad I got. If anyone on the Coast wanted to see me any more they could come after me. I wouldn't go back if I was begged to. I kept prodding at my anger, telling myself Hannah'd a felt different if she'd a knowed I had all that money.

With more money than I could ever a made in any five years of my life, I rode toward Monterey wondering where to go now, what to do next.

I put my horse up at the livery barn, thinking I had to get out of Monterey quick. Monterey was too close to everything that tugged at me. A softness for Hannah kept on plucking at every mad feeling I got.

I made my way to the Pacific Ocean House, to the same table where I'd sat facing Hannah less than a year ago. Now I was facing nothing.

"Two coffees," I told the boy. It was what I'd said before, when one of the coffees was for Hannah. I paid up for both of 'em. I couldn't touch either.

The boy was standing near the door and I asked him, "When's there a boat for San Francisco?"

He come walking over to the table, friendly boy, he seemed like. "We got weekly boat-service now. One's going out in about an hour, next one—in a week."

I told him I was obliged to him, walked out and went back to the livery barn and told the fellow to put up Ranger till I come or sent for him.

I got to the boat and sailed off for San Francisco. The first five minutes was all right, and after that it was bad. Something was wrong with my stomach, and I liked to turned wrong side out before we tied up at the San Francisco wharf on Montgomery Street. I couldn't walk straight when I got off the damned boat, went bobbing up the wharf as if it was swinging like the boat done.

I was looking for a place called Kearny Street where the boat captain'd told me I might find me a place to stay. It was raining. I went up Montgomery Street with so many people, so many kinds of people, all jamming along, crowding each other off the wooden sidewalk.

Seemed like in a rain some of them people would of stayed in wherever it was they lived. They was even thicker when I made the turn and come to the street named Kearny.

Never seen so much mud, horses, wagons, hoopskirts and fancy fixings, all my life. Made me dizzier than the boat done. Whips was cracking, curses flying. There was sailors with beards, Chinamen with yellow faces, tall dark men with their heads all wound up in silk rags. Was queer how so many of the same sort could all of got their heads cracked. They must a all been fighting together, though they was peaceable enough now.

I smelled food and found I was hungry as all get out. Hadn't et a thing since I got on that rocking old boat near three days ago. I turned into the eating place. When I saw the price-card on the wall, I got up and walked right out, but I might as well a stayed there. Next place things was just as dear, and I was hungrier. I made out a skimp meal, and paid a dollar for it.

I was standing in front of the place, wondering how I'd find a place where I could camp and cook myself up a bait of beans, when I felt something kind of crawling in my pocket. I damped right quick and had hold of a skinny boy about sixteen years old.

The ornery polecat had been fixing to steal my money, if I'd a been toting it in my pocket! When I got through shaking him, I give him a toss out into the muck of the street.

People went by, paying no more notice than if it had been just a everyday thing.

That town was a dizzy place. People stepping on my toes if I didn't keep them drawed back, poking their elbows in my ribs as they shoved past, made me feel more lone than walking any trapline in the back country of the Coast.

I stood there, not knowing which way to turn. The loneness started to come down on me. All that day over the wild trail after I left, tossing up and down with me on that tipsy boat, clear above all the rattle and muck of Kearny Street, there was some words of Hannah's that I couldn't get away from. Right now I could hear 'em, clear as the June night she said to me: "Your high wild land seems close to heaven. Could we make our lives good and have fun here, so we wouldn't be strangers in heaven when we get there?"

There was no going back to that June night. There was no trail at all for me and Hannah. I'd got too far off for her ever to walk with me again.

I got a wild urge to go back. I wanted it bad, but I couldn't start.

It was a queer thing to be Zande Allan, wanting something and not trying to get it. Even my feet dragged back, but I made myself go on. Carrying my bedroll with my gold safe in it I elbowed my way through the crowd and walked slow along Kearny and stood on the edge of the crowd trying to make up my mind what to do next.

I might of stood there all night, trying to think, if I hadn't felt a big hand slap my shoulder and heard Tony's brother Frank, the one I got the cattle from, say, "For God's sake! You look like old Comisa Joe. What you doing in San Francisco, in them mangey buckskins?"

I was pumping his hand like it was a handle before I ever thought what I was doing. "I come up to buy some clothes and stuff," I said. It was the first I'd thought of such a thing, but why not?

"How's mining?" I asked him.

"It's worse than San Francisco."

"Mining must be hell," I answered him, and we both stood there and laughed. When we stopped our laughing, I told him, "If it's that bad you won't be mad that I've got some money for you."

He said, "I got money. You think I'm asking for money?"

"Easy, Gallo," I said. "I owe you three hundred dollars for stock I got back from them Indians. Thirty of them cattle's getting fat on my pasture right now, and I was wondering how I was going to get you paid for them."

"*Thirty?*" he said.

I took a quick look at him. He wasn't aiming to make out I'd got off with the other sixty.

"It's a long story," I told him. "But I'm getting blamed sick of standing up in this town. Where does a fellow find a creek to make camp, in all this muck?"

"You can bunk with me," he says. "I got a room down on Broadway till the end of the month, and then I'm going back to the ranch and find me a wife. The dry spell is broke, Tony wrote, so there'll be feed again. I'll start over. These town people are crazy, don't know how to live."

"I'll pay my share and be obliged to you," I answered him, glad he wasn't asking to buy his cattle back. We went shouldering our way along Kearny Street together, me hoping that Broadway might have a tree or a bush or something growing on it.

It was the worst street of all. Noise, fights, music-playing, all day and all night, women grabbing at a man every minute, till you had to curse 'em to get rid of 'em, and then they stopped and cursed you right back.

Best you could say of the place where Gallo was staying was that it had a door, and you could bolt it and keep strange people out. The town was like a sink of wickedness. Me and Gallo walked together so's not to get hit on the head and carried off to serve before the mast in the cargo vessels bound only the devil knows where. I'd told him about the reward money I was packing in my roll but I never let on I knowed about his uncles. He had nothing to say about his relations, only said it wasn't safe to carry money in this town.

Frank took me up Montgomery Street to the Wells Fargo place, where the sign that they had in gold letters said, "Banking, Exchange and Collections." I hated like hell to put my money in there, but the town was lousy with thieves.

After the slick-looking fellow in the round-tailed coat showed me how it went into a big iron safe, and how I got a receipt for it, and proved to me they'd been keeping folks" money in there since 1852, I handed over the $1,500 I had weighting me down, and got a book to write orders for money on. I said nothing about what I had in my money-belt.

Next day I went back and asked him to give me my money. He done it, when I'd wrote him out a order for it. Once sure I could get it back, seemed like the best thing to let him keep the money. If I had it on me and got killed, Hannah and my son might never see the color of my gold.

My first week in the city was enough to start me planning to go back, even if Hannah'd never speak to me again. One thing left to me I was sure of, my own hills. Come summer, winter, fall or spring, with them I knowed where I was at. But each day seemed like the next would be a better one to go. Whole month went that way.

I'd made up my mind I'd get Ranger the silver-trimmed saddle I'd wanted all my life, but that stove I'd saw over to Frank's place kept coming back to my mind. I was walking up Market Street when I seen a place all fixed up to sell tools and stoves, so I turned into it and started looking around. There was a lot of stoves. I fixed on one with nickel trimmings and I bought the whole works, pipes and all, ordered 'em shipped by the *Sierra Nevada* when she come next November.

This here fellow selling stoves told me it could go on the train to Salinas City, then go by wagon-freight to Monterey. He showed me how the stove could all come apart for packing. I hefted it. It'd pack on a couple of animals all right. I could take it right down the Coast with me.

The freight charge was the same, either way, but I wasn't going to trust this train-freight too far. I told the hardware fellow just how to go about getting the stove off the *Sierra Nevada* at Big Creek, happen the train changed its mind about hauling stoves.

He had a pink paper printed with a picture of the very stove I'd bought. Showed how drafts turned to make the oven get hot and save the wood, all about caring for the stove. He give me the paper, didn't charge a cent for it. So I up and bought a handy pot for heating up water, with a long spout for the steam to come out of.

More I bought, the more I felt like buying. I thought about

Pa being so set up because he was the savingest man in Monterey County and I waved my hand careless, pointed to a counter and says, "I'll take some of them plates—six of 'em, and three of them there round pans marked 'milk pans.'" I shelled out more'n a hundred dollars for all that stuff. I felt fine when I walked out, folding the picture of the stove to go in my pocket. I had a urge on me to go find more things, spend money.

Bold as brass, I walked into a place that sold nothing but ladies' fixings. There was a unrolled bolt of blue stuff and I made for it. It was the very blue of Hannah's eyes, and it rustled like ripe cornstalks when the fellow measured it. I bought a ten-yard length of that blue shot-silk for Hannah, and a good decent black for Ma. The hell with Mr. Avery. He wasn't the only one could buy presents.

That blue goods was what did it. I decided right then tomorrow I'd get that train for home. I walked down Market Street and was turning over onto Kearny, when I saw the store that sold nothing but books.

Books.

I didn't have a Bible to my house. If I *could* fix things up with Hannah—winter evenings when the fire was blazing high, and the little chap was tucked in his trundle bed, it would be a fine thing to be sitting at the table, the Book open, reading the good words.

I went in and told the man I wanted a Bible. He had stacks of 'em—all sizes, all prices. All them books standing on shelves give me a turn, but I didn't let on. I said, "You got a Bible with pictures to it?"

He had. There was Noah, and the real Ark, there was the serpent, wound round the tree, and his tongue stuck out to scare a child out of his senses. If ever a book could help in bringing up a child to be good and right-respecting, this picture Bible was the book.

It cost me five dollars, and I never spent money gladder. The book fellow sold me a doctor book. He told me, and I could see the straight of it, that living far from doctors and all, this was a fine book to have in the home.

That's what he said, "A fine book to have in the home." It told all about every sort of sickness and hurt that could come to man, woman or child, and a lot of things to do for ailing animals.

First I thought to take two of them, and bring one to Ma, but when I found they cost five dollars each, just as much as a Bible, I stuck to the one. Ma could borrow it, if she had need. I got a Mission hymn book with pictures for Iowana instead.

I was spending a lot of money. I had new clothes a Chinese tailor was making for me still to be called for and paid for, and my ticket on the train. The money in my pocket was going fast. So was the cash I'd been carrying in my money belt. Having money put in the bank give me a feeling that it wasn't my money any more. I stopped on Montgomery Street and asked that white-faced fellow in the cut-away coat once more if I could have my money if I wanted it, and he said, "Of course, Mr. Allan, of course."

Him calling my name like that made me sure it was all right.

I waved my hand at them little bars and said, "Long as I can get it when I want it, you keep it for me. You sure it don't cost nothing?"

"We are glad to oblige you, Mr. Allan," he says, polite as anything, settling his glasses onto his nose and smiling at me as he asks, "Are you staying in the city long?"

I got a better opinion of him. He knowed I was no city fellow. I put my elbow on the ledge of his cage as I told him,

"Nope, leaving here tomorrow morning, and not sorry, either."

I got the banking book out of my pocket and asked him one of the things I'd been worrying about. I says, showing him the first page of my book, "Now whenever I pay for things I just write in how much money I'm paying out, I sign my name right here, and then it's an order on my money that you're holding for me here, is that it?"

He said it was, told me again that the captain of the *Sierra Nevada* would take one of these checks and give me hard money change if it was coming to me. So I left the money and walked out, kept on going.

I had the two dress lengths, the three books, and I didn't have a pack-sack with me. I was almost wishing I hadn't bought none of it when I saw the big valise in the window of the Chinese shop on Dupont Street. Say, you could a put Hannah's valise and Ma's little satchel both inside this one. The Chinaman took it out of the window and I smelled it. It was leather, all right, no fake to it. I got it paid for, wondering if I'd have enough cash left for new clothes and my railroad ticket. The big satchel swinging again' my leg made a good creaking sound as I swung along down Dupont Street to where my clothes was waiting for me to try on.

The Chinese man was a queer-spoken fellow, but his words was easy enough followed once you got used to the swing of them.

He was smiling polite as he held back a curtain, saying, "In here, please. You try on now."

I ducked my head to go under the curtain, and as I come into the back room, I seen a tall bearded fellow in ragged buckskins walking toward me and wondered what he was doing in here. Then I seen he was carrying a big valise, same as me. 'Twas me, in a looking glass, full length.

It give me a turn. No wonder them slicked-up folks twisted their necks to give me a second look. I'd get my hair cut. I'd wear them clothes out of the tailor's place.

I got my black suit on. The cloth was smooth as fur. There was a white shirt and a black neck-scarf to go under the collar. I give only a short look to the mirror, frowning like I wasn't quite sure it was just right. I felt shame to let him see how tickled I was.

"They'll do," I told the Chinese fellow. I took the bank book out of my buckskins, wrote out a ticket for the clothes I had on and twenty dollars more. He took it, turned it over, said, "Sign here, please, Mr. Allan," putting a yellow ringer to the back of the slip. I signed. When he handed me my buckskins in a neat paper package, he hand me two ten-dollar gold pieces.

I put it in my money pouch, but *he* said, "Obliged to you, Mr. Allan. Come again."

That bank book was all right.

The barber got through with me and I went down Broadway, found Frank waiting for me in the room. He looked at me like I was as pretty a sight as ten fat head of prime beef, 'spite of me looking bleached where the beard had been. He hooked his thumbs to his belt and drawled out, "Well! Say! That rig's first rate. I'll order one just like it; take my pick of the Valley girls."

I laughed, too, but I kept thinking, hoping. By this time Hannah'd be used to the baby. She'd see I made a better figger of a man than the gaunt, whiskered fellow she'd had a mad at.

I slipped off my good coat and set it straight across the back of the chair.

Then the thought come to me that Hannah wasn't the woman to be took in by a new, good coat. Seemed like the starch went out of me.

XII

In the morning Frank Gallo was set on going to order a suit. I told him no train was going to wait for him or anyone else. But he was bound to go uptown so I picked up my new bag and made my way to the ferry. I gnawed my lip and wanted to push that poky old ferryboat, but, landed in Oakland, I found I'd got there in good time. Fact is, I'd been waiting for about an hour when people lugging valises started coming along.

Another half-hour, and here comes Gallo, whistling to hisself and pleased with the world.

He comes up, gives me a poke in the ribs and says, "New stagedriver over to Rootville's got a daughter. Uppity little piece, about seventeen, and yella braids wrapped around her head. Never give me a look, but when my new suit comes—well, I'll lay odds she's Mrs. Gallo by next Christmas."

"I never bet."

He went off into laughing like I'd said something funny. I never did find out what ailed him, for right then the train come puffin' up and liked to scared me much as it done the teamsters' horses.

There wasn't enough fences in this town of Oakland to keep the cattle up. The boys that was hired just to do that run out of the depot and chased cows off the tracks.

What with cow-bells jangling, dogs barking and horses either standing on their hind legs or trying to kick the wagons to pieces behind 'em, it was worse than a round-up. I wasn't looking for the wild toot of the train's whistle or the great puffs of smoke and steam that come belching out like the whole contraption was fixing to blow up. It might of been better to put up with the boat-sickness.

I saw a new part of the country, found out how a train looked, but I'd a been as well off on the boat. There's a train sickness, plaguey as the boat kind.

But the train went fast. Once out of Oakland and clear of cows, it went flying. I didn't have no company for the trip. Soon as we got on the train Frank spied a lone young woman; bright red hair she had, and he got a seat by her. Soon I heard her say she was visiting relations at Soledad and then they was both talking like old friends.

A couple times we took on wood to fire the engine, but mostly we kept on going. After we passed San Jose City, there was still five lone men of us left.

We got to talking. I found out one of 'em was going to get a team in the livery barn at Salinas City and was fixing to drive over to Monterey. I asked him could I pay fare and ride over to Monterey with him.

Spite of his hard hat and gold chain across his front he was hearty, told me I'd be more than welcome.

"More than welcome."

I took hold them words, thought I'd say them to Hannah when I told her about the new stove. Hannah'd like the sound of them words much as she'd like the set of my new black coat.

Seemed like I could a run home quicker than trains and teams would get me there. Frank was not acting like he found the trip long. Seemed to me like I should a took that bet about him marrying the Rootville girl.

At last the time come for me to go. The train man called

"Salinas City." I said, "See you in Rootville at Christmas, Frank," laughing as I picked up my valise. He never let on he heard me.

I walked down the steps of the train, into Salinas City. For a minute I tried to think how it must a been with Hannah, coming all that unknown way across the plains and mountains. She was a strong, brave woman, and quiet. She'd never spoke of her train trip at all.

I couldn't picture how her trip must of been, so I started looking at what I could see in Salinas City. Wasn't much of a town, but what there was to it seemed livelier than Monterey, not so many Spanish to it.

The roads was deep mud, dark, too, but this Mr. Parker I was with knowed his way. He invited me in to have a meal with him at the Abbot House, wouldn't let me show the color of my money.

"No," he says, waving it away. "You're paying your share of the livery team, and I'm glad of company. It's a long drive over at night, roads bad, and lean bear around the Laguna."

It was a long drive, but we'd a made it before daylight if hadn't happened we got mired at the foot of Long Hill, just past the Laguna. We had quite a wait before a freight wagon come along.

Sitting there in the dark, shivering in the cold wind, I said to Parker, "Fellow knows where he's at with a trail, but when you haul wagons along a road, anything is like to happen."

He bit off the end of another one of them black stogies, pushed a crumb of it offen his lip before he answered me, "Roads is what will build up this country of ours, you watch and see."

There'd never be any roads building up the Big Sur country. But I didn't tell him that. We was talking about the cattle business, when the freight wagon come along.

Spite of a drizzling rain holding back the light, it was full daylight when we pulled up at the Pacific Ocean House. I figgered to sleep till noon.

At noon I et, and found the hotel'd put me up a passel grub to eat on the trail. My new suit was safe in my satchel, folded smooth, and I'd put on my old worn buckskins. I got Ranger paid out of the livery barn, bought a couple good-looking mules at the Presidio, and then went over to the place by the dock where the train freight from Salinas City was stored. I couldn't believe my stove would be there, but I found it at the freight depot, all crated up pretty as you please, and the pans and stuff was there, too.

It looked fine, but it had to come apart in a lot of pieces before I could get it packed. Even with two mules I had a big load.

The rain had cleared, and when I rode out of Monterey and up the Carmel Hill, all the pines was glistening, the raindrops turned into rainbows by the thin spring sunshine.

I got to Wild-Cat Canyon by sundown. As the last sight and sound of towns and people faded away, the trail narrowed, my own kind of trees and free wild places closed around me. The headlands stood black again' the last sun-glow over the ocean, and the quiet mountains waiting to be climbed seemed to fold on and on forever—all pointing the way to my homeplace.

Every time I topped a rise, I could make out a campfire burning down at the Mal Paso. I got there, and found Comisa Joe, the old market hunter, frying up a big spiderful of fresh deer liver.

I pulled the animals out the trail, unpacked and fed 'em. I was glad to squat down beside Joe, share the fire and the deer liver. Old Comisa Joe was the best scout Fremont ever had; never was such a hand with working buckskin, but likker, that

240

was his trouble.

Money was still burning my pocket, so I bought a good pair fringed buckskin pants from him, and what he called a bearded shirt. 'Twas a hunting shirt with the fringe laid in across the breast, and fine-looking work it was, too. I handed him out the eight dollars he asked, thinking he'd be drinking in Monterey by daylight. Sure enough, he lit out for town, and I stayed at his camp, letting the mules rest good.

It was slow work, moving two pack animals along the narrow trail. By the time I was at the ford on the Big Sur another day was most gone. The water was still belly deep at the ford, and roiling fast. Seeing the river so deep and dark, I knowed the grass was tall and strong on my hill pastures.

Acrost the river, I rested and fed the stock again. I knowed them willing pack beasts was overloaded but they'd do all right long as they took their own time. At best it would be late night before I'd turn off the Coast trail. It would be deep past midnight before I'd be opening my own gates.

At Red Fox Creek I stopped the beasts and unstrapped my valise. There was half a moon and the light was good when the south wind didn't push the thin scud of clouds over its face. If that south wind hung on 'twould be raining by the morning. Save my life I couldn't make up my mind whether I'd put on my good store suit. By the time I'd told myself I'd left in buckskins, I was drawing up the lacings to the shirt I'd bought from Comisa Joe.

Two miles now.

Two miles can be longer than two hundred.

My hand was wet when I took down the first barred gate; I wanted to shout when I let down the bar to the next one and stepped the pack animals over. I come to the latched gate, and remembered how I'd left. Maybe me and Ranger'd never come there together again, me feeling proud when he nosed the gate open.

I stood outside my own gate and it come over me all of a sudden. I'd been working my way around to the spot I stood in every year since I'd set out to be head man over the folks I lived amongst. Seemed like I was a stranger-man to my own self.

A feeling of loneness liked to knocked the breath out of me. I was a lone man. It was my own doing.

Hannah done right well with things while I was gone off across the mountain after cattle, spite of her being so big and clumsy. She was better off without me.

I could leave her to herself. I could give her that.

I led the two mules up and started to unpack. I'd leave the things right by the gate. Hannah'd know I'd been there.

Lifting off the first part of the stove, I couldn't help wishing I'd told Hannah how I'd been figgering to do with that grizzly hide. Thinking how I'd planned about her feet and that fur, I put my face again' the pack I was unlashing. I'd owned up to myself, at last, why I was starting to sneak away from my own place again. It was the same thing that sent me racing off, near crazy, almost two months ago. I didn't have the gumption to humble myself and tell the straight truth. But until I could make myself own up to my lies, I wasn't fit to live with my own self, much less with Hannah. What held me back right now was my doubt that I was big enough to tell my wife how small I'd been.

I straightened up and jumped back quick when I heard Hannah's voice, right close by.

As I looked around I seen she had my old musket in her hand. She set it to lean on the rail at her side the fence and said again, "What you doing, Zande?"

I wasn't going to have her know she'd nearly caught me

bawling. I covered it, saying short, "See for yourself, can't you?"

"With a south wind blowing, you'll have to move that stuff before long. It'll get wet."

What she said riled me. How come a prairie woman to tell a Coast man that a south wind blowing up meant rain? Beside, Hannah sounded like she was speaking to a stranger.

Standing there, fifty pounds of pack in my arms, I was trying to think up a answer. She picked up the old gun without looking at me, went up-trail toward the house, calling sharp, "I'll heat up supper."

In a minute the smell of a fresh drift of smoke held close to the ground by the low gray clouds come rolling down from the house. The smell of smoke. She'd kindled it with greasewood, laid pine, and some lilac to the top. It was all there in the smell of the smoke, plainer to me than any of them printed city signs. I smelled it deep. It was like a smell could hold the core of every lonely feeling that ever come to a man in all his days.

I started fastening up the pack ropes I'd loosed, trying to act like the drops falling on my hands was rain.

I couldn't make it. I clutched the pack-saddle. Loneness tearing out of a man must be some like the pain that hits female creatures when they bring out life. The pain burned like fire, but it cleaned, like fire cleans brush from the hills and you find solid ground where underbrush was too thick to get footing. Truth is solid ground. I'd tell the truth to Hannah, all of it.

I started telling myself, "Best get over to the shed and get this stuff unloaded before she calls supper."

I didn't look for her to let things I'd done pass by without a word. I didn't want; wouldn't be right.

But I never hoped she'd say, "I'll heat up supper."

Her saying the south wind was blowing up and the gear would get wet if it was left at the gate showed she was looking after things, which anyone would expect. *Supper.* That's a different thing. Them words opened the door, the house.

I'd a liked to pray God to let me know what to say, what to do. But I'd went back on Him too often. I'd have to do my best by myself. I picked up the valise. I put it down. I opened it up, took out the dress and books. I put 'em back in again, and shut the bag.

Halfway to the house I turned, went back to the shed again, opened the valise and took out the old worn buckskins. I'd go into the house the way I left it; no new finery on me, no presents for Hannah.

If she wouldn't take me for a husband-man again when she heard the truth about me, I'd leave all them things in the shed, the picture of the stove showing how it was got together right on top of the other things. She could get Iowana or Ma to help her put it in place. I'd tell her about putting the grizzly hide by the bed, but not about putting her feet to warm while she sung to the child. Such things is for a man to think, not to say.

The comb hanging by its string above the washing place seemed like a friend; the wood bowl I'd burned and whittled out to hold water, the gourd with the long handle—they was all near as my hand. They was home. First I'd ever noticed that since Hannah and me got started on being married together, I'd been thinking of my shack as home. Before that, it was always "the shack," or "my cabin."

Since that time I'd tramped on all the trail-sign that shows a man's feet to the place where his house starts to being his home. If there was any way back, I was going home.

I give thought to that notion, trying to squint at myself in the piece of bright tin tacked above the wash place. Wasn't light enough to see. I was bound to get my hair parted straight as Hannah had it fixed when we started to the barbecue. When my thumb said the part was straight, my hair wet enough to lay flat, I walked to the closed door.

Reaching to pull it open, I pulled my hand back.

I knocked on my own door.

Hannah swung it open quick, a look of surprise to her face, but her voice was low, "Your supper's ready."

I was setting at my old place by the table before I could even see the room, and then it didn't seem to matter. I didn't want to ask her why she had firelight and candlelight, too. I was only thinking about Hannah's eyes. She'd changed the room, but not like her eyes was changed. She looked square at me when she opened the door and told me supper was ready. There was no more for me in her eyes than if she'd been looking at a table. No more than there was in all the eyes that didn't see me, when them folks was shoving past me on Montgomery

Street. Her hands put food on the table like a woman does for her man. Her eyes didn't see me.

I put food in my bowl. I broke a corn-dodger. I never took notice of the sweet ripe smell there is to new-baked meal. It was like I was eating ashes. There was nothing I could think to say. But I could go through the motions of eating.

The awful loneness I'd brought onto myself come home to me more'n when I stood outside my own gate. In a room that had fire, food, the woman I'd married, I was alone.

Hannah stood facing the fire, her back to me, not busy with her kettles. Just standing still.

The quiet deepened in the room and I got afraid that if I set my spoon down on the table board, it would make a noise like a redwood tree falling in a deep canyon. If I said a word, it would tear through that quiet like a gunshot. How could I start to tell her the truth if she wouldn't talk at all?

I couldn't stand it. That wife of mine. No woman has the right to hold such deep stillness.

In spite of me not wanting it that way, my voice come harsh and loud as I said, "Set down, Hannah. There's things to be talked out—"

No woman, a rattler rather, she whirled around to face me, her eyes flashing anger as she said, "Yes, I lied about my age. Yes, I lied about it the second time. I'll lie about it again if it suits me to. And—if you call me a liar, I'll call it right back at you."

My heart give a jump. She remembered the first words I'd said to her when we both set down to that table in Monterey.

I'd been so fearful I'd not looked at her any more than I'd seen the room. Now I seen again how straight she stood, poorer than when I'd seen her first, poor 'most to gauntness, her head so high, her breasts so round with their flood of milk.

I seen her standing hot-mad and slim, facing me in the firelight and my mouth went dry, making me whisper, "The child, Hannah, where's the child?"

With a curl to her lip she said, "What's that to you?"

I hid my shaking hands under the table.

"Our child, Hannah. Yours and mine."

A stone could a been standing there in the room for all the move or sound she made.

Then she come over and set down at the table across from me. I knowed she was there by the small scrape the stool made as she slid into it. I wished I could a had a sight of even her hands, but seemed like I couldn't raise my eyes.

Finally she let out a long breath, and I raised my head as she lifted her hands from her lap, clasped them together on the table in front of her. They didn't tighten up none, and her voice was easy as she said, "It's long past any child's bed-time."

I was scared to ask more, I set quiet, looking down at my plate.

She stood up and walked toward the bedplace. As her hand reached out to shove the curtain back, she stopped and looked back at me.

I knowed the room was changed, but I hadn't looked to see what changed it. Now I looked at that curtain. It looked neat, all patched together in little squares. The thing that hurt me past bearing was the little blue pieces with the white stars to them. Hannah's wrapper. I'd never seen her in my mind, all them miserable months I'd been away, but I seen her blue eyes shining above the stars on her clean blue wrapper.

"You shouldn't a cut up your wrapper to make a curtain to hide a young one from the light, Hannah."

There wasn't anger, there wasn't sorrow, only evenness to the way she said, "I'd cut up a lot more than that for my children, Zande. But I'm through with you telling me what to do. I'll do what I think's best."

I pushed back the stool I'd been hunched on, walked over to her quick, and caught her wrist in my hand. "No, you won't, my girl. Not if I'm here. Say the word and I'll go. You got the right. But if I stay here—if we're here together we'll both—" I stopped and caught myself. "We'll *all* do what I think's best."

Like she was listening to something I couldn't hear, she said, "Quiet, Zande!" Then she turned back to me like she'd just noticed I was there, and give me a long steady look. "What *you* think? You don't think. You don't know how!"

I was mad, having it slapped at me that-a-way, but she was right.

I took her hands, and she let hers lay in mine, not taking herself away—just not being there. I stepped a mite closer to her and said, "But that don't mean I can't learn. I learned a lot of thinking since the night you told me to quit wanting what a boy'd want and start after the things that belong in the man-part of life."

I seen her eyes glisten bright, but she looked down quick, hiding from me. "You remembered that?"

It was no lie about me learning to think. I caught her neat with my words: "Like you remembered what I said to you in Monterey."

Her head come up quick, and there was a hint of her old way in the mouth she made like she tasted something sour. "There's too much to remember. What we got to do is forget."

I wanted, to say to her, "Forget and forgive is good words to make a team out of." I couldn't say it.

Seemed to me her hands moved inside mine, like they might be taking notice I was there, but I couldn't be sure. Maybe she was wanting to take them free. I let go. She put 'em

248

behind her back and said in a quick, thin sort of way, "Well, the child. Do you want to look at it?"

I nodded my head and stumbled back to my stool by the table, so's to get my face hid out of the fire glow.

She stepped beyond the curtain, and let it fall behind her.

Looking down that grizzly's throat was nothing to waiting for Hannah to come out from behind the curtain. It was the same feeling that two-headed calf of Ramirez's give me. I'd be served right if I'd fathered a monster. Hadn't Hannah herself feared such a thing so deep she thought to kill herself?

Hannah come out, walking quiet, a short little bundle in her arms that would of gone into a pack-sack. She put it on the table, peeled back some of the covers from the top and said, "There."

She turned quick and went back to the bedplace, leaving me alone with this damned bundle. Made me uneasy. What scared hell out of me was seeing it wrapped in cream-colored stuff. Flannel. I sweat, remembering what I'd done with the flannel.

All to a sudden there was a quick, strong move in the wrapping, and I seen a hand come up out of it. The whole hand didn't look much bigger than my thumb, but it reached up, opened and shut its fingers like a real hand.

I half stood up, leaned forward, and looked where the flannel stuff was pushed back. There was a fuzz of red hair, a blur of red face, a mouth working like it was trying to eat.

This was no two-headed monster. This was a red-headed Allan. Its face was turned one side and I could see Pa's ear cropping out plain as if 'twas on Pa's head. My son. I wanted to pick it up, to put my finger along the funny little fist; to heft that little red-head gnawed me like hunger, but I couldn't do it. I still had the truth to tell to Hannah. I told myself I'd had no chance yet to tell her.

I wiped the sweat off my lip and looked up when Hannah come out from the curtain. She was carrying what I thought was a bundle of more wrappings for the child on the table.

She put it down. I heard a thin wail from the bundle, seen it move. I stepped back, my mouth 'most too dry to whisper, "Where did you get that?"

No more than if it was a cutting of hay or skins tacked to the shed, Hannah said, "You ought to know. It's yours."

I jerked open the collar of my shirt, felt my wet hand slide again' the wet skin of my neck. I swallowed, asked her, "Twins?"

She give me a look I wouldn't of took from her a year ago. It said, plain as words, that I was a gawk. So did her lifted eyebrows and the way she said, "Twins? Of course. What else could they be?"

I squatted down on my heels, steadying my back again' the

good stout boards I'd rived to make the wall. What a woman I'd had the luck to find, been the fool to run off from. "Twins," she said, like it was a thing could happen any day. No man of the Coast before me ever got two boys to one time.

Hannah went about her own business, paying no heed to me. I kept watching her. Going over to the fire she laid her finger 'longside a small iron kettle, then lifted it, held it close to her cheek. That was Ma's kettle. She used to lift it, test it just like that when Mel was little.

Watching Hannah do the same was a feeling like having two hands on life, one reaching back, one feeling for years still far to come. It filled me with glory and it made me ache with shame. It wasn't honest for me to be here. I swallowed, tried to fix the words to tell her about Maria. My mind grabbed at the thought of the stove, the stuff I'd brought and I stammered, "The mules, Hannah. I got 'em broke to plow." I could speak of the animals. She'd already seen them.

She was reaching for the horn spoon, picked it off the shelf by the chimney, looking close at it like 'twas more to her than plow-mules. Maybe she hadn't heard me. I spoke up, "Will be needful to have hay-feed for the cow, grain for the fowl, too."

She didn't answer. She picked up one of the babies, took it over to the block beside the fire. From the sound of her step and how her skirt swished, I knowed she was putting me in place. But when she dipped the spoon into the kettle, brought out the warmed milk, she made soft coaxing sounds to the baby, like a mother-bird at feeding time.

Soon she carried that one behind the curtain, come back and picked the second one off the table. This time she unbuttoned her dress front, turning so's I wouldn't see the baby catch hold her nipple. Hannah bent close over the baby, turned her head up and looked at me. There was naught but love and sorrow to the way she said, "I ain't got enough milk for them both. Have to nurse 'em every other time. Wasn't for the cow I'd a lost both of them."

I seen what was bothering her. I meant it when I told her, "I'd never have grudged getting you a cow if I'd a knowed how it was going to help."

Hannah got up, hanging onto the baby like it was thistledown. Walking quick she took it back to sleep with the first fellow. Then she turned on me.

"Get me a cow?" She clenched her hands, stepped so close she was all but stepping on me. "Like you got me a clothesline! You—" Her eyes was flashing and she blowed out her breath with a mean sound to it. "I live plain," she says, dragging out every word I'd said to her in Monterey and giving a nasty twist to it. "No frills and I got no mind to change."

She swung half around, walked to the fireplace and turned to face me. "Well," she said, her voice thinner and higher than I'd guessed it ever could go, "you just take your cows and your clotheslines where they're wanted. Go offer 'em to Maria Demas, why don't you?"

My crazy temper—that buzz like red color and red sound, mixed hot inside my head—took holt of me. For the first time in my life I fought it back, beat it down.

When I could I said, "There's hard words to stay quiet and take."

Her answer come bitter as poison on coyote bait, "No one's asking you to stay."

That was so. Hannah hadn't asked me to.

But I had to. Life was here. It was in the firelight on Hannah's face, the shine on the bowl of the spoon I'd whittled out, the table smoothed from use.

Hannah took a bundle of stuff down off the shelf, set down

on the block by the fireplace, and picked up her needle. Now was the time for me to tell her all the truth. I never faced so black a job. I'd get it all set in my mind and find that I was getting ready to tell her that if it hadn't been for her listening to, looking at Avery like she did, I'd not got messed up with Maria. Seemed like the straight truth wasn't in me.

I got to my feet, crossed the room and slid down beside her, reached out and caught her long hand, so busy stitching criss-cross trails to shut me out.

Finger by finger I took my free hand and closed her fingers around mine, held her folded hand between both mine and put my head again' her knee.

She didn't draw back.

I got courage to say what I'd never been able to out and tell her before:

"I love you, Hannah. I'm hard-headed and a great fool, and I'll 'most drive you crazy sometimes. But I'll always love you."

She didn't answer. I was scared to look at her but this was truth. I had to make her see I meant it. I said, "Words won't work for me, seems like. I wanted to tell you long ago, but I was scared you'd think 'twas comical—"

She never moved. I couldn't stand it. I dropped her hand and grabbed her shoulders, shook her, "God damn it, woman, I've fell in love with you!"

Her hair shook loose. I heard the bone pins dropping on the stone hearth before she went limp again' me. I felt her shaking. I'd finished everything, yelling at her, when she was broke with grief.

Gentle as I knowed how, I took my thumb and finger and turned her face up.

She was laughing. Laughing! Hot blood went pumping through me as I pulled her to her feet, tightened my arms around her. My mouth went hungry for hers, to get the taste of her laughing into me, but she cooled me smart as if she'd throwed a gourd of spring water on me.

There was that strange smile, that knowing look, as she pulled back, looked square at me and said, "That's not news, Zande. Why did you think I was waiting for you? That I ever come back here after the barbecue?"

I felt my damn cowardly backside cringe up but I had to say it. "I laid out with Maria. Up to the feed shed at the barbecue."

She drawed back so's to look full at me. "I thought you'd come to feel it was right to own up. I saw your leg go out that window, Zande. I saw Maria, too."

Shame held me numb. I stood there, too shamed to say one word.

All the tiredness plain on her face, she lifted one shoulder, let it drop. "I'd thought never to come back here, Zande. I was bound to get through with that barbecue someway and then— I was going to leave. Wasn't till you run off with Maria that the anger left me, the lonely ache took hold."

I couldn't believe I'd heard her straight. "Maria? I never run off with Maria. I went after cattle—and by God I got 'em!"

Hannah got a look to her like she didn't want to own to what she had to say. "I know, Zande. Iowana didn't want to talk, but I—" She spread out her hands and her face went pink but she looked full at me. "—I kept at him till he told me." Her voice was mighty soft as she said, "I was proud of you."

Maybe the doubt showed on my face for she answered in a voice that stirred me deep: "You said, 'Long as you live, you're Mrs. Allan and I'll stand by you.' I believe that. I couldn't do less for you than you'd promised to do for me. That's love."

The look on her face was strong as the mountains, soft as

new grass. I had to hear it.

"You mean we're home, together, now?"

She slid down in front of the fire, pulled her knees up close under her chin, nodded her head.

I wanted to stay down there beside her, sit where I could smell the sweet-fern smell of her hair, take her deep into my arms. But shame kept me still. It was like that little fog of white lace I'd tore from her the night I first took her for mine was still there, just above the ashes. My mind could see it there so plain, I was a feared she'd follow my look, see it, too.

She tilted back her head and looked at me. Her eyes looked bluer from the tired blue look under them, and then her smile come so gay I couldn't see the tired look.

"Sit here and warm your back," she said, patting the warm hearth stones. "I don't want you 'way over there while I talk to you."

I didn't want to talk to her. I couldn't trust myself closer. I stammered, "I got some stuff in San Francisco—"

She sounded sort of put off. "Did you?"

I talked straight on, "And something for Ma, too." Her eyes were too bright for me, her face eager, her hands raised and held out for me to pull her up from the floor.

"I'll get the stuff."

I was outside, telling myself rough and hard that Hannah held rape was rape whether folks was married or not. I'd damned near lost her once, but this time I'd keep it in mind every minute. I had a woman worth waiting for.

In the dark of the shed I had to feel for the pink paper that showed the picture of the stove all set up. No trouble finding the valise. I could smell its new leather plain as new rain, and I went off up the trail listening to the small leather squeak it made when it struck my leg. I damned near dropped it, though, when I suddenly heard the tune I was whistling between my teeth. It was the *Dance of the Little Bears*. I hoped Hannah hadn't heard it. Set her thinking about Avery...them flannels...

She was lighting a new candle, fixing it in a miner's candlestick drove into the boards beside the chimney. I wondered how come she got such a thing, but I'd find out later. She come over to the table looking for all the world as much a little girl as Alice Ramirez when she put out her hand and stroked the shiny leather.

There wasn't a mite of longing for herself when she put both hands to it, stroked it soft and put her face down to it, saying, "It's brand-new, Zande! So strong and good. It will last you for life."

"That's so," I said, fumbling clumsy for the catch to open it. I dumped the wrapped-up stuff on the table, and she looked at me like a half-tame doe will watch a man just before it runs.

I had to sound rough, "Well, open 'em up. Open 'em up if you want to see what's inside."

She picked up the first one and set down on the stool by the fire, holding it close to the candlelight so's she could see to pick the knot out of the string. She wound it neat into a ball around her finger before she folded back the paper, let it slide to the floor, and jumped to her feet, shaking out a fold of the stuff, feeling it between her fingers, before she held it again' her shoulder.

When I see her eyes shine like two blue stars and how the soft stuff flowed over the cup of her breast, I gripped the table with both hands and told her, "You become that blue-colored stuff mighty well, Mrs. Allan."

She had both arms around the stuff, holding it like she held them bundled babies, a shake to her lip as she said, "Oh, Zande— Oh, my dear…you thought of me—"

I bellowed, "Thought of you! By God, woman, I ain't done naught else for nigh a year! That's a hell of a way for a man to run his ranch."

Sounding sassy, she wrinkled her nose at me, "It's been good for you."

"Well, there's a picture Bible in this here one," I said, handing her the Book, "that ought to be good for both of us."

She caught me up, "*All* of us," she says, firm. Hannah's a lot like Ma, some ways.

"And this here's a book for bellyaches," I went on, shoving the other book at her. The way she was looking at that Bible, 'twould take all night before I could get to show her the stove. I had the paper with the stove picture hid under my hand, waiting for her to get half scared looking at some of them pictures in that doctor book. She didn't.

I reached out, shut the book and put it on the table, telling her, "That ain't hardly no fit picture for a woman creature to be staring at. Look, this here is what I got for Ma."

I'd slipped the string, knots and all, off the paper, and I pulled the black silk up for Hannah to look at.

It was just black stuff, and oughtn't to take but a glance. Then I could show her the stove.

Hannah give it a long look. "That's extra nice, Zande. Your Ma's a good woman; she's real fine and about all she's ever got for it is hard work."

I hadn't thought about that, but it was so. I blurted out, "Maybe Ma won't think much of it. She ain't ever saw me since I dumped them there flannels of Mr. Avery's into the outhouse."

Hannah's eyes got wide, her mouth hard and straight. She looked at me like I was one of them slimy things a fellow rinds when he turns over a rotten redwood.

All to a sudden her face changed, and she doubled up, laughing like crazy, laughing till she dropped on the stool by the table, and rocked with laughter.

She tried to say something two or three times, and she went off into that laughing streak again. Finally she rubbed her eyes with her knuckles, fished a square of stuff out of her wrapper pocket and blowed her nose. She looked me straight in the eye and said, hard as any man could, "Zande Allan, you ought to have your tail kicked straight off. Of all the—"

There she was, whooping with laughter again.

I guess I got the damnedest woman in the world for my wife. Keep me busy all my life trying to figger her out.

She was sober as a justice, though, saying, "Well, I hope that's the last of such nasty tricks. It was plain filthy of you, and you know it. You better try to live up to such a mother as you got. Kept her mouth shut, she did."

There come that far-away look to Hannah's eyes and she said, "Poor Mr. Avery. Well, I did wonder what Ma boiled and boiled and sunned and sunned that stuff about—"

She started laughing again, gasping, "Oh, dear, oh, my," till I felt like a fool.

I cleared my throat and says, "Why the *poor* for dear Mr. Avery?"

I couldn't help feeling a load lift off my chest when she said, "He's dead, poor man. Died in Los Angeles. He never got to the warm islands. But Mel did. He started a letter back and Arvis brought it in when he went over to Jolon. Ma got it about a month ago. The boat Mel went on sailed, even before the letter started up here, so Mel must be walking on the coral beaches right now."

It all seemed too far away to think about. Half my mind was wondering if we'd ever see Mel again. Maybe not. He was too soft for these mountains. The other half my mind was wondering if this was the right time to show the stove picture to Hannah.

I unfolded my hand, spread the picture out so's the whole print of the stove would show at once, and I fought the proud down out of my voice, couldn't get the best of it.

"Look, Hannah, this is for you. I got it in the shed, and I'll set it up tomorrow. Got the tin pipes for it; too—"

It was a good thing I'd sort of wore her down with showing her dress-lengths and them books. If I hadn't, I guess she'd a gone clean crazy. It was, for a minute, having a humming bird and a band-tailed pigeon in the house instead of a woman. I liked it. I tried wiping the grin off my face with the back of my hand, but it wouldn't stay off. She was out of breath and well-nigh wore down before she could say a word. Even trying to talk started her to jumping and whirling again, breaking up her words so I could scarce follow them, but I made out "...cook for a whole threshing crew and no trouble at all...get it up for the christening party..."

I reached out my hand and caught her, held her as she started for the door. "Here. Come back here," I said. "It'll keep. Tame down, or I'll throw it over the cliff."

She had me by the shoulders, shaking them, tumbling out words so fast they rattled me. "Iowana can help...tomorrow... have to get it set up the first thing, so I can get used to it by the christening. If your Pa spits at it I'll kill him—"

"For God's sake, Hannah, shut up," I told her. My arms wouldn't stop reaching for her, so I walked round the table, away from her. "You fixing to hold a christening for them?"

"Yes." She give me a shy sort of look. "It means a lot to me. I want them children to get a right start."

There was a chuckle trying to shake me but I hid it. "Late for that, ain't it? They already got 'em a ornery crooked stick for a father."

Hannah frowned me down. "Not one word again' them children. They're healthy and they're handsome; there ain't none better."

She was right. I was puffed with pride in my family but I couldn't let on. I asked her, "Who all's coming to the doings?"

Hannah's hands clasped together, her eyes was shining. "I'll bake *two* cakes, great big ones. I got eggs already laid by, and Arvis brought down some honey—" She looked up like she'd just remembered something. "Everyone's coming. Your Ma is seeing the word's passed along."

Hannah stopped talking, watched me for a moment and then she told me, "I asked Maria and her husband."

I didn't believe it. I didn't feel so much mad as flabbergasted. "You never asked that wench!"

Hannah nodded her head. "Yes, I did. She come back here on Valentine Day. Zande, I wanted to shoot her when she come up here—"

"Why didn't you? You should of."

"That's how I felt when she come." Hannah took a breath that split between a chuckle and a choke. "Zande, Maria isn't expecting." My wife's face colored up. "I wasn't half so mad at her, once I found that out. She even told me she'd come back to get a charm from her grandmother to help her. Her eyes was full of tears when she saw my children. Tony wants a son awful bad, she told me so."

If my face didn't tell Hannah how proud I was that she'd give me two at one time then Hannah's eyes wasn't as sharp as I knowed they was.

But I had to speak out on what was eating on me. "She damn near wrecked my life, but that was much my fault as hers; I don't hold that again' her, much as I do again' my own self." I shook down my temper, said, "It's her stealing my land I'm never going to overlook. I don't want her on my place."

Hannah's head come up. "Careful now, Mr. Allan. This is my home, too. And you'd not feel so snug about Maria if she'd been having a child next August and you was shaking scared it might say "Allan" to the whole Coast."

She give a sniff, but her voice softened some as she told me, "Maria didn't take land of yours. It was vacant land, anyone had the right to it as much as you."

I could feel my patience stretched thin as I said, "And I didn't feel kindly to you for helping her fence it, neither. How come you to do such a thing?"

Hannah's voice was crisp as the blue silk on the table. "Arvis helped me make garden. He told me what out of all them seeds I'd brought in my trunk would grow in the winter. Anyway, I thought it was his land; that it would be nice when he'd marry and I'd have a near neighbor. Of course, I'd help any neighbor, and he's only a boy."

We both looked hot and sharp at each other for a minute and then I give in. "What's done is done," I said. "Maybe she'll sell the land to me. I don't want her poking around here the rest of time."

I felt better when Hannah said, nodding, "I don't either." Her look got troubled, she said, slow, "Maria won't sell. When she said it was her land I asked her to, but she wouldn't..." She took a deep breath, half laughed. "Well, she isn't coming to the christening, so you don't have that to fret about."

I put my hand light on Hannah's shoulder. "I don't have one thing to fret about—yes, I have. What you plan to call the boys?"

"Boys?" she says, with a curl to her lips. "Why boys?" Then she softened and said, proud-like, "We got a boy and a girl, Zande. A whole family!"

I lied hearty, "That's my best news yet." Even as I said it, it come sneaking over me that it wasn't a lie. It was truth. A girl. Another Hannah, a little new one, to grow up in my own country, tie me even closer to my own woman. "Could we call the girl for you?"

She tossed her head. "Hannah? That's too plain. I had figured 'twould be nice to call them both after things in these hills, but you pick out names to please you."

I had to half turn from her lest she see how shook I was. I said, "You're a great hand to do a man a kindness. I'd like to have me a boy called Martin; that'd be after you and your folks. Would you think it right to call the girl Blaze?"

Hannah's head tipped one side, she sounded puzzled as she tried the name like it was a taste in her mouth. "Blaze?

Blaze? That's a cut on the side of a tree, helps travelers find their way back through the wilderness—" Her lips parted and her eyes was lighted as she whispered, "Was that what you meant?"

I nodded.

Hannah said soft, "It's a pretty sound: Blaze. We've got names for both of them now."

We stood close together. The fire was down to coals. Daylight was already coming strong enough to show the crumpled papers on the floor. Hannah went over and pinched out the candle, opened the door.

Over her shoulder she called back soft, "There's pink in the sky and the dawn wind smells of sweet clover. Come taste the morning with me, Zande?"

I heard a faint mew from one of the young ones, but I slid out the door quick, shut it close again' the sound.

We walked together down toward the madrone tree. Its smooth trunk was already picking up the first red streaks to the east.

We stood there together, looking down to the sea.

The way things was now, me and Hannah and the boy— Blaze, too—could never stand at the tiptop of the ranch and know that all the streams flowing between us and the sea was ours. A corner had went out of it. It was Maria's. She'd be one to hold on to it.

I could see trouble, maybe, in the years ahead, but for once in my life I could see the minute. Here was the softest pink morning that ever spring shook out over the mountains.

"The morning has a fine taste, Hannah," I said.

She looked a little troubled. "I bet you want your breakfast."

I turned to her, bold. "Hell with breakfast," I said. "I'm not hungry for food."

She didn't answer, just walked along the trail to the spring, and I followed her. She'd dammed up the overflow ditch to her garden, and there was a good pond, still in the morning calm, and holding the pink and gold of the sky. It was a good sight, and when one of them big sea-cranes that roosts in the canyons come winging down seaward, trailing his slow shadow across the pool, Hannah turned to me, her face as lighted as the sky.

"The morning's younger than we are; but let's be happy." She chuckled, "The babies are asleep, but they won't be long."

I never said a word about the whimper I'd heard. I reached for her hand, and she pressed her shoulder again" me, saying in one of them ways of hers, as if it didn't mean a thing, "Iowana piled a lot of clean new straw out beside the shed yesterday."

I don't think so fast, but my God—

"Mrs. Allan," I says, "I'd like to have a look at that straw."

She give me one of them looks that curl a man's toes back, and she says, "Well, why not?"

I grabbed her hand hard, and laughing like a pair of fools, we run up the trail to the shed—running under a gold sky, into a gold world spread everywhere around us.

For the first time in my life I felt to home in the world I was borned in.

The End

ACKNOWLEDGMENTS

Delia Bradford, a plein air painter born in Big Sur to artist parents, painted the covers of the three books of the *Big Sur Trilogy.* (www.deliabradford.com)

Roger Rybkowski of Adpartner graphic design, edited, designed and prepared the *Big Sur Trilogy* for publication. (www.myadpartner.biz).

Gary M. Koeppel, educator, artist and entrepreneur, resurrected the first two novels and rewrote the third unpublished manuscript to create the *Big Sur Trilogy.*

Robin Coventry, now passed, many of whose illustrations of Big Sur homesteads populate and embellish the written storytelling in the *Big Sur Trilogy.*

Photo archivist Pat Hathaway provided numerous historic photographs that were converted into black & white sketches to embellish the *Big Sur Trilogy.* (www.caviews.com)

Coast Publishing in Carmel, California publishes art books, novels and limited edition art prints and sculpture. (www.cstpub.com)